The Forgotten Prince

The Forgottten Prince.
Copyright © 2022 by Eileen L. Maschger

Published in the United States of America
ISBN   Paperback: 978-1-957312-56-9
ISBN   eBook: 978-1-957312-57-6

All rights reserved. No part of this publication may be reproduced, stored in a retrieval system or transmitted in any way by any means, electronic, mechanical, photocopy, recording or otherwise without the prior permission of the author except as provided by USA copyright law.

The opinions expressed by the author are not necessarily those of ReadersMagnet, LLC.

ReadersMagnet, LLC
10620 Treena Street, Suite 230 | San Diego, California, 92131 USA
1.619. 354. 2643 | www.readersmagnet.com

Book design copyright © 2022 by ReadersMagnet, LLC. All rights reserved.
Cover design by Kent Gabutin.
Interior design by Ched Celiz.

THE FORGOTTEN Prince

By Eileen L. Maschger

ReadersMagnet, LLC

*To my favorite editors.
Celidah, you transformed my imaginative spark
into a bonfire of creativity, passion, and excitement.
And to my Michelle, you bring order to
my chaos and clarity to my madness.*

*Special thanks to Allison Day-Zitnak for
her illustrations and beautiful artwork.
Further appreciation is extended to Celidah Porter
and Michelle Spano as contributing editors for my books.*

Chapter

Once upon a time, in the great kingdom of Marconia, where the land was much greener and richer than you have ever known, lived a handsome young prince. Although he was diligent in his studies and remembered everything he was taught, the prince was always thinking of something better to do. He loved to laugh and run and get lost in the nearby woods. When he appeared to be focused on his studies, he was actually scheming about how to sneak down into the kitchens, fool the chef and help himself to the sweet, delicious pastries that were readily available. He never met a joke he didn't like and he never missed the opportunity to point out some ridiculous thing he could exploit for fun. His parents tolerated most of his nonsense, for when all was said and done, he excelled when his education was tested. Whenever the prince was faced with a difficult political matter he was asked to resolve by his father, the king could not help but be proud of the prince's ease and confidence. His solutions were ingenious and the king and queen knew, despite his shenanigans, he would grow up to be a generous, good king in their stead.

The prince's most loyal and trusted friend was a simple son of a huntsman who lived, secluded, in the nearby forest. The boy was only a few months older than the prince, and they met by chance during one of the prince's unsupervised jaunts into the woods. Ever since then, the two boys were inseparable, and the forest, along with the castle grounds, became their playground. Side by side they were quite the pair, ready for any obstacle thrown in their way. Rarely the one was ever seen without the other. The prince and his friend were never bored when they were together, as they sparred often with various weapons. Late-night heists to the kitchens were much easier with two thieves instead of one. And the two boys being boys, got into all sorts of mischief, most of which they were able to get away with.

The Prince's friend generally had a serious and confident manner. But, when a sword was in his hand he became someone altogether different. He was fearless. Fighting was always a good sport for him. He relished it and was always sorry when the game was over. His excitement opened up creative venues allowing him to see his opponent clearly, and work a perfect solution to defeat him. His dream was to be a soldier in the king's army, and his dream was fulfilled at the young age of seventeen. Everything he learned, he perfected. With each passing year, his skills grew increasingly unmatched, even by older more experienced soldiers. This earned him profound respect and honor with his fellow fighters. His quick wit and undaunted manner made him an excellent warrior, but his heart was what made him a leader. Amidst his many one-on-one battles, he was somehow aware of his brothers in arms, where they were, who they were fighting, and how he could help. He was known for swooping in on a fight when the odds were most bleak, and save a fellow soldier from his untimely end. Instead of waiting for praise, he would immediately help his brother back to his feet and dutifully charge towards his next opponent. A man of such skill and character did not go unnoticed by the king and queen, and by the age of twenty-one, he became the leader of the entire Marconian Army. The young general happily accepted this honor and led his men with all the pride and responsibility one would expect from a valiant general. But, at the end of the day, he always found time to visit the prince for a few good laughs and friendly company. All in all, the castle dynamic was full of fun merrymaking, and the kingdom prospered because of it.

Alas, life could not always be fun and games. One day the king and queen grew very ill, and on the eve of the prince's twenty-first birthday, they passed away from this world. It was unfathomable to describe the pain the poor prince was in at the moment he learned his parents were no longer with him. All he wanted to do was shut himself up in his room, refusing all pleasantries of his life, from food to friendship. Had he been any other boy, no one would have blamed him for responding in such away. However, he was a prince. And, although he was never officially coronated, he had all the responsibilities of a king bearing down on him with crushing weight. The luxury of mourning his parents' death on his own terms was not to be, for looming just past the eastern border of his kingdom lurked a fearsome tyrant. He saw the prince's grief as an opportunity to broaden his borders in pursuit of conquest. The vile king's army was assembled and stormed the young prince's kingdom with no mercy.

The prince leaped into action to collect intelligence and plot counter attacks. But his thinking was not as clear and calculated as it used to be. The prince was reckless and determined to eradicate his foe regardless of the price. When his councilors continually questioned his orders, and voiced concerns for the men who would be in the thick of battle, the prince gave up the desk overflowing with papers and donned his armor instead. He insisted on fighting alongside his army to give them the confidence, and assurance they needed to do what was required. As a result, the prince's uncle was summoned to assume the position behind the desk. His uncle was all too happy to oblige and came straightway to the castle while the prince was off to war.

With wrath that had never been seen from him before, the prince rallied his troops with a fearsome war cry that made the very ground tremble. The mighty men of Marconia fought bravely, but the prince fought as if he were possessed by a demon. Every flick of his blade drew copious amounts of blood from his foe. But the prince was greedy for more as he rushed into the terrible masses of his enemy recklessly, impatient for the opportunity to fight. He never flinched. Even when an opponent managed to gain the advantage, the prince raged on and on without concern for his wellbeing. He craved the opportunity to inflict pain on his enemy and delighted in engineering new, gruesome ways to torture each offender. His army was simultaneously inspired and horrified by their prince. Thanks to him, the Marconian army was not only able to hold their attackers at bay but steadily push them back to the border they emerged from. However, the terrible, unhinged mindset of the prince troubled them. Even the general could no longer ignore how the rage of battle consumed his friend like a disease.

Back at the castle the prince's uncle, Lord Robert, sorted through intelligence and military strategy to carefully plan possible attacks that would be forwarded on to his nephew. In truth, he was a blessing to have amid the chaos of war. In a remarkably short period, the prince and his uncle had eradicated the enemy with only one battle left to decimate their threat.

The prince wanted the complete annihilation of his enemy. He wanted to end the war and show all other powers watching what happens to those who threaten Marconia. So, he took three hundred men of his army to flank the opposition. It was a brilliant strategy that would force their opponent to spread out their numbers to defend on two different fronts.

The final battle ensued, and the army fought with full hearts and spirit as defenders of the realm. The enemy was sent into a hasty retreat, and the valiant army of Marconia celebrated their triumph. But their elation was brief when they realized the prince and his troops were nowhere to be found. A search was organized to find them straight away, but what they found was worse than anything they could have imagined. All three hundred men lay slaughtered in a grotesque, merciless fashion several leagues from their prescribed position. Only one of the men had survived, their beloved prince. When asked what had happened, he had no recollection of what transpired. Try as he might, his memories were hazy, and he could not explain the carnage that lay around him.

Rumors of what happened during the attack swarmed like mosquitos, becoming more unsettling and frustrating with every word. The most popular of these rumors was that the beloved prince lost all control, allowing hatred and anger to overcome him. It was said he turned on his loyal men to satisfy his blood lust. Of course, the prince fervently denied this theory. But, the more he insisted he was innocent, the more his people believed his guilt.

The kingdom turned to Lord Robert, demanding justice for the lives of the three-hundred. With the ease of any king, Lord Robert executed the prince's sentence with authority and wisdom. The prince was banished from the castle and stripped of his birthright as leader of the kingdom. The young prince was left with nothing, except the clothes on his back. Many called for the prince's death, but the wise uncle insisted enough blood had been spilled. As a compromise, the prince's name was deemed evil and no man, woman, or child was allowed to speak it. The prince became a living ghost as he wandered throughout his kingdom, a mere shadow that was ignored, and eventually forgotten.

Lord Robert became King Robert, and the kingdom rejoiced as he assumed the role as their new leader. But the new king had set up an elaborate façade to hide his real intentions. As the years passed, King Robert's true nature was revealed. He was viler and terrible than the neighboring tyrant that the Marconian army had originally saved them from. The people began to whisper fond recollections of their former, now disgraced, prince. Prayers and hopes began to hang in everyone's hearts, wishing he would return to set things right. But their prayers remained unheard as the young prince was lost to the winds. No one knew or could even speculate where he had gone, leaving them to their ill fate under the iron clutches of King Robert.

Chapter

"Boooo!" The crowd clamored at the cast of actors in a sudden wave of noise.

The town square was filled with onlookers, passersby, and children leaning their heads out of upstairs windows. All were watching an elaborate performance by the traveling gypsy troupe. A tall, muscular man clothed in bright blues and greens strutted confidently toward the front of the stage; and stretched out his hands to the crowd.

"Yes! I know, right?" The crowd was hushed to a loud murmur. "It's tragic, dramatic, horrific… and a whole lot more words ending in 'ick'!"

The man paced the entire length of the stage to ensure the entire audience had his attention.

"How could the young prince let this happen? Does he not care about his invaluable kingdom and devoted subjects?"

The mass of people lifted their voices with an uproarious jumble of opinions:

"No, he doesn't!"

"Why would he leave us?"

"Where'd he go?"

"He has a royal obligation!"

Once again the storyteller stretched out his hands, and the noisy crowd dimmed to a hush.

"Ladies and gentlemen, have no fear." The man's voice was commanding and soothing. "We are not just any band of traveling gypsies, are we?"

"No!" shouted the crowd, much happier than before.

The storyteller puffed up his chest with pride. "Ladies and gentlemen, we are the White and Red Troupe!"

The crowd whistled and cheered with all their might when the troupe's name was announced.

"We always seek to offer you a show, unlike any other performer who graces your magnificent square." He paused to allow more cheers to swell, and add to the overall effect of the show. "We would never simply leave you with half the story!"

The crowd gasped with excitement. Their anticipation was at its peak, now that they knew they were about to hear something extra concerning a tired old story.

"As many of you know, our fortune tellers are the most gifted in the land—dare I say, the world?"

The crowd offered more cheers of encouragement.

"Now settle down everyone, and pay close attention. The next thing we will show you is a prophecy from the most powerful seer among us. The loved and feared, Brizo White."

The audience "ooh-ed" and "ahh-ed" as they whispered to one another to listen up. All eyes were fixed on the now lone man on stage. He was grinning wildly, feeding off the energy of the crowd. He spoke slowly and evenly, losing the flashy embellishments he had been using a moment ago. While he spoke, performers acted out the scenes behind him; adding more effect and entertainment to his words.

"There will come a time when the heat of the sun will be too great. Our wells will run dry and the crops will not grow. It will be a time of great struggle, that death himself shall walk among us.

And, in the summer of that year the Red Bear of Marconia will awaken, and shadows of his strong arm will gather in hidden corners, awaiting the day of his unleashing. The ghost's heart will beat again. He will find strength from his misery and remember his courage.

The mighty bear will roar, and his subjects will thirst for the same power and glory their nation once carried. They will raise the cry for freedom, justice, and all that is good. And the long-forgotten prince will fight, ladies and gentlemen. He'll fight for his people. He will fight for his birthright, his love, his beloved country. The Red Bear will clear the weeds that have choked our land and exterminate the parasites that have infested our homes. And all will begin to heal once more!

But heed my words. If the Bear of Marconia roars and his people remain silent, then their silence shall be their doom. The poison that has leached into our hearts will overpower us. And we too will become just like our prince—forgotten ghosts with only a distinct memory of who we once were and will never be again!"

The crowd roared with excitement as the man twirled off the stage with an elaborate flourish of his coat allowing the audience a full view of a glorious battle acted out by more members of the troupe. The crowd was captivated as they watched the good king fight his evil uncle to reclaim the kingdom for all that is good.

Until now the townspeople had been entertained by the gypsies with dancing, magic shows, forms of daring escapes, tricks, and music. The fight scene at the end of the story was the grand finale putting everyone in joyful moods which they expressed with applause, heartfelt thanks, and, most importantly, money. The scene ended with a glorious triumph over the evil king, complete with confetti and a small show of fireworks. The final bow was made and the crowd cheered with gratitude for the gypsies' performance. Reluctantly, the crowd dispersed to return to their normal business. One by one the children jumped out of their high perches in trees and on rooftops, then ran off to find something new to occupy their time. The troupe gathered up the performance gear and any loose coins that didn't make it into the collection buckets. Then they headed out of town where their wagons were parked, a small piece of home no matter where on a map they were. They would unload, nibble on a late lunch, and rest a bit before arrangements for dinner would need to be made.

Chapter

The storyteller still wore his blue and green coat as he gathered up his supplies, and any other spare coins the troupe might have missed. As he tied up his remaining pouches of flash powder, one of the troupe's principal dancers strolled up beside him. She wore a long red dress that was snug around the bodice. The skirts were hitched up past both her knees, allowing the dress to twirl and flourish for effect. The high skirt also provided room for her to move freely, show off her balance, and mesmerize onlookers with her clever footwork. Half of her dark hair was pulled up out of her face, while the rest hung in long, tangled curls past her shoulders.

"Fantastic show, Spencer," Her voice fluttered in the air like low flute notes—soft, mesmerizing, and beautiful.

"Your sister wrote the stories, Rosie. You should congratulate her," Rose always congratulated him after a show, and Spencer looked forward to it every time. He thought she was the most beautiful woman he had ever met, and she always looked the most attractive after a show. Hair tangled, skin glistening, cheeks flushed, and her body... he looked away to clear his mind.

Rose crossed her arms at him slightly upset. "True, but you are the one who brings her stories to life. I would think you earned a little credit. Never have I seen a crowd so involved as today. That should mean something, doesn't it?"

Spencer smiled warmly at her, "Coming from you, it means everything."

Rose smiled back just as warmly but quickly looked down to pick at her dress while her feet shuffled.

His smile only grew bigger when he shook his head at her. "Alright, now tell me the rest."

"What do you mean?" Surprise overcame her.

"Every time you come to congratulate me you always follow it up with a list of things that I need to fix."

Rose's eyes widened in protest, "I do not!"

Spencer arched an eyebrow at her.

"I don't always..." She started again only to be distracted by him choking back a laugh.

"Alright, fine." She threw her hands in the air as she started listing things to change for the next performance. "Tricks should be moved to the beginning to draw more people in, and we should put in some comedy before the music. That way the energy stays continuous..." Spencer nodded in turn, mentally noting every suggestion. "... and why did you use different knots for my daring escape? It took me a full minute to get free. You need to stick with the easier knots we always use; I was almost late for my cue."

"Not this time." Rose blinked at his answer. Spencer always listened to her critiques, but never came right out and said 'no' to her.

"Why not?" She was genuinely interested now.

Spencer smiled as he cupped her chin gently with his fingers. "We wouldn't want to make it easy for this beautiful flower."

Rose shook her head free, upset. "Come on now, we're not on stage anymore."

Spencer shrugged, letting out a long sigh, "The new knots take you longer to solve. The longer you struggle and squirm the more suspense it adds for the crowd. If it's too easy the people watching get bored. All in all, it's a better show for the audience."

Rose understood what Spencer said, and was even more annoyed that she agreed with him.

"Well, you could have warned me," She mumbled.

Spencer slung a knapsack over his head and onto his shoulder, grinning at her. "What fun would that be?"

She rolled her eyes at him, but couldn't stop a smile from curving her lips. Whenever Spencer put on his mischievous grin, a playful twinkle touched his eyes that always made Rose swoon. Rose spun gracefully on her heel to turn away from the man. As she walked, Spencer easily kept up with her, stride for stride.

"Rosie, I thought perhaps… since it's still warm for a winter day, you might join me for a picnic in the woods tonight."

"Sounds lovely," she answered honestly. Then she remembered herself, and her tone hardened again. "I'm sorry I can't. I have lessons."

Spencer furrowed his brow and nodded in stern sarcasm, "Right, your lessons. The ones that are so important."

Rose grew defensive, "They are important. Zoe has so much more to teach me."

Spencer rubbed his face with his hands, no longer trying to hide his frustration. "Rosie, you already know how to read the cards. You've done it for Zoe countless times when she wasn't feeling well. You're just as good as her, maybe a little more because you don't just give them the good news. What more could your sister possibly show you?"

Rose paused as she searched for the right words to use. "Things, important things only she knows."

Rose rolled her eyes at her own pathetically unconvincing answer.

"Fine," Spencer shrugged. "Keep your secrets, but do not think for one second I don't know what's going on with you."

A slash of panic cut into Rose. "What's going on with me?" She asked carefully.

"You're avoiding me," Spencer answered obviously.

Rose relaxed a little. "I am not avoiding you. I'm with you right now."

"Every time I try to do something with just the two of us, you always have a lesson to run off to."

"That's not because I'm avoiding you. They are real lessons."

"You don't have to make up excuses for me, Rosie. I get it."

Rose turned serious, "No, you don't."

He stopped abruptly, drawing her attention, and glared skeptically at Rose. She looked away, avoiding his eyes. Rose could see the congregation of wagons not far off in the distance, and wished she was already in her wagon, not having this conversation.

"Maybe I simply do not share the same feelings for you that you obviously have for me," she muttered. It sounded like a confident statement in her head, but in actuality, it came out uncertain and poorly rehearsed.

"There's something you should remember, Rosie," Spencer waited for her to look him in the eye before continuing. "Your prophetic sister is not the only one who can tell when you are lying."

Spencer continued on his walk at his normal pace now, forcing Rose to quicken her step to keep up. There was no chance she was going to allow him to have the last word about this.

"You just have all the answers, don't you?" Rose was angry—angry that Spencer caught her, angry that she had to lie, angry that she did have feelings for him, angry about... so many things.

"Not all of them, but I wish you would trust me with more." His gaze burrowed into Rose as if digging for clues. Rose felt nervous. Spencer did have a remarkable talent for piecing together the truth of things. What scared her was that she wasn't ready for him to know, and it took every bit of power she had to not tell him. She calmed a little when his eyes softened and he smiled sweetly at her. "It's alright, Rosie. I'll let your classes be another one of your secrets, for now."

He veered off in a different direction towards his wagon with a satisfied smile.

Rose couldn't believe it. She hated how easily the man got under her skin. Worst of all, it felt like he could hear her thoughts, begging him to let the issue drop, and he did. He could read her like an open book, and that angered her even more than his smug face.

"You have secrets too, you know," she shouted after him. "Dark, scandalous secrets!"

Spencer waved to her without looking back. "Enjoy your class, Rosie." He called back pleasantly.

Rose balled her fists as she stomped toward her wagon in the opposite direction. Her home was painted a snowy white with dark brown trim. Ordinarily, it would look out of place among all the other brightly colored wagons, except for ornately painted vines that swirled all around the trim, invading onto the sides of the wagon as well. The decorative vines were littered with painted rose blossoms of dark red and creamy white. The personal touch only made the simple white wagon more inviting and special. Hanging on both sides of the door were two planter baskets. One held a small rose bush that bloomed red, the other white. This was the home of the two matriarchs who led the White and Red Troupe, Brizo White and Egiro Red. Everyone in the troupe was used to calling them Zoe White and Rose Red—twin daughters of the first matriarch, and as inseparable as ever. When their mother passed away, they took on the responsibility of the troupe without hesitation. All the performers were happy in their little caravan and proud to have a home with a famous band.

Rose ignored the beauty of the wagon as she stormed through the brown door, slamming it unnecessarily behind her.

Chapter

Rose flopped onto a chair and cradled her head in one of her hands, slowly massaging her temple. On the table next to her was a single candle, and a deck of tarot cards that were well worn on the edges. This was Rose's favorite deck, and most often used. The cards had a softness to them and felt comforting in her hands as she shuffled.

Another woman, the same age as Rose, watched wide-eyed at her dramatic display. The woman sat crossed-legged on a bed that was tucked away in the back corner of the wagon. Her hair was long like Rose's but was so fair it appeared white. Her skin had an unnatural paleness to it and appeared hollow and empty like someone in desperate need of a good meal. When she spoke, her voice was soft and slow like the song of a bird.

"I would love to know the story behind this display."

Rose lifted her head to look at her twin sister, Brizo White. Her annoyed glare betrayed her as Rose's lips curled with amusement. Her sister, Zoe, was always fascinated with stories. She wasn't able to leave her wagon as much as she wished, due to her illness. Instead, she found solace in listening to all the stories among everyone in their troupe, and compile them into a written history of the White and Red Troupe. When that wasn't enough she took pleasure in writing her exciting thoughts into a delicious plot that might end up as a new performance for the next town.

Rose sighed to herself, "It's just Spencer. He, he… that man vexes me!"

"Again?" Zoe looked down to hide her smile.

"He says I'm avoiding him. He thinks these classes are just an excuse I use to not go on a picnic with him."

"Spencer asked you to go on a picnic with him?" Zoe sounded thrilled, but Rose was impervious to any excitement.

"Yeah, he did," she shrugged. "The whole thing is so stupid."

"I'll say. Why are you here and not out with him?"

"Because we have a class, Zoe. A whole lot more rides on this than a picnic with Spencer."

"That depends on how you look at it," Zoe mumbled.

"What?" Rose honed in on her sister.

"What?" Zoe asked back, innocently.

"What did you say?"

"I said, you can go if you would like. We can do this some other time."

Rose stared at the door, toes twitching as she considered her options. For a moment she entertained the idea of leaving the wagon to enjoy a picnic with Spencer. Instead, she shook her head.

"No, if I go now he's going to make a big thing out of it. It will only add to his argument that the classes aren't real, and that's not true." Rose hated to lie to Spencer, even when it was only withholding the truth.

But to do something purposely that would convince him he could be right, well, that was just as bad.

"If that's what you wish," Zoe spread her hands in acceptance. "Remember, you cannot avoid him forever."

Rose rolled her eyes as she shuffled her cards again. "Enough about Spencer. Can we focus on our work?"

Chapter

Zoe mused over Rose's frustration. Her sister was solid as stone, always confident, never rattled by what life threw at her except when she was around Spencer. In Zoe's opinion, Spencer was different than the usual caravan gypsy. He had a past that he took great care to keep secret from everyone, everyone except Brizo White.

Ever since the age of eight, Zoe was able to see things about people. Each person she met would be accompanied by small visions that gave away information about them. People in love would have a trail of hearts following them, and flames for those who were angry. When Zoe looked at Spencer she saw a glistening sword with a red banner flowing behind him on a phantom breeze. This vision seemed odd for Zoe. When Spencer joined the troupe, ten years ago, he refused to touch a sword. He even shunned the blunt wooden prop swords used for practice and performances. Luckily, he had a silvery voice that commanded the attention of everyone which made him perfect as a storyteller and eventually the director of their shows. He was able to make people hang on to his every word, convinced that what he would say next would be brilliant. A talent that came a bit too easily to him, in Zoe's opinion. Without a doubt, she knew Spencer's past was an interesting story, but she chose to leave him to his secrets, as she had her hidden secrets as well.

By the time Zoe turned twelve, her visions became more detailed. She was able to see each individual's future in a way no other fortune teller ever could. At first, Zoe was terrified by what she would see, but her mother insisted it was a gift. Zoe was convinced that learning how to control her gift would give her the chance to use her power to help favorably shape people's destinies. At least, that was what her mother convinced her she would be able to do. At the mature age of nineteen, Zoe's visions grew larger and more intense, concerning major events, and would come unsolicited to Zoe at random. All the members of the troupe had come to know Zoe as a seer of the future, and everything she saw would always come to pass.

The gift was a family trait, passed on to the firstborn child of the gift bearer. Zoe and Rose's mother also wielded this power. She passed on as much knowledge as she could to Zoe concerning her powers and its possibilities. The most valuable piece of information was a warning. Their mother warned them of evil, power-hungry tyrants who would give anything to have a visionary in their control. What better way to ensure their fortunes and successes to amass more prestige in the world! This is why their mother started the White and Red Troupe, so they would never be in one place for too long, thus protecting her and her daughters from any covetous eyes. When their mother grew ill and passed on, Zoe took Rose's hand and made a vow.

"We will never leave each other. You will never be alone," Zoe promised.

"Never, as long as we live, I will be there for you," Rose promised, just as sincerely.

Zoe had come to balance all these kinds of visions and her own life rather well. She worked hard not to think about what she saw for too long. After all, the visions were about other people's lives and rarely concerned her. Then, a couple of months ago, one of her visions kept returning to her over and over again—a vision that was meant specifically for her.

The first time she saw it, she was sitting in her wagon one night, enjoying her evening tea, when she started to remember what life was like when she and her sister were little and her mom was still alive. Every night the two of them would make up stories by the warmth of the stove while their mom sat in her rocking chair, usually working on something in her lap. But what Zoe saw was not a memory—it was a vision.

Rose and Zoe were sitting around the wagon stove enjoying a warm, delicious dinner; while their mother sat in a chair nearby, knitting. Zoe had successfully scarfed down everything in her bowl to move on to the delicious cookies Mom had made for them earlier. While Rose was still munching on vegetables, Zoe had the entire tray of cookies on her lap and was already working on her second and third cookie in her hands. Jealously, Rose asked for some cookies too only to have Zoe scream angrily at her sister that they were all for her. Their mother's happy attitude grew very serious as she spoke to her little girls.

"What one has, the other must also," the older woman spoke in a loving but firm voice.

Then the woman turned and spoke to Zoe directly, eyes intense and all gaiety stripped from her face.

"Don't you ever forget: What one has, the other must also."

Her mother's voice boomed as the stove went cold, and the wagon grew dark and ominous. Zoe instinctively looked to her sister for some kind of comfort but found none. Rose sat with her arms folded and a satisfied smile on her face, completely oblivious to the change in the room. Zoe looked back to her mother but found her chair empty. An unsettling chill ran up her spine when she tried to make sense of what was happening. Instantly Zoe doubled over as a sharp pain pierced her side from the inside. She breathed deeply hoping to soothe her discomfort, but every breath only worsened the pain. It spread throughout her middle and down her legs. She called out in agony when she crumpled to the floor. Rose continued to exist in her own world where everything was fine. The pain finally overtook Zoe, allowing her one piercing scream before all went black and it was over.

The vision terrified Zoe. Her mother had spoken those exact words to them so many times, but never so intensely as in her vision. And never has she felt so much pain and despair in her visions that affected her directly. The words were never spoken directly, but she had seen enough visions to know two things: she needed to teach Rose how to use the gift of prophecy and far more terrifying, what would happen if she continued to use her own.

Chapter 6

Rose regarded Zoe as she shuffled her cards. At first, Rose was a little jealous of her sister. She had never seen anything special about anyone the way Zoe could, aside from the random tarot reading she tried on a stranger that happened to be true, Rose didn't have any prophetic visions. Her mother sat her down one day and assured her that the gift was inside her as well. Rose was told not to worry about the matter because, with time, her gift will manifest itself. Later, their mother passed away due to a tragic accident, and the only comfort Rose could find was from Zoe.

Almost immediately after their mother was gone, Zoe also grew more and more sickly. The stronger Zoe grew in her gift, the more tired she became. Over the next decade, Zoe became weaker and weaker, until the day when she stopped wanting to leave her wagon altogether. Venturing outside for a stroll was more of the main event than a casual thing to pass the time. Rose was sad when Zoe stopped performing in the troupe's plays and was even more heartbroken when her sister no longer risked heading out to even watch the troupe perform the very stories she worked so hard to write. Writing was what made her happy anyway, Rose reminded herself. It kept Zoe's mind focused and gave meaning to her life. Instead of just being the sickly matriarch, she was a vital part of each performance that ensured the success of the White and Red Troupe. And, from what Rose could tell, her sister was happy with the arrangement.

As for Rose, she was happy to not have her gift yet, especially if it meant sacrificing her health and life. Rose busied herself with taking care of Zoe, making sure she didn't overexert herself and making sure she had everything she ever needed. One thing Rose insisted on was her sister having enough rest. So when Zoe would drift to sleep, Rose would quietly sneak off to attend to other duties. She would be found developing a new trick with her knives, talking with Spencer about how to upgrade their performances, or helping other members of the troupe with their own families, among other things that required her attention. On those rare days that everything seemed to be taken care of already, she would eagerly disappear into the woods. Rose delighted in tracking the animals, climbing the rocks, swimming in the pools of water, and any other adventurous thing she could think of. They were all welcome distractions that provided relief from the constant worry she had for her sister. All in all, she was satisfied with her life.

Rose knew the exact day her active, satisfying life was disrupted. It was when Zoe had a vision that disturbed her, and insisted she taught Rose how to use her gift. Since then, Rose and Zoe had spent much of their free time working together to jumpstart her gift. Most of their time was spent sitting at the table while Rose casually shuffled and laid out her cards over and over, hoping to trigger something inside.

Zoe encouraged Rose to use her cards, much to Rose's relief. Rose was comfortable with her tarot cards. She had done so many readings since she was a little girl, that she was able to use and interpret them very well. It was a — small skill she was happy to remind her sister about, from time to time. More often than not, a childish squabble would end with Zoe shouting at Rose that her gift of prophecy meant she would always know the outcome of the argument, so she would always win. To that Rose would confidently shout back that the cards never lied, and were just as prophetic as any of her sister's visions. Rose knew her talent with fortune-telling would never compare to Zoe's gift of prophecy. But there had been times when Rose's readings were so intuitive that even Zoe would rub her chin in thought. So when the time came to try to spark some kind of gift in Rose, her sister insisted she used her cards as an outlet.

Chapter

Rose closed her eyes after cutting the deck, took a deep breath, and tried to focus.

"Clear your mind," Zoe calmly spoke to her sister. "Get rid of every thought except for the one question you want to be answered."

None of this was new. Rose always started this way before reading the cards for anyone. She imagined using her gift would need to be done the same way, or at least starting out the same way. Rose focused harder, almost in a strain of desperation that today would finally be the day. Nothing came. All she saw were flashes of nothing.

"Maybe you're trying to ask a question that's too complex. What's your question?"

"I was only trying to see what's for dinner tomorrow. I didn't think that was too complex."

Rose rubbed her stomach in distress as it rumbled loudly. She was hungry, and the smell of stew on the stove was only making it worse.

Zoe smiled as she filled a wooden bowl to the brim for her sister, then filled another bowl for herself. She sat down across from Rose.

"No, dinner for tomorrow is not too hard of a question, but I wonder if it's not powerful enough either. What you eat tomorrow doesn't matter, whether it's fish or rabbit. Something a bit closer to home might help. Something deep, and important only to you. Something you would do anything to know the answer to."

Rose looked around the wagon as if an appropriate question was written on the walls for her to choose from. Then it struck her. There was one question she never allowed herself to dwell on because she never thought it was possible.

"Okay, I think I have one. Deep breaths, clearing my mind, and focus on my question."

Rose mindlessly shuffled twice, cut the deck, and began to deal the cards. Her mind was a black space void of thought when she heard a soft voice whisper in her mind.

"*Will I ever find true love?*" The whisper echoed softly in the empty space repeating over and over, gradually getting louder each time. The echoes layered on top of each other, bouncing off of every word, turning her simple question into an uproar of voices demanding answers. At the precise moment, Rose didn't think she could bear the noise any longer, all went silent and the darkness was gone.

Rose looked around and found herself standing on top of a hill. One by one, various soldiers materialized around her in the middle of a gruesome battle. Fear overcame her when a swinging mace barely grazed the top of her head causing her to duck instinctively. Rose let out a small shriek as she rolled away from the fight as best as she could. Then a familiar voice caught her attention. Spencer stood a few yards away from her. Only, he didn't look like the Spencer she knew. He was clad from head to toe in sturdy armor and chainmail with dark red paint splotched all over it. In one hand he held a battle hatchet and in the other, he wielded a heavy, broad sword with the letter 'M' engraved on it. He shouted her name in desperation!

"Rose, get out of here! It's too dangerous!"

"Never!" she called back, "I'm not leaving your side!"

"Don't argue with me, Woman! Run for-!"

Rose froze in terror when the next thing she saw was Spencer being stabbed in the chest

and falling lifelessly to the ground. She screamed in pure agony as the world around her, once again, dissolved into darkness.

Rose flinched at the sight of Zoe eating her stew across from her. Zoe watched Rose carefully, then glanced at the cards that were dealt. One card glared obviously at Zoe. It had two people standing with a glorious cupid leering above them: the Lovers.

"Did you see something? Or feel something? Did it work?" Zoe softly pried.

Rose blinked as she looked around. She was back in the wagon, complete with smells of stew and a warm stove. She was unaware of the cards that were dealt as she looked at her sister.

"I'm not sure. I think I saw something… a glimpse, maybe." She looked down at the cards, and immediately recognized the two lovers facing her. Rose swept them up in one fluid, easy movement with her hands returning them to the deck. "It all happened so fast."

Zoe arched an eyebrow at her sister with concern. Rose swallowed a spoonful of stew, nervously wondering if there was a way her sister had seen the same vision as she had. She dismissed that notion, realizing there would be no reason for Zoe to ask about the vision if she could see it herself.

Zoe spoke smoothly, ignoring Rose's discomfort. "If you saw something, even a glimpse; that's still something. You're starting to use your gift." Zoe smiled with pride for her sister.

"Not very well." Rose shrugged, trying to erase the vision from her mind.

"Nonsense, our gift is just like any other muscle in our body. The more you use it the stronger it will get."

"Then stop using your gift. If you're not prophesying then you can't get any worse," Rose begged.

Zoe looked ashamed. "My gift is a part of me. Asking me not to use it would be the same as asking me not to breathe. Besides, my gift and my path are linked; I cannot turn back now."

Rose's eyes grew wide. She was not ready to lose her sister, nor was she ready for her vision to come true. Rose rubbed her face and shook her head, trying to shake off her troubles.

"I think that's enough of your lesson for one day." Rose stretched as she gathered up the bowls to wash and Zoe grabbed a towel to dry. "It's time to get some fresh air."

"Yes, I believe you're right," Zoe agreed as she dried off a bowl. "Please, try not to be out too late."

"I won't because you're coming with me."

Zoe dropped the bowl in surprise. "Excuse me?"

Rose picked up the bowl and handed it back to Zoe. "You have been in this wagon all day. It is still fairly warm, and there is plenty of light. You will be fine. We are going for a walk in the woods."

"Rose, you know I can't. I need to build up my strength…"

Rose cut her off, "*What one has the other must also.* Mother's words are for both of us. You want me to tap into my gift, then you need to be a part of my life too. No negotiation."

Zoe rolled her eyes at her sister. "Let me put a few more layers on."

Chapter 8

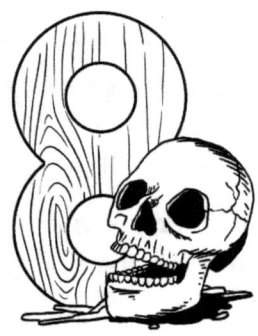

The afternoon turned frigid quickly once the clouds curled their way around the sun, blocking its warm rays from the women. By the time they made it back to the caravan, occasional flakes of snow started to dot the air around them. And when their soup was warming up over a freshly stoked fire, the flakes had turned into thick clumps of cottony white that easily cloaked the wagons in a soft blanket of winter. The snow was no concern for the two sisters. They knew winter was upon them, and preparations had already been made to keep the troupe warm and fed for the season.

The white-and-red-flowered wagon was cozy that night. Zoe was bundled up in her blankets telling her sister Rose a story while watching her cook. Occasionally Rose would interject with interesting plot twists, or humorous answers the characters had to say. Rose loved complicating her sister's story to keep things interesting. Rose's interruptions never bothered Zoe. She would continue smoothly, turning the many complications into a successfully entertaining tale. This was a fairly common routine for the two when they weren't weighed down by important matters of the troupe. It was a game their mother taught them long back when they were little. The game would draw the entire family together, and a feeling of love and unity would always follow. Those were happy times that the girls held onto, and insisted on continuing after the loss of their mother.

The night was like any other night for Rose and Zoe as they slurped their soups eagerly. Then, their dinner was disturbed by a timid knock at their door.

Zoe looked at Rose surprised, and a bit intrigued by the distraction. "Are you expecting anyone?"

Rose couldn't deny a dark feeling growing inside her. She glared at the door and tensed as if something dangerous lurked behind it.

"No." She spoke slowly while she considered countless options regarding who it could be. She inched toward the door while her fingers touched a knife hidden behind her back. Her heart raced. It was only a common knock at the door, but Rose felt uncontrollably uneasy. She grabbed the latch and was grateful for something sturdy to control the shake in her hand. Her heart beat even louder when she mustered her courage and threw open the door.

What they saw caused both grown women to gasp in fear. Rose instinctively stepped in front of Zoe.

Zoe ducked under her blankets squeaking, "It's a bear!"

Huddled at the bottom of the doorsteps was a large mass of brown fur with snow frosted all over it. Rose waited for the heap of fur to move in some way, but it remained still. Her nerves had settled, and she was confident enough to approach their visitor even if it was a bear. Slowly, cautiously, she reached out her hand to the beast. The fur was cold, wet, and not at all what Rose expected. She grabbed a handful of fur and pulled. Rose was relieved to find out it was only a bearskin cloak.

The cloak revealed nothing but bones, and a skeleton face bleached white. No eyes, no organs, only a simple skeleton you would expect to find dried up in an old tomb somewhere. Rose leaned in closer and jumped when the head abruptly turned around to face her. The eyeless glare bore deep into Rose's soul, terrifying her, but also inviting her to come closer.

"*Egeiro,*" It hissed.

Rose felt a connection with the skeleton, although that was absurd. She had never seen it or heard its voice before now, but she knew she was linked to it somehow.

Almost in direct confirmation, the skeleton spoke again. "*You know my name. Say my name.*"

Rose yelped, dropping the cloak from her hand, not believing what she just witnessed. She covered her ears, shaking her head, refusing to hear any more from him. She saw the skeleton's bones shake with joy as it started to laugh. Rose trembled when she could still hear the skeleton's laugh in her mind.

"Rose, what is it?" Zoe had come out from under her blankets and placed a concerned hand on Rose's shoulder.

Rose jumped at her sister's touch, then looked back at the shapeless form in front of their door. This time, what she saw was much different. The bearskin cloak remained the same but underneath was a man with coppery skin, short dark hair, and a small scruff that prickled around his face. Confused, Rose cautiously bent over and touched the man's face to confirm he was not the skeleton she saw earlier. He was very much real; his skin was warm but only slightly. Her fingers felt down to his neck to check for a pulse.

Zoe gasped at the sight of the man underneath the layers of furs. "Is he alive?"

"Barely, I'll need your help to get him inside."

The two women strained under the weight of the massive man. Rose was grateful for his short stature because a taller man would have been much heavier. They dragged and tugged the limp body until he was positioned directly in front of the stove. Rose took his bearskin along with several layers of jackets to the other side of the wagon. She easily brushed off the snow and laid them out to dry from the weather. Zoe burned some herbs for the man to breathe in as he slept, and put on a kettle of water to warm. Rose thought she saw Zoe gaze thoughtfully at him.

"Who do you suppose he is, Zoe?" Rose asked.

Zoe furrowed her brow. "I don't know."

Rose dropped what she was doing to direct her full attention to her sister. "What?"

"I honestly don't know."

"How can that be? You can always get a read on someone."

"I know!" Zoe sounded a bit upset that she couldn't do something as simple as an aura read, something she had been doing since she was eight. "Every time I think I see something, it gets fuzzy and shifts into something else that eventually blurs out into another blur! Nothing is definite."

"Has that ever happened before?" Rose asked.

"Never," Zoe sighed as she combed the man's hair out of his face with her fingers. "The only thing I can tell you is: he is important."

Rose moved to stand next to her sister in comfort and took the opportunity to stare scrupulously at the man. "Important how?"

"I don't know, I just have a feeling." She looked up at Rose. "Don't you?"

"I feel…" Rose's words trailed off. She froze in discomfort when the image of the laughing skeleton invaded her mind. She pushed it away just as abruptly. "I feel like we need to be careful with this guy."

Zoe nodded in agreement as a soft moan left the man's lips. He squeezed his eyes tight then opened them wide at the sight of two women hovering over him.

"Am I dead?" he whispered. The two sisters exchanged glances. Zoe smirked. Rose was unimpressed.

"If not for us, you would be," Rose answered.

The man slowly sat up. "Well, thank you for your kindness, ladies, but I really should be on my way."

"In the middle of the night, in your condition?" Zoe spoke calmly. "Not likely. What you need is rest."

Rose stared down at their guest, "Yeah, and just what were you doing out in a snowstorm anyway?"

"Rose!" Zoe hushed her sister and gave her a firm look.

"I'm looking for someone." The man answered reluctantly.

"Who?" Rose insisted. The man glanced back at Rose angrily before masking it with a practiced smile.

"Someone who can help me," he answered.

"We can help," Zoe persisted. "We have already saved your life. What more do you need?"

The man smiled at Zoe before answering. "You are very nice to offer, but I can take care of myself."

He tried to stand but dizziness took over and he fell back to the floor with a loud thud.

Rose laughed, "How? You can barely stand up!"

Zoe wouldn't relent, "This really is the best place you can be right now. Our troupe has some of the best healers in the nation."

"Troupe?" the man asked.

"Yes," Zoe confirmed. "You are among the White and Red Troupe. My name is Brizo White, and this is my sister Egeiro Red. But, everyone here calls us Zoe and Rose."

The man's face was locked with surprise, or was it relief, Rose couldn't quite tell.

"You're Brizo White?" He asked.

Zoe blushed, "Yes I am."

"And you want to help me?" His voice shook with disbelief.

"Yes I do," Zoe smiled.

The man gave a wary glance at Rose then smiled back at Zoe. "I suppose I could stay until I'm a little better."

Zoe beamed, "Excellent, let me get you a bowl of soup."

Zoe eagerly eased herself up to grab a bowl of soup, while Rose settled down beside him. She was emotionless, calculating, and full of questions.

"Who are you?"

The man stretched out his hands in front of the stove to warm them.

"My name is Lee."

"And how did you come upon our caravan… Lee?" She tried his name out on her tongue. It didn't sound right. She knew he was lying, but there were other questions to be answered.

Zoe appeared with a warm bowl of soup wrapped in a towel. Lee took it eagerly. He paused, just long enough to savor the aroma, then ate a heaping spoonful.

"Mmm, this is delicious," he nodded toward Zoe, 'Did you make this?"

"No, Rose did," Zoe's shoulders sagged noticeably as she looked away from him. Lee nodded his appreciation to Rose then turned back to Zoe.

"Well, you were the one who offered me some, that makes it extra special."

Zoe blushed. Rose couldn't believe how her sister was acting. She was being far too welcoming for a mere stranger at her door. All Rose wanted was a little caution from the great Brizo White .

"Do I taste a hint of cinnamon?" Lee asked, peering at Zoe through his heavily veiled eyes.

"No," Rose answered sharply.

"Yes," Zoe answered at the same time as her sister. Rose turned toward Zoe with surprise painted on her face. "I added some to the bowl because I think it tastes better."

"Too much spice is not good for you, sister," Rose pleaded. Zoe and Lee ignored her entirely.

"I knew it tasted wonderful because of you." The two of them laughed quietly together, while Rose was getting a headache just being in the same room as them.

She tried to change the subject. "Why don't you tell us where you're from?"

Lee decided to answer Rose, only after seeing genuine interest from Zoe as well. "I'm from here, meaning Marconia. But I'm not from anywhere in particular. I tend to move around a lot."

"That sounds so lonely," Zoe whispered to herself. The sadness in her voice was not overlooked by Rose who looked contemplatively at her sister.

"You know, Zoe, I think it's past time for your evening cup of tea. Remember what happens when you skip it?"

"What happens when you skip it?" Lee asked innocently.

Rose looked back at him seriously, but Zoe gave him a nonchalant smile.

"It helps me sleep." Zoe shook her head dismissively. "It's alright. I'll be right back."

Zoe went to the back of the wagon. In a matter of minutes, she was expertly grinding up dried herbs in a stone bowl. Rose turned back to Lee and decided to toss out all formalities.

"Exactly what are you doing?" She asked in a hushed voice, so only Lee could hear.

"Doing? I'm not doing anything?" He answered ridiculously.

"You are flirting with my sister!"

"Is that what I'm doing?" Lee pretended to be ignorant.

Rose gritted her teeth as she struggled to speak quietly. "You better start speaking plainly, or I swear I will use all my gypsy knowledge to curse you in so many ways."

"What if I don't believe all your hocus pocus?"

Rose leaned in closer, glaring at him as if he were an insect. "You strike me as the kind of person who does."

Lee sighed, "I'm already cursed. I doubt there is much more you can do to make my life any worse."

Rose eased up, only slightly, when she heard the sincerity in his last answer. "You underestimate me," she spoke plainly.

Lee shifted as he looked away from Rose. The woman held her ground silently demanding him to speak.

"Perhaps I do have a special interest in your sister," he admitted.

Rose was still suspicious of the man. He was hiding something from them, and his secrets gnawed at her. "Back off, you are not Zoe's type."

Lee simply winked at her with a boyish grin, "Maybe, but she could be mine."

"You conceded, selfish, overconfident…"

"Tea?" Zoe appeared with a tray of cups and a bright smile just for Lee.

"Oh, not for me, thank you," Lee answered politely. "Tea is too bitter for my taste."

Zoe's smile dimmed, "But this blend is on the sweet side, and I brought plenty of sugar."

Rose interjected, "Zoe, he says he doesn't like tea. Maybe he could…"

"I suppose if it helps with your nightmares, it can help with mine as well," Lee spoke over Rose as he gave Zoe a warm smile. Zoe smiled back, relieved, and then blushed while pouring him a cup. Lee faced Rose triumphantly. "I wouldn't want to be rude to such a generous hostess."

"Do you have trouble sleeping too?" Zoe asked as politely as possible.

"Yes, I tend to have… nightmares," his cheeks flushed with embarrassment.

Zoe spoke softly to Lee. "What kind of nightmares do you have?"

Lee hesitated for a moment, "Just faces. They might be memories. I'm not sure entirely, but I haven't slept well since they started."

"When did they start?" Zoe asked.

Lee smiled and answered a little too confidently, "About ten years ago."

"I'm so sorry," Zoe handed Lee a cup of tea.

Rose simply scowled at him. If she could make him disappear with her stare, he would have been gone by now. Instead, Rose settled on asking him more questions. "So Lee where are you from, and where were you headed?"

"I come from all over Marconia. I grew up here and have seen almost all of it." Lee's face turned serious. "I always plan on leaving the borders of Marconia, but something keeps pulling me here. I suppose because it's my home it's too painful to leave."

"Well, don't you worry," Rose feigned compassion. "When you are feeling better there are some nice cities nearby. I'm sure you can-"

"I cannot afford anything in the cities," Lee looked pointedly at Rose, "cursed, remember?"

"Never mind your money." Zoe dismissed the tension in the room. "You are welcome to stay with us as long as you need. Assuming you are willing to help with the work, of course."

"I would love that, thank you," he nodded to Zoe with appreciation.

Rose was beside herself. Never had she felt so ignored by her sister until now, and she couldn't take it anymore.

"Zoe, will you come to speak with me alone, right now?" Rose didn't give her sister a chance to respond as she grabbed Zoe's arm. She pried her sister away from Lee and pushed her to the other side of the wagon. Once out of earshot, Rose scolded Zoe in a sharp whisper. "I've changed my mind. He can't stay here!"

"Why not?" Zoe asked, softly with no aggression whatsoever.

"What do we know about this guy anyway? I know we are supposed to be compassionate to strangers, but this is going a bit too far, don't you think? What if he's dangerous?"

Zoe looked at her sister curiously. "Is there something you're not telling me? Have *you* seen anything?"

Rose blinked awkwardly at her sister. She wasn't sure if she was being mocked for her inability or if she was genuinely interested that Rose could have seen something. Either way, Rose did not feel comfortable telling anyone about the skeleton, or whatever it was that she thought she saw. They were always told that death was a dark, perilous part of the gift and they should never be tempted to venture in that direction. She didn't want to see it, but it was there and it recognized her. Rose's recollection made her shiver with worry.

"No, it's only a feeling," She lied. "This man just feels like bad news."

"Interesting," Zoe continued to study her sister. "The feeling I get around him is nothing but good. This man is important, and he needs to be here with us."

"So, what I say doesn't matter!" Rose threw up her hands in frustration. "You're the expert here, so it's your opinion we will be following?"

Zoe put a hand on her sister's shoulder. "Calm down, I didn't say that." Rose took a breath to contain her anger. "It's interesting that we have two completely different feelings. I always thought if your gift started to manifest it would just confirm everything I would see. Are you sure there isn't something you're not telling me?"

Rose decided not to risk lying again, instead she pursed her lips. She peered at her sister expectantly, wishing she had some kind of solution to all of this.

Zoe's eyes searched in front of her as she pondered the issue. "When it is all said and done, sending him away will only go against my instinct. We both know what happens when we don't listen to our instincts." Both women nodded in acceptance, a grave seriousness overcame them as they remembered their hard lesson concerning the matter. "But we cannot ignore your worries either, or something worse might happen."

Rose was relieved her sister finally believed her and was starting to act like herself again. Zoe continued with the solution.

"The best place to watch an enemy is in plain sight. And what plainer place could there be than right here with us? It will be easier for you to keep an eye on him." Zoe emphasized, "As for me, I will have more time to verify my suspicions, and piece together what his role is concerning us. In the end, he needs to be here."

"Fine," Rose grumbled, arms crossed and defensive. "But he's not staying *here*. I will find someone he can bunk with." Rose half expected her sister to argue that as well. Instead, Zoe nodded.

"That may be for the best." Zoe agreed. "We wouldn't want you murdering him in his sleep due to a bit of flirting on my behalf."

Rose looked at her sister with surprise. She thought Zoe was allowing herself to be played by this man; instead, she was encouraging it. Rose relaxed a little, apparently Zoe was already playing her own little game.

"You shouldn't be giving me any ideas, sis." She allowed a small smile to show she understood.

Zoe turned back to talk to Lee, all smiles and excitement. "It's settled, you will stay with our troupe. Rose has even offered to find you a more comfortable place to stay during your visit."

Lee responded graciously toward Rose, "That is very kind. Honestly, thank you." He sounded pleasant enough, but the look in his eyes mocked Rose with his obvious victory over her.

Rose nodded emotionless at the stranger, simply running through the motions of protocol and generosity, even if was forced.

Zoe topped off Lee's cup of tea. "So Lee, why don't you tell me about your travels? Is there anything of interest you have seen?"

"Sadly no, my travels have been tiresome and melancholic. I had hoped to hear more about you and your troupe. I'm sure you have many exciting tales to tell."

The two began a long conversation about everything and nothing, complete with smiles and flirtatious glances. Rose wanted nothing to do with them. She needed to be somewhere, *anywhere*, but there. The two didn't skip a beat when Rose threw a heavy jacket over her shoulders to leave the wagon in search of a place for Lee to stay. She slammed the door shut, eager for the empty quiet of the snow that lay outside. But the wintery peace was not in the cards for her tonight. The frigid cold turned her thoughts to the bone-chilling laugh of the skeleton. No, she corrected herself with a shudder, it was the laugh of Death rattling around in her head.

Chapter

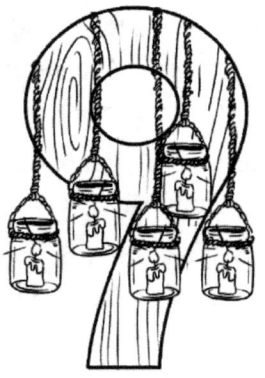

Rose banged on the door of a bright green carriage with dark blue cloudlike swirls painted all over the molding. It was a rather simple decoration by comparison to the other wagons nearby, but it suited Spencer perfectly. He always seemed to save his creative flair for the stage. The door cracked open just enough for Spencer to peek outside.

"Rosie," his voice was always kind when he spoke to her. Spencer opened the door a bit more, so she could see his entire face cemented with concern. "It's late."

"I need your help," Rose uttered quickly. He studied her while waiting for Rose to tell him more. "Can, um... can we discuss this inside?"

Spencer's eyes twinkled as he opened his door the rest of the way, inviting her in. Rose hated how his eyes twinkled like that. His face always remained stoic and hard, but when his eyes lit up they captivated her in a way that forced her to smile. All right, she didn't hate it. She *loved* it when his eyes brightened towards her. What she hated was how much control it had over her. At times that small look would cause her to forget everything she had been meaning to say to him. Other times a glance like that, even from afar, made her feel warm and her heart flutter.

Rose needed to keep her wits for this. She specifically avoided eye contact with him, but it didn't help. His handsome face with a smooth grin invaded her mind. That very look he only reserved for her. The door closed with a loud thud leaving the interior lit by numerous candles glowing in jars that hung from the roof like tiny chandeliers. Rose admitted it was a clever idea, and just as beautiful. She loved seeing every jar lit like this although she would never tell him openly. He casually leaned against a chest of drawers with his arms folded, waiting patiently for Rose to tell him what was happening.

"There's a stranger in our camp," she began. "He calls himself Lee. There was a knock on our door and there he was, half dead. Zoe offered him a place here until he felt better, but there's something about him I don't trust. I tried to find out details, simple things like where he's from or what he does, but he just calls himself a wanderer."

"So, you would need me to…" Spencer was waiting for her to ask the favor she needed from him.

"Can he stay with you for a few days until he's able to move on?" Rose said a little too rushed.

"No."

Rose threw away all pleasantries and spoke bluntly. "Come on, he's almost frozen, hasn't eaten in days, exhausted, and he needs our help."

"You just said you don't trust the man," Spencer pointed out.

"True," Rose admitted, "but it is still our way. We never turn away those in need."

"Let him stay with you then," Spencer shrugged at the obvious solution.

"Are you crazy? There's no room for all three of us in that little wagon. And I'm sorry, I do not want him around my sister any longer than needed. She keeps staring at him as if he were someone important, and he…. Ugh! The way he makes her laugh, and smile… no, he cannot stay with us."

"You don't want your sister smiling and laughing?" Spencer was having a hard time piecing together what Rose was saying.

Rose turned a dark glare on Spencer, "This guy is a little too smooth to trust. He's confident and flirty, and he already has Zoe wrapped around his little finger. I don't want him around her any more than he has to be."

Spencer nodded his understanding, "How about he stay with anyone else, then?"

"No, it has to be you. You're the only one I trust to keep a sharp enough eye on him," she stated.

Spencer's shoulders dropped, "Why is it, whenever you need a favor, you always look to me."

"I do not. There are plenty of other people I look to for help." Rose was trying not to be insulted.

"Really?" Spencer was surprised, "Name one."

Rose panicked as her mind fumbled for a name.

She stuttered for a moment then uttered, rather hesitantly, "Garrett."

It was the first name she could think of. He was no one of real consequence to her. Garrett was just another member of the troop, but she knew by Spencer's darkened mood that she should have named someone else.

"That oaf?" Spencer scoffed. "You wouldn't ask him for the time of day out of fear that he would mistake it for a confession of love."

"That's not true," Rose argued more confidently. "Just last week I asked him to hand out fliers announcing our show."

"That does not count," Spencer stated. "He has had that job for a while now. And I recall you saying you gave him that job just so you could avoid him for a day."

Rose took in an offended gasp, "I gave him that job because he is good at it. The townspeople love him!"

The room went silent, and Rose knew she said the wrong thing by the look Spencer fixed on her.

"What did you just say?" Spencer whispered with disbelief.

Rose looked away, embarrassed, then mumbled, "The townspeople love him."

"No," Spencer answered with forced restraint. He was angry and Rose knew it. "The villagers love me. I'm the one they come to see."

"They come because Garrett gathers them up for you," Rose countered.

"And, I'm the one who *keeps* their attention." Spencer was shouting now. "It's a harder job than you think, Rosie. But if you think the villagers love Garrett so much, then why don't you make him the lead storyteller?"

"Maybe I will," Rose shouted back.

"Oh please, Rosie. You know he wouldn't last one minute on that stage. You cannot trust that guy with such important responsibilities! The harder he tries to please you, the worse he messes things up. There's no comparison here!"

Rose crossed her arms in satisfaction, "So, Lee can stay with you then?"

Spencer held a finger up to Rose, "Except that." He turned around and flopped down on a chair in the corner of his wagon.

"But you just said…" Rose started, but was interrupted by Spencer.

"You tricked me to get the answer you wanted to hear. If you have to cheat, then my answer is still no," Spencer lectured.

Rose should have known he would say something like that. Over the years Rose had perfected the technique of wordplay for things to go her way. It was a trick she learned from her mother and had served her well. No one seemed to realize they were being played, except Spencer. He picked up on her tricks rather easily. Spencer never misses a thing. But because they were friends he had no problem calling her out, which both impressed and infuriated her.

"I tricked you because this is important, Spence. Zoe may have a good feeling about this guy, but I have a bad one. There's something off about him."

Spencer was quiet for a moment in thought, then a smile formed on his lips. "So, this is really important to you?"

"I believe that's what I just said," Rose answered.

"And you immediately thought to come to me," he reiterated.

Rose sighed with relief, glad he finally understood, "Yes Spence, I know I can trust you."

Spencer's smile grew wider, and his eyes turned mischievous, "Goodness, Rosie. If only there was a specific word that is commonly used to express how you are feeling towards me, right now."

Rose folded her arms across her chest, unimpressed, "Contempt?"

Spencer shook his head in surrender, "I love you too, Rosie."

Rose spoke calmly but was having a hard time keeping cool. "Please focus, Spencer. I just know we would all be safer if he was staying with you. Nothing escapes you, so he won't be able to trick us out of anything. Besides, we both know you have plenty of room in here for someone else."

"For someone else, no. But I always have room for you," he spoke softly.

Rose tried not to blush, "If you have enough room for me, then there will be plenty of room for someone else."

Spencer gave her a shrewd smile, "No there won't. Think about it, exactly how many late nights do you spend in this wagon?"

Rose's eyes narrowed, "I don't like what you're implying, Spencer."

Spencer was the perfect example of calm, "I'm not implying anything. You come up with a lot of excuses to find your way over here, all in the name of your sister's privacy. Now, how's that going to work if a third person is taking up some space?"

Rose rolled her eyes, "OK, yes! I spend a lot of time here. That's not so surprising. You're the lead storyteller who organizes our shows and I'm one of the matriarchs who makes all the arrangements for you to perform your shows. We work very closely together with a lot of late nights."

"That may be how it starts, but how it ends…"

"Stop!" Rose cut him off abruptly.

It was no mystery what Spencer felt for Rose. She knew it, he knew it, and everyone in the troupe knew it. Other men her age had long since avoided her because they always figured the two of them were together. The few who knew the truth still avoided Rose because they were too scared of what Spencer might do if they made a move. If Rose was being entirely honest with herself, she had to admit she enjoyed those late nights with Spencer. It was the only time, aside from being alone in the forest, when she felt like herself — not a matriarch, not a caregiver for her sister, not the one who had to have all the answers and resolutions for every problem, just herself. When it all was weighed out, she didn't have the luxury to be just herself very often. Too many people needed her attention and help. To entertain the idea of a relationship, along with all the other responsibilities she had to manage, just wouldn't be fair to either of them.

Rose calmed her voice and tried to be serious with him. "Look, I know this stranger won't want to try anything with you looking over his shoulder. And if he does, I trust you will be able to stop him from harming anyone."

Spencer blinked at her. "You may not have noticed, because you're so busy keeping an eye on Garrett, but I don't use swords. I'm not exactly the best choice to have as your protector." The words seemed uncharacteristically hard for Spencer to say. Instead of wondering about it, Rose simply allowed a small amount of sympathy for the man.

"I have noticed, and I know you are the most capable man in this troupe to take on this responsibility, even without a sword."

An easy smile touched his lips. Spencer got up to move closer to Rose. He towered almost a head above her as he looked down into her eyes. Rose had to tilt her neck back to stare defiantly at him. He caressed her chin with his fingers.

"So you *do* take the time to notice me," he whispered.

Rose drew in a deep breath, allowing him to remain close a moment longer.

"So, that's a yes then?"

Her smile was small but full of pride, knowing he would agree.

"Of course," he answered.

Seeing that sparkle in his eyes was too much, so Rose turned to head for the door.

"But, what exactly do I get out of this?" He called after her.

Rose turned around sharply and slightly offended. "My heartfelt gratitude should be enough."

"Afraid I'm going to need a bit more than that," He eyed her hungrily.

"You know, Garrett would do this out of the kindness of his heart."

"Garrett would offer you his left arm in exchange for a lock of your hair," Spencer snarked.

"That's what gentlemen do," Rose quipped.

"Well, I'm no gentleman, so I'd settle for a kiss." He couldn't hide the hope in his voice.

Rose focused all her energy into remaining calm and in control. "You would settle for many things from me, Spence."

Spencer bowed his head in surrender, "Your heartfelt gratitude is all I require, my lady."

Chapter 10

ose led Lee across the camp. Any other night it would be a bustling walk with music and laughter along with several cooking fires giving off the most delicious aromas of dinner. Tonight, thanks to the heavy clumps of snow falling from the clouds, all was quiet. Most of the families were tucked away in their wagons staying cozy by the heat of their small stoves. Zoe was no exception. When Rose returned to her wagon to collect their curious new visitor, she found Zoe struggling to stay awake as she enjoyed her tea with Lee. Rose was immediately troubled when she found her sister in such a state and chided her when Zoe insisted she didn't want to cut short her time with the charming young traveler. Even in her exhaustion, Zoe was stubborn enough not to give into Rose's desire for her to rest, that is, until Lee agreed to come by to see her again tomorrow.

Rose kept trying to work out the game her sister was playing with him, but couldn't figure it out. Zoe was acting entirely childish. This made Rose feel even older since she always saw her sister as steadfast and level-headed. Zoe would never allow herself to be drawn in by anyone so easily. The weight of Rose's responsibility for Zoe rested heavier on her frame. She couldn't imagine what Zoe saw in this man to make her melt so easily. About the only positive thing about him was the genuine look of concern he had while carefully watching Rose escort and tuck her sister into bed. She also caught a glimpse of worry in his eyes when he saw how instantaneous sleep overcame her. Lee had opened his mouth to speak but remained silent, lost in his thoughts. Rose was grateful for his silence. She was in no mood to answer questions about her sister, and Lee had already tested her limits of patience and composure. Besides, more questions from him tonight would only magnify her suspicions of his motives in her camp. The deafening tone of Death still irritatingly resonated from Lee, and the soft rattling laugh Rose had heard continued in her head. Rose flexed her shoulders to try to shake the feeling from her. Lee was not someone she needed to fear. Soon Spencer would have his watchful eye on him, and whatever mischief or manipulation Lee had planned would be thwarted by her dear friend. She smiled to herself, glad she was able to convince Spencer to accept this important task—a task she trusted only him to do.

Spencer smiled warmly when he helped Rose up the stairs and through his door, then immediately grew tense. He crossed his arms defensively with a cold, unwelcoming stare for Lee when he entered his wagon. Lee looked up and flinched at the sight of Spencer. The exchange between them felt like lightning, as they continued to stare each other down in silence.

Their tension did not go unnoticed by Rose. She looked to Spencer, "Do you know each other?"

"Pretty sure I'd remember a man named Lee." Spencer's tone mocked Lee's name openly while his stare remained fixed on the shorter man.

Rose felt awkward and didn't want to stick around long enough for Spencer to change his mind about his new roommate.

"Well, it's late." Her eyes continued to flicker back and forth between the two men for some kind of acknowledgment. "Goodnight, Spencer."

Spencer managed to tear his stare away from the stranger to return her awkward smile. The door closed leaving the two men to their agendas.

* * * * *

Lee inclined his head before offering a small bow of respect to his new roommate.

"General," he said.

Spencer remained stone still with his arms still folded across his chest, "Your Highness."

Lee returned Spencer's cold stare, refusing to back down. Initially, he couldn't believe his luck. He had been lost in the storm but managed to find a door to a family that saved him from a cold, lonely death. On top of that, it was the door to the home of the one person that could give him some clarity. Luckier still was that the lovely woman had asked him to stay. Of course, her sister had offered numerous protests; but in the end, he was allowed to stay with them. Lee remembered feeling victorious over Rose, thinking that in the end, her sister, Zoe made the final decisions.

He remembered Rose's threat from before while standing face to face with the one man in the entire kingdom he wasn't ready to see. The wanderer had truly believed his life couldn't be cursed any more than it already has. When he met Spencer's disapproving glare, he was fully aware that Rose had made good on her promise. Perhaps she wasn't as powerless as he thought.

Chapter

The days became shorter during the winter, yet Zoe could feel time stand still every minute she was around Lee. Ever since she got her first real look at the stranger at her door, Zoe felt as if something awakened inside of her. When he left to settle in Spencer's wagon, she was saddened by the possibility of not seeing much of him during his stay. Lucky for Zoe, Lee seemed to gravitate toward her as naturally as bees to honey. At first, it was a series of small serendipitous meetings in which they would catch up on the latest news, then be on their way. Those meetings grew longer and longer because neither wanted to leave each other's company. Zoe found it difficult to contain her excitement one day when Lee sought her out purposefully, with the only intention of spending time with her. She loved being around Lee. He was always so pleasant, and thoughtful in his conversation. He had no fear of debating an issue with her or teasing her for the sake of a laugh they both shared. Lee had taken to helping one of the troupe's artists with painting new backdrops for their performances, at the encouragement of Zoe of course. So, occasionally he would bring in a rough sketch of his latest work to share with her. Zoe couldn't remember the last time she was this happy, and she looked forward to her time with Lee every day.

The only problem was Rose. Zoe couldn't talk much about her time with Lee without Rose grumbling on and on about how he was bad news. The very moment Lee was welcomed to stay with the troupe, Rose and Spencer had been on edge. Zoe could feel the burning glare from Rose when Lee was nearby, carefully watching, hoping for any opportunity to pounce. Rose was all too eager for a reason to kick him out of their welcoming troupe. Thankfully for Zoe, the opportunity never came. Lee was a perfect gentleman when it came to her. Often, Rose would try to explain how horrid Lee was when she was not around. But Zoe was always quick to dismiss her sister's comments. Surely Lee was just as respectful with everyone else in the troupe as he was around her.

Spencer's attitude mirrored Rose's. He was hardly ever found out of the eyesight of their guest. When Lee arrived, he had become more careful and focused than ever before, a feat Zoe had not imagined possible. Rose's and Spencer's attitude toward Lee was so similar it made Zoe laugh. For someone so insistent that Spencer is not the man for her, Rose and he sure acted like an old married couple far too often. Zoe had made a promise to her sister a long time ago that she would never be alone. Now with the inevitable fortune that Zoe's health would be getting worse, she wanted to ensure that Rose would have someone to turn to as well. Spencer was the perfect person to fill that void for Rose. He was the only person Zoe knew who could distract Rose long enough to calm her down just so she would take a much needed mental break from the day. Of course, Rose would never admit to it and convincing her that Spencer is a necessary part of her life turned out to be a harder task than Zoe imagined. It's not like Spencer would turn down the opportunity. He was so enamored by Rose that this dislike of Lee could easily be an elaborate ruse to place him in Rose's good graces. But seeing Spencer visually tense when Lee was around kept Zoe alert. As with many things concerning Spencer, there was more going on that neither he nor Lee was telling.

Zoe was happy for the warmer weather of spring. She enjoyed the fresh air, but couldn't stand the cold as well as she used to. Now that spring had arrived she could venture outside if only for a short time, to escape the all too confining walls of her wagon. Today, she offered to grind up different shades of dried flowers to make more paint for Lee's new project. She settled down in a sunny place on a woven mat with her grinding stones set comfortably in front of her. Beside her, several glass jars sparkled, waiting to be filled with vibrant powders to be mixed in oil later. Zoe had just finished crushing onion peels and flowers to fill up a jar with yellow powder then began working on orange. She had managed to crush up the flowers and spices into small manageable pieces to work into a powder when she felt a presence close behind her. Zoe wanted to smile but instead pretended to be unaware of Lee trying his best to surprise her.

After a few long moments, his voice came from directly over her shoulder. "What are you doing?"

Lee's voice was soft and casual, and despite Zoe's anticipation of him she still started in surprise. She smiled then shook off her nerves to face him. His face was hovering over her shoulder in perfect view of her work, and now was nearly nose to nose when he turned toward her. Zoe studied his golden eyes for a second before looking away, slightly embarrassed.

"I was making some more paint for you," she answered as relaxed as she could manage.

"Oh?" Lee sat down next to Zoe, now much more interested in her work. "But how could you possibly know what colors I need?"

Zoe smiled back at Lee, "Master Day told me."

"Ah yes," Lee sighed. "Master Day does have a tight eye on my work."

"That's her job," Zoe laughed. "In the end, she has the final say when it comes to how the scenery should look. You answer to her."

Lee nodded his head, "Right, right, it's just… you could have asked me."

"But I wanted it to be a surprise," Zoe answered sweetly, then frowned as she started to work again. "It is not much of a surprise anymore, though."

Lee held a new jar open for her to pour some of the orange powder in. "It is still appreciated, thank you."

Zoe grinned while grabbing a new handful of plants to grind up.

"Also, I never thanked you for talking to Master Day on my behalf," Lee continued. "She told me you were the one who suggested she take me on as part of her team."

"I may have mentioned you to her, but your work is what kept you on her team," Zoe responded.

"Still," Lee shrugged, "I never would have considered it without your help. These aren't exactly what I would call the hands of an artist."

Zoe muffled her laugh. "I was always told that everyone has the hands of an artist. It all just depends on the medium they use."

"I don't understand," Lee nudged her to elaborate.

"Well, some people use paint, others use clay, fabric, food." Zoe stopped working to look at Lee again. "Some artists use words or weapons. Even small acts of kindness can be an art form."

"Who told you that?" Lee looked at her skeptically.

Zoe nodded assuredly, "My mother did."

A corner of Lee's mouth curved in amusement, "So what is your medium?"

"At the moment," Zoe's eyes searched for her answer. "Flowers, I suppose."

Lee gave a low chuckle, "Well, they will make great colors."

He reached over to grab a pinch of powder to look at it closer. His hand brushed the side of Zoe's fingers causing her to drop the stone with a puff of orange smoke.

Lee's smile only grew wider. "Am I making you nervous?"

Zoe took a deep breath then decided to answer honestly, "Increasingly, but that doesn't mean I don't like it."

They both shared a warm smile that would make the sun jealous. Zoe loved it when Lee smiled, especially when he smiled at her. She had a feeling it was something he didn't do often; in a way, it was something he reserved only for her.

Zoe rubbed her hands on her knees to muster some courage, "Why don't we go somewhere to get away for a bit."

Zoe's heart was filled with excitement, but she could see worry seep into Lee's eyes. Her mirth deflated as she tried to interpret what he was feeling. She couldn't believe how foolish she was acting. All she wanted was something a bit more than the casual friendship they had formed, but apparently, that idea scared Lee. She turned back to her work to busy her hands again. She needed an excuse not to look at him anymore.

"Never mind," she added quickly. "That was a silly thought. I shouldn't presume too much. I have plenty of work to do here anyway."

Lee placed his hand on hers to halt her work, then leaned in closer with a small smirk.

"You don't presume too much. I fear you presume too little concerning us." Zoe was about to ask him to explain, but he continued without pause. "But, that is probably my fault. I'm so concerned with how I could mess things up, I don't even try to…"

Zoe watched Lee fade away into his thoughts for a moment. She was afraid to speak, thinking it would distract him. Suddenly, Lee looked up with a new resolve in his attitude. His eyes were sharp and his smile sure.

"Yes, let's go somewhere." He placed some lids on the jars, and Zoe allowed herself a small amount of excitement.

"Where?" She asked innocently.

"We won't go far. Just to the other side of the camp to give you a change of scenery." Lee answered, knowing Rose's looming glare was watching his every move.

"Oh," Zoe answered trying not to sound disappointed.

Lee smiled confidently at her, "I want to show you the project I've been working on for Master Day."

"Oh?" Zoe was immediately interested, and her excitement grew again. "Is it a new backdrop?"

Lee's eyes grew mischievous, "Now don't you try to ruin any surprises now."

They gathered all the jars together into a large sack that Lee settled on his shoulder. Zoe laughed when he bowed low taking her hand to help her up. Then, he curled it gently around his arm to help her cross the camp.

Chapter 12

Rose's teeth clenched as a low growl rumbled in her throat. As of late, her sister would meet up with Lee almost every day. That didn't make seeing the two together any easier though. It made Rose's blood boil to see her sister laugh with such a repulsive man. She couldn't understand how Zoe didn't see straight through this gentlemen-like act Lee put on. Lee treated Zoe with the utmost respect and reverence one would offer a queen. Not that Lee knew anything about how to act around a queen, she reminded herself. Still, Rose could not deny, the act was very convincing. A little too convincing.

When Zoe was not around, Lee was straight up dreadful. His attitude was dark and depressing, and he easily drained the joy out of any conversation. She was relieved when he started working with Master Day. His attitude improved a little and he wasn't loafing around all day. Still, he grated on Rose's nerves to the point where she avoided him, but the nagging worry about her sister drew her back in time after time, to watch out for Zoe. She had promised her sister when they were young that she would always be there for her. Rose took that promise seriously to this day—even now when it meant saving her sister from her misjudgments.

In Rose's opinion, Zoe was being far too accommodating for Lee. What had started as a visit for only a few days had turned into an all winter long stay. Rose was beginning to wonder if he planned to stay for the spring as well. The thought of an even longer stay with Lee upset Rose so much she quickly grabbed a jacket and supplies so she could disappear into the woods.

She didn't venture too far this trip, just far enough to be out of earshot of the daily bustle of the troupe. After gathering a few berries for her to snack on she found a familiar cliff face and started to climb up to her favorite retreat. It wasn't a hard climb, easy enough to get up or down in case of an emergency. And the perfect place to be alone. However, upon reaching her destination she immediately saw her favorite spot had already been taken.

"Spencer?" She scanned the area for anyone else. "What are you doing here?"

"Keeping an eye on Lee," he gestured downward to show a perfect eagle-eye view of their entire camp and all that was happening among the group. "What are you doing here?"

Rose hesitated before she answered him. "Avoiding Lee. I often come here when I want to be alone."

Spencer gathered up his pack as he started to stand, "Oh, well I will be out of your way then."

"No," Rose protested a little too loudly. Spencer looked up in surprise. "It's okay. I don't mind being alone with you. That is if you don't mind me joining you."

Spencer motioned to the spot next to him while settling back down on a large rock.

"Are you hungry?" he asked.

Rose pulled out her pouch of berries and frowned. "I was able to find a little bit on my way up, but the pickings were rather slim."

"They weren't slim when I climbed up." Spencer blushed as he pulled out his own, nearly overflowing pouch of berries. "Help yourself."

Rose smiled and added a few of his berries to her bag. "So, what's he doing?"

"Just touching up the paint on some of our props." Spencer pointed downward to help Rose get a fix on their guest.

"Does he know what he's doing?" she worried.

Spencer gave a small laugh, "Yes, he's not a bad artist, and I find it lightens his mood when he paints."

"Impressive," Rose nodded in appreciation. "He should paint every day."

They both laughed as Spencer promised to have more scenery drawn up to keep Lee busy from now on.

"So, after all this time do you think Lee is panning something?" Rose asked.

"Absolutely," Spencer muttered.

"How do you know?"

Spencer smirked at Rose, "Because he has been here all this time."

Rose's eyebrows lifted, "But, you don't think he is dangerous?"

Spencer shook his head. "I have not figured that out yet. He seems harmless, but I worry one wrong move and he could lash out violently at someone."

"Like what?" Rose asked nervously.

"I do not know. It is probably best if he keeps painting for now. And perhaps, fewer growls from you would be helpful," he jeered.

Rose blushed, "No promises. He is awfully close to my sister, after all."

Spencer chuckled, "Fair enough."

They sat in silence for a while, but the silence only made Rose uncomfortable.

"Has Zoe given you any new stories to direct for the spring?"

Spencer sighed, "Rose, relax. It's just you and me up here. We don't have to talk about business all the time. We could get crazy and try to have some fun."

"I don't have time for fun. There is too much to do to keep this troupe running," she retorted.

"That excuse is getting tiresome, Rosie. Everyone has their part to play and everyone in the troupe pulls their weight. I know you have the time."

"What would you suggest we do?" Rose sighed. Then she continued with mock excitement.

"Perhaps we should chase each other, jump, skip, sing, and climb trees as if we were little kids again?"

"I wouldn't be opposed to climbing a few trees, since you don't enjoy it when I chase after you."

Rose rolled her eyes, "We're too old to climb trees; it won't end well for us."

"The last time we climbed a tree together, I thought it ended up pretty well."

Rose blinked, surprised by his response. "That was one kiss," she whispered. "It was one kiss that happened so long ago I can't even remember."

"Two years ago," Spencer began to speak using his storyteller voice to adorn his words and emphasize his point, just for Rose. "You were climbing a tree to get some honeycomb. You lost your footing and fell into my arms. Then you proceeded to thank me with those sweet lips of yours. It sounds like a good ending for me."

"You let me crash to the ground, and I stopped breathing. Then you tried to blow air back into my body to save me!" Rose sat straight and proud that she was able to correct his preposterous story.

Spencer leaned in so close to her, she could smell the campfire smoke off his shirt. His eyes sparkled.

"I thought it was too long ago to remember?" He asked calmly.

Rose's pride melted away to reveal a small amount of terror sweeping over her. She was caught. She knew the moment he recalled as clearly as he did. The climb, the fall, his breath. Then, just as he said, a proper 'thank you' with a kiss from her — a long, soft kiss, the kind that held layer upon layer of emotion and feelings. She lost her balance as she allowed her memory to take over. For a moment, she was lost, lost in the possibility of having more with Spencer. She enjoyed being lost and wanted to drink in that moment for as long as she could. Spencer caught her in his arms, jolting her back to life… real life.

Her face hardened again, breaking free from his embrace.

"Really, Spencer?" She asked, furious that he was able to slip past her barriers again. "Are you ever going to give up on me?" An idea struck causing her to rummage through her pack.

"What are you looking for?" he asked peering over her shoulder.

Rose drew out her deck of tarot cards. "These!" She declared with excitement.

"What are you going to do with those?"

"I'm going to read your fortune," she stated.

"No, you're not," he countered.

She looked at him. "Yes, I am."

"No, you're not," he said stubbornly. "I know how your fortune telling works. Your cards will not work for you if the person you are reading does not want to hear their fortune."

Rose huffed at Spencer even though he was right. One thing Zoe and she would always remind their patrons to do is to have an open mind, and an open heart for them to see the person's future, that is, of course when they relied on their cards. When Zoe relied on her gift it didn't matter how the person felt. Rose felt envious of Zoe at that moment, wishing she knew how to use her gift to see Spencer's fortune.

"Why not?" she asked.

"Because my future is something I imagine to be very personal. It may not be something I want you to know all about."

"But Spencer, what if I see a beautiful woman in your future."

"That's not much of a stretch because, at present, I'm already with a beautiful woman," He smiled.

Rose turned a shade of red in embarrassment. "I'm talking about possibly seeing someone else in your future for you."

"Then I will be pleasantly surprised when it happens. For now, I'm content right where I am."

Rose wanted to be upset but she couldn't. The truth was, she was also perfectly content with him just as he was, working closely with her as an adopted gypsy storyteller. Now that she thought about it further, Rose feared that if he had agreed to her little game, all she would see was the vision of his death again. Her blood ran cold as she recalled the scene so vividly. The faint laughter of her new skeletal friend tickled the back of her mind.

"Very well," Rose returned her cards to her bag gravely.

She looked back down at the camp to spy on what Lee was working on now. She found him kneeling next to a fair-haired woman who was lying on the ground with bright red splotches staining her clothes around her middle.

"Is that Zoe?" Rose shouted as her anger got the best of her.

"Is that blood?" Spencer added.

"I swear, Spencer, he is going to die. I will kill him myself," Rose vowed darkly while scooping up their bags.

"Don't worry, I'll help you," Spencer agreed.

They raced down the cliffside and back to the camp to search for Zoe.

When they finally found Zoe, Rose was astonished to hear her sister and Lee laughing loudly with each other.

"What on earth is going on here?" Rose demanded.

Zoe looked up at her sister and wiped tears of joy from her eyes before answering. "I offered to help Lee with his painting. One thing led to another and we were caught up in a paint war with each other."

"Hey, you started it!" reminded Lee as he snickered behind his teeth.

"No, you started it when you spattered my face with the blue," Zoe responded.

"That was an accident, and you knew it. You were the one who painted on my arm with the green for fun," he laughed.

"Explain the blood!" Rose interrupted.

"Blood?" Zoe looked at Lee, "Are you bleeding?"

"No, are you?" he asked.

"No," Zoe confirmed. Then she looked down at herself to see the copious amount of red paint that spilled all over her. "Rose, this is paint! We were playing around and I grabbed the bucket to throw on Lee, but instead I lost my balance. I fell backwards spilling the paint on myself. It was an accident."

Spencer chuckled at the situation, but Rose shot him a sharp look to quiet him. This was not something to laugh at.

"You lost your balance?" Rose asked seriously, turning her gaze back to Zoe.

Zoe knew from her sister's tone that she feared the worst. "It was nothing, I tripped is all. It's nothing to worry about."

"Nothing to worry about?" Rose was fired up. Spencer pulled Lee up from his knees and took him out of the way of the storm that he knew Rose was going to start. "I thought you were dead or dying, and you say it's nothing to worry about?"

"It isn't, Rose! We were just having fun," Zoe answered.

"You think it is fun to give me a heart attack because I think my sister is dead? You think death is funny?" Rose shouted. The skeletal laugh started up again, causing Rose to flinch.

"No one is saying that, Rose," Zoe spoke softly.

"This isn't right, Zoe. You should be conserving your energy. Not wasting it all to the brink of collapse with trivial things like this!" Rose lectured.

Zoe was having trouble catching her breath. Rose was right about her using up all her energy, but she didn't back down either. "I don't consider a little fun to be a waste, sister."

Rose glanced over at Spencer, who was strategically placed in front of Lee, so Rose could not see him. Her friend simply kept his mouth shut, his face silently agreeing with Zoe. The anger inside of Rose calmed a little, and she bent over to help her sister off the ground.

"Come on," Rose said as she threw Zoe's arm around her shoulders. "Let's get you cleaned up."

Spencer turned to face Lee, who held an expression somewhere between anger and fear. "What do you say about the two of us getting out of here for a bit, at least until Rose cools off."

"Gladly," Lee accepted.

Chapter 13

Zoe's clothes were soaking in a barrel of water just outside the wagon. Rose shook her head and accepted the fact that they will have a faint pink hue from now on. The two of them washed the paint from Zoe's skin as best as they could. Then Rose offered her sister clean clothes to change into.

As her sister changed Rose couldn't stop pacing back and forth in frustration. "I don't like you spending so much time with Lee. There's still something about him I don't trust."

"Something about him?" Zoe repeated back at Rose. "You can't stand anything about him. What's bothering you today?"

Zoe was able to hide her rolling eyes, but the obvious jab from her sister struck a little too hard for Rose's tolerance.

"You mean, aside from the fact that he's a liar?" Rose folded her arms defensively. "That man isn't being very forthcoming about anything concerning who he is or where he's from. He's hiding something."

"Everyone has their secrets, Rose, even you. It's unfair to hold this against him too harshly." Rose's mouth hung open refusing to agree with her sister, no matter how true her words were.

"Besides," Zoe continued, "I've already told you, there's something important about him. He needs to be here with us." Zoe emphasized each word as if trying to stamp it into her sister's brain for good.

Rose knelt next to Zoe to plead with her sister. "Tell me, then. Tell me what you have seen. What is so important about this guy, and why does he have to be here?"

Zoe shook her head weakly. "My word used to be good enough for you."

"That was before you started to teach me to rely on my own gift. To come to my own conclusions."

Zoe gave a small smile. "I didn't realize you were paying attention to me."

Rose smiled back at her sister. "Yeah, well, I do pay attention. I've come to trust your word, sister. But, not today, and not when it concerns Lee." She spat his name as if it tasted like poison in her mouth.

"I promise, I haven't seen anything. It's just a feeling. He's important, and he needs to be here."

Rose pushed away from Zoe, flopping back on the rug, exasperated. "My goodness, how this man has a hold on you! I'm starting to think you made all this up just because you have a crush on him."

"Made up?" Zoe shouted back defensively. Rose might have felt sorry for her words, had her sister not stuttered all over her own. "What do you take me for, a lonely beggar who will say anything for a copper?"

Rose opened her mouth to respond but was silenced as Zoe continued.

"And what if I am fond of Lee?" This time she was confident, glowing with all the authority of a grown woman. "Can you blame me? He's the first man who hasn't turned away running once he learned about my gift. He talks with me. No, he argues with me, teases me, questions what I say, and in turn, forces me to think harder than anyone has. He doesn't pick and choose his words for fear that I'll get upset and waste my energy. When was the last time anyone talked to me without dripping with reverence and tact?"

Rose opened her mouth again in protest, but Zoe cut her off again.

"Excluding you, Rose." Rose remained silent, allowing her sister to finish. "When he's around, I feel like… myself. I haven't been allowed to be myself in a long time, sister. It's a good feeling. So yes, I'm going to try to keep him around as long as I possibly can, so I don't forget who I am."

Rose was feeling more miserable with every word. She had no idea this is what Zoe was feeling and worse that she had never considered the matter before. Did Zoe even have a crush on Lee, or is this just how her sister acts normally to normal people? Did Rose even know her sister as well as she thought?

Zoe smiled warmly at her sister as if reading her thoughts. "And, if I do have a crush on Lee, I would hope my sister would be happy for me that I finally found someone I can open up to."

Rose relaxed when a few of her worries vanished from her mind. "Zoe, I am happy for you. I'm just being careful."

"You're being my sister." Zoe smiled. "I will never be mad at you for that."

"Secrets never stay secret long, Zoe." Rose loved her sister, but she still would not allow herself to trust Lee, even for Zoe. "One day his secrets are going to catch up to him, and we are going to catch the brunt of that mess."

"He's a good man. He won't harm or ruin this troupe." Zoe's eyes were so sharp that Rose shifted uncomfortably under her stare. "Besides, you already have Spencer watching him."

Rose's eyes flicked up to meet Zoe's in surprise.

"Yes, I know about that." Zoe's lips twitched into a knowing smirk when she saw Rose shift uneasily. "If you don't trust me, don't you trust Spencer? He has never let you down."

"I trust my gut first."

"Over Spencer?"

"Spencer can't even handle a sword, never goes near them. Even if he suspected foul play, he couldn't do much to stop it." Rose gritted her teeth. She was horrible at lying.

"Rubbish! If that's how you felt, then you would have given the job to someone else." Zoe argued back.

"Just because he's my first choice doesn't mean that he couldn't miss something. You overestimate his abilities."

"And you underestimate him, Rose," Zoe said poignantly.

"Why are you making this about Spencer? This is about you being more careful around Lee." Rose crossed her arms protectively, daring her sister to continue her argument.

Zoe leaned toward Rose as she opened her mouth to offer her rebuttal in kind, but no words came. Zoe simply froze as her entire body went rigid. Her eyes stared off at nothing and her pupils dilated causing her light blue eyes to look uncharacteristically dark.

"Rose Red, Rose Red, will you beat your lover dead?" Zoe's voice was emotionless and distant as if she was speaking into a tunnel.

The first time Rose had seen her sister act this way, she was terrified. She had no idea what was happening or what to do to help. Helplessness was a quality that Rose always wrestled with. Through the years Rose had come to understand that this was how Zoe received her visions. At her most powerful moment as a seer, her body was at her weakest. It still terrified Rose after all this time, but at least she knew what to do.

Rose didn't touch her sister for fear of disturbing her vision. But she did draw close with her arms outstretched to catch Zoe just in time when she slumped over the edge of the bed. Then, Rose tenderly leaned her sister back onto the pile of pillows. Zoe's breath was short, and all her energy was drained. She was weak, but the episode was over. Rose sighed in relief when Zoe was acting like herself again.

"The truth, Rose." Zoe took a few breaths before continuing. "Do you trust Spencer?"

Concern and fear drowned Rose's eyes as she focused on her sister. Zoe had just mentioned how angry she felt when everyone is extra careful around her because of her health. Now, Rose had angered Zoe to the point where she had a vision, and all her energy drained within seconds. The pain Zoe was in, right now, was entirely Rose's fault. As her sister, she should have known better.

Rose breathed her answer softly, "With my life."

"Then ease up on Lee. He is not a threat." Zoe's eyelids fluttered closed and she drifted off into a much needed, deep sleep. Rose tucked the blankets snuggly around Zoe, then tiptoed her way to the door.

Chapter

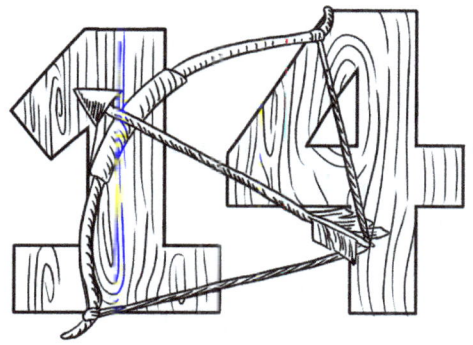

Rose closed the door behind her softly to not disturb Zoe. She considered her sister's words carefully, then she considered her own visions, trying to make sense of the two. Zoe had always kept any vision about Rose to herself much to Rose's dismay. Rose was curious to know if she was making the right decisions or taking the risks she needed to. This was the first time Rose had heard Zoe recite a vision about her while she was listening in. Now she understood why Zoe kept those visions to herself. Rose's head was a blur of 'what if's' or possibilities of what such a simple line could mean. She closed her eyes to clear away those thoughts and focus her mind. In a matter of minutes, all was quiet again except for a faint laugh she heard echoing in her head.

    Rose opened her eyes to see where the sound had come from. In front of her, she could see Spencer and Lee slinging bags and bows over their shoulders. Spencer fixed a couple of knives to his belt, and Lee tightened his boot strings. Anger and a little jealousy burned inside her, as Rose's eyes fixed on Lee. She was not going to let some stranger steal away her sister, and certainly not Spencer. He was too valuable to … the troupe.

She gathered her nerves in a convincing display of calm as she approached them.

Spencer smiled at her with his special smile and offered a nod of respect. "Hello, Rosie."

His deep voice threatened to subdue her anger for a moment. She gave him a half-smile, not allowing herself to be distracted.

"What's going on?" Rose eyed Lee suspiciously.

"We are going out for a bit," Spencer answered vaguely.

"Out? The sun is going down soon. What could you possibly have to do?" Rose's forehead wrinkled in confusion.

"What is it to you?" Lee mumbled behind her back.

Rose turned to face Lee. "I'm the matriarch of this troupe. It's my responsibility to keep track of everyone in it, for safety." She emphasized the last part so her reasons were clear.

"We will be fine, Rosie. We are just doing some night hunting. I'll keep an eye on Lee."

"It's not Lee I'm worried about," Rose spoke softly as she scowled over her shoulder.

Spencer smiled broadly, tilting his head to one side. "You're worried about me? I thought you didn't care."

Rose tried not to blush then sighed in exasperation. "I'm worried you won't catch much. I'm the better shot, so I should go with you."

"Not this time, beautiful. This is a man's trip." Spencer answered a little too quickly.

"Man's trip?" balked Rose.

Lee gave her a sideways glare. "Yes, meaning just us."

Rose shot an icy stare at Lee, not missed by Spencer. He smirked at her, amused.

"Rose, this time is going to be just Lee and me. We have some things to do, nothing important."

Rose blinked in disbelief. She glanced back at Lee while stepping closer to Spencer. Her voice lowered, so only he could hear.

"You never turn me away from a hunting trip. You usually insist on it." Spencer shifted uncomfortably. "What's different this time? What aren't you telling me?"

Spencer was noticeably irritated, "Nothing, we're just going hunting. It is not a big deal."

"It will be a big deal when you come back empty-handed, and by the end of the week, the troupe is hungry. All because there isn't enough food to share."

"I said, we will be fine." He spoke forcefully which caused Rose to hesitate in surprise.

Lee chimed in, gloating, "Don't worry, Rose. I'm sure there are plenty of other things you had planned to do without us today."

Rose's countenance darkened as the two men started to walk away.

"Right!" she shouted after them. "You know, I did have plans this evening. I was going to do a bit of hunting myself."

Spencer froze mid-step and looked back at her.

Rose allowed a smile while twirling one of her knives in her fingers. "See, I was planning on leaving shortly after you. And, since I know you will be out, I'm probably going to follow the same path that you take. Oh, don't you worry. Most likely I'll hang back a bit, so I won't ruin your man's trip."

Spencer slowly walked back to her. "Not much of a hunting trip. Unless, of course, you're hunting me."

"Nah," Rose smiled bigger. "I'll do fine. All I have to do is pick off all the game you scare away." She glared up at him defiantly.

Spencer was no longer amused with the woman. All his mirth had melted way into a cold stare that challenged her glare. Both were locked in an impasse, wrought in stubbornness. The man finally shook his head as he took an extra jacket from his pack. Rose delighted in her small triumph when he draped the garment over her shoulder. She would have smiled but instead retained her stare in defiance.

"Don't get in my way," he ordered.

"Don't get in *my* way," Rose shot back, clearly offended.

They joined back up with Lee, who was shaking his head at the two of them. He mumbled to himself when Rose walked past.

"Rose Red, Rose Red, will you beat your lover dead?"

Rose's head jerked as she faced Lee, "What?"

"What?" Lee asked, barely befuddled.

"What did you just say?" Rose demanded.

Lee shrugged, "I didn't say anything."

Rose was rattled. "Have you been talking with Zoe?"

"Of course I have," he smirked.

"About me?" She tried not to sound desperate.

"Why would we talk about you, when there's so much more to say about us?" Lee's smile was malicious.

Rose winced in disgust, "Forget it."

As much as she tried, Rose couldn't forget what she heard. Twice she had heard those words, and both times while angry with Spencer. She heard a faint laugh again, taunting her. Rose tried to zero in on the sound, but it was gone as fast as it came.

Chapter

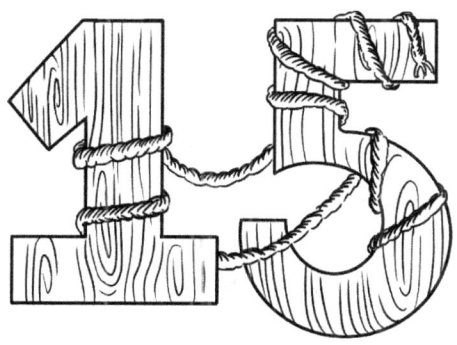

hey walked deep into the woods. It was much farther than Rose felt necessary. She wondered when they would eventually stop so they could track a few animals.

"So," she loudly whispered to Spencer, "are we ever going to hunt on this hunting trip?"

Lee couldn't suppress a laugh that agreed with her. "She does have a point, Spencer. Where exactly are we headed?"

"There is a spot farther ahead I have wanted to try." He answered.

"Farther?" Rose breathed through her teeth.

"You could have stayed with the troupe as I told you to." Spencer smiled. Rose merely stared icy darts at Spencer's back.

"Well, she's here now," Lee spoke up, rolling his eyes. "There is no sense in making her suffer for it."

Spencer missed a step and turned to Lee. "Seriously?"

Lee lifted his hands in surrender. "What? She can hold her own. It's not so bad having her around."

Spencer hissed as he continued. A few flecks of pink clung to the dark sky while the sun slowly drifted down past the horizon. Rose and Lee walked side by side as Spencer forged the path.

"You don't have to defend my actions to Spencer," Rose muttered to Lee. "But, thank you."

"Yes, you sound very grateful," he retorted, sarcastically.

"I am. I said *thank you*," Rose insisted.

"Yeah," Lee's face was suddenly emotionless. "I heard you."

Rose gave him a wary look. The man seemed burdened with his thoughts. She allowed a longer, unbiased look at the man. His dark hair cropped short and swept back revealed rather soft, gentle amber eyes. She would even call them kind, were it not for the dark shadow his thick brow cast from being furrowed low in concentration. His jaw was set strong, and his lips drawn into a small frown. Attitude aside, Rose could see why Zoe thought he was handsome. Maybe Zoe felt sorry for Lee and thought loving him would be the cure. Whether that was true or not, Rose was starting to feel sorry for the man. More was going on than he was telling them. She sighed deeply when the matriarch in her started to surface. For reasons she could not explain she wanted to help him, even though he was displaying every reason a person should avoid him. A smart person would simply leave him to his own devices. Unfortunately, Rose knew the smart thing to do wasn't always the right thing. She took a calming breath, not knowing exactly what she should say.

"Are you doing alright, Lee?" She tried to ask as pleasantly as possible. No sense beating around the bush when you're not exactly sure what you're looking for.

Without skipping a beat, he answered flatly, "I'm fine."

The words shot out at her like knives. Lee must have known he wasn't convincing because he turned to look at Rose who was taken aback.

"Why?" His gruff voice softened slightly.

Rose hesitated, "No big reason. You just... um... you have a face."

"A face?" He looked at her like she was ridiculous.

"You have the 'mush' face." She tried to explain, and failed miserably. "You look like there's a lot on your mind."

Lee sighed loudly, "This is just my face."

"No one's face looks like that for no reason. Something is going on with you," Rose insisted.

"Even if there was something, why would I tell you?" He asked, skeptical.

"Because I care about you," Rose surprised herself with her answer.

"Really. I thought you didn't trust me. Weren't you the one who asked Spencer to keep an eye on me, so I don't do anything stupid?"

Rose eyed Spencer's back. She would have a discussion with him about why he cannot keep his mouth shut when it comes to personal secrets. Or, perhaps, it was Zoe who told Lee he was being watched. Of course, he could have figured it out on his own. She dismissed that last thought as silly and settled on having a firm talking to with Spencer when she had time. She heard the faint, skeletal laughter in her mind again.

"True," she spoke slowly. "I asked him to watch you because you're obviously interested in my sister. You're just getting the same treatment as anyone else."

"Oh, so if I was a prince with all sorts of airs and riches, nothing would be different?"

"Don't talk nonsense to me. Speculation holds no weight, as far as I'm concerned. All I know is what I see, and I don't see any reason to trust you with my sister, yet."

"And you see and know everything, don't you?" He openly mocked her.

"I see enough. I imagine you're the one who knows everything." She countered.

"And don't you forget it," The man actually smiled.

Rose shook her head, "My goodness you are self-centered and smug. I'm glad I asked Spencer to watch you."

Lee was losing patience with Rose. "I'm smug? What about you? You have me pegged as someone horrible. You don't know me. You don't know anything."

Rose was unrelenting, "I'm trying to get to know who you are. But every time I ask you something, you get all upset or avoid the question. What am I supposed to think, that you are all rainbows and butterflies?"

"You're no peach either, you know." Lee refused to let up in this argument. "You are as prickly as they come, and you expect me to open up my life to you? I thought matriarchs were supposed to be smart."

Rose stepped closer to Lee, threw all caution to the wind, and slapped him before he realized what was happening. Fire blazed in his eyes as his fists clenched. Rose immediately felt terror mixed with regret for what she had done. She had unleashed something that she didn't think he was capable of. She stepped back to give him space to control his anger. It didn't work. He started to charge towards Rose, who was now paralyzed with fear.

In the split-second Rose had to think, she tried to work out what she should do. How could she subdue Lee's attack without hurting him? More importantly, how could she subdue him without hurting herself? Her options were slim, and she struggled to respond in time.

Before Lee could lay a hand on her, Spencer had already leaped into action. While Lee's attention was focused on Rose, Spencer threw his hiking bag at Lee's feet to trip him. Then he crashed his full weight at Lee landing heavily to the ground. As Lee lay stunned from the fall, Spencer quickly grabbed the man's arms and pinned them securely behind his back. Lee struggled to break free with no luck.

"Let go of me, Spencer!" Lee howled.

"Never going to happen." Spencer spoke calmly.

Rose relaxed and planted her hands on her hips. "Ha! I'm the prickly, dumb one? I'm not the one being tied up." Rose watched Spencer wind coarse rope around Lee's wrists. "Why *are* you tying him up? We were only arguing."

Spencer looked at Rose after tying the knot. "Yes, you were," he smiled. "It turned out to be a far better distraction than I had planned."

"Distraction," Rose's face twisted in confusion, "from what?"

Just then, two thick arms took hold of Rose from behind and pinned her arms to her body. She screamed, kicked, bit, and clawed to break free but to no avail.

"This is a feisty one!" The man's voice scratched as he spoke to Spencer. "I can imagine having lots of fun with her."

If Spencer was bothered, he didn't show it very well. He handed Lee off to a second man with straw-like hair. The man stared down at Lee with complete disgust. Spencer walked over to Rose to tie up her hands as well.

"Don't imagine too much. She goes along with Darien."

"Darien? Who's Darien?" Rose blurted out, unable to think of anything better to say.

The men easily ignored her while the first one whined in dismay, "What? Why?"

"Think about it," Spencer explained calmly. "If she escapes, she'll run and tell someone what happened. Which means people will come to rescue Darien, and we will be wanted men."

The man's scratchy voice growled, "If she escapes."

Spencer chuckled when he pulled the cord tightly into a complicated knot. "Trust me, she would find a way."

Rose glowered behind her shoulder at Spencer. "Yes, take a long look at what happens to the crazy people who trust this backstabber."

Lee chimed in, "Yeah, and you thought I was going to be the one to do something stupid."

Rose directed her glower back at Lee, "Really? Bigger problems to deal with! And why does everyone keep calling you Darien?"

Spencer put his hands on her shoulders and leaned his face in close next to hers. "I'm very sorry about this, Rosie. In all fairness, I did tell you to stay home. We only needed the prince."

"Prince?" Now Rose felt like she was the one who had just been slapped. Anger and disappointment boiled up inside her. She jerked her head to look at Lee… Darien. "You told us you were a poor beggar who had nowhere to go!"

"Focus Rose, we have bigger problems to deal with." Lee calmly redirected his anger back to Spencer, who seemed to be enjoying himself thoroughly.

"Yes, I was trying to do us all a favor by making Darien disappear. However, having a chance to trick you as well—that was a welcome perk."

Spencer reached out to caress her cheek, but Rose recoiled and spat at him. She felt a small feeling of triumph until she realized Spencer's smile only grew bigger. Rose wondered if this was all some kind of game to him. Exactly how well did she know Spencer? And why was Lee not at all surprised by the ambush? Did he know Spencer had something up his sleeve? If he did, how did she miss the signs that Spencer would betray them? The thought that Lee was able to see it all before she could angered her almost as much as being captured.

"Right then," Spencer took out a handkerchief to wipe his face. "We have important people waiting for us. Time to start walking again."

Rose didn't budge. "What makes you think I'll do anything you say?"

Spencer considered her for a moment. "You're right," he acknowledged. Then, in one fluid movement, he swept her up and settled her easily on his shoulders. Spencer turned and trudged towards the faint sounds of a village nearby with the prince and the two men following close behind.

Chapter

Spencer led the group into a large abandoned building. On the main floor, walls and doors were up to give the appearance of rooms and hallways, but above them was all open scaffolding. There was an elaborate network of interlocking beams that might have borne the load of a second or third floor. They entered a room where one man placed all of Rose's knives, and any weapons Darien had on a table tucked snuggly against the wall. They were each shoved into a chair facing away from each other. Then the two men began to tie their prisoners into their seats as Spencer watched carefully from another corner in the room.

"This is incredible," Darien muttered, more disappointed than angry. "After all we have gone through together, everything we've done, I would have never imagined this would be the kind of man you would become, Spencer. Where's your loyalty and sense of honor? I thought I had my friend back. I trusted you!"

"I trusted *you*! Remember how that ended?" Spencer's voice boomed with authority, daring Darien to respond. He didn't; instead, Darien clenched his jaw angrily.

Rose leaned her head back to be closer to Darien. "Exactly how long have you two known each other?" She asked gently to not upset the broken prince.

"We grew up together," he mumbled in response.

Rose nodded her head while processing the new information. Escape was the only thing on her mind, and brute force was out of the question. Perhaps she could get through to Spencer.

"Hey, I'm not a part of this history you have with Darien." She spoke confidently. "So I probably shouldn't be here for the next installment. If you let me go I won't tell a soul; I'm perfectly fine with him disappearing."

The scratchy voiced man answered her. "Now that you're here, Spencer can't make that decision. Your fate is in the boss' hands now."

Rose turned to look back at Spencer. "You mean, you're not the boss? That's funny, I never pegged you like someone's lackey."

Spencer casually propped himself against the wall with one foot, arms crossed, and still as a statue. Rose had never seen him as serious as he was right now. She couldn't help but wonder what was going through his mind to lead him to trick her. For a moment, Spencer looked tortured. His eyes were full of sadness and longing. Her face softened into concern before she spoke again, not to her captor, but her friend.

"Spencer," he glanced up at her, "please."

He pushed off the wall and walked over to her, never taking his eyes off hers.

"Those knots won't do men." He crouched behind Rose to re-tie the ropes even tighter with more complicated knots. Then he looked at her, calmly. "We wouldn't want to make anything easy for this beautiful flower." Then he smiled with an all too familiar sparkle in his eyes.

Rose found it odd that Spencer would choose to use that particular line now. It was what he always said to the audience when they were on stage, right before she would perform one of their escape routines.

"You have a lot of nerve to think you can still charm me as your prisoner." The confidence in her voice surprised even her.

"I can't help it." Spencer shrugged. "When I look into your eyes, it's hard to turn off the charm."

"You're crazy if you still think you have a shot with me, after all this."

"Meaning I had a shot before?" Spencer's eyebrows raised as Rose pursed her lips, annoyed.

"It's never going to happen," Rose said flatly. "There's no coming back from this."

"Where's your imagination, Rosie? This is why Zoe is much better at writing stories than you." Spencer spoke as if they were the only two people in the room.

"I'll use my imagination for my own needs, like getting even with you." Rose jabbed.

Spencer's eyes lit up with excitement, "Oh, I look forward to that. I would love for you to entertain us with a show."

She scoffed at him, "I'm sure you would."

"Only if you are… *up* to the challenge, of course."

Rose stared at him confused. Spencer was so serious, so angry a moment ago; and now he was flirting with her as if they were back at the caravan. He had reverted to his same routine using the same old tricks. She was about to say something else when a squat, little man entered the room. He appeared to be completely hairless except for a fiery, red beard and mustache that were waxed into three sharp points. His clothes were rich, and he carried with him a finely crafted longsword with gold inlaid around the hilt.

He zeroed in on Darien, grinning wide from ear to ear. "You found him!"

"Peter." Darien's voice was filled with loathing.

"Who's Peter?" Rose asked in a hushed tone.

"He's one of my uncle's stooges," Darien whispered.

"Your uncle?" Rose asked.

"King Robert," Peter announced. Rose turned her attention to him. "The rightful ruler of Marconia."

Darien spoke up again with some gathered confidence. "I'm surprised my uncle didn't come to do his dirty work himself. Instead, he sends you. I can't help but feel a little insulted."

The bearded man looked down his pointed nose at the prince. "You think the King himself would leave his castle for trivial matters such as this? It's a shame all this time hasn't made you smarter."

Darien simply made a sorry face to play along with Peter's rouse.

Spencer took the opportunity to redirect the conversation. "Yup, as promised, I found your rather pathetic prince. He's all yours, assuming you have what you promised?"

Peter looked up at Spencer as if he were about to berate him as well. Instead, he took the sling that held the magnificent sword off his shoulder and handed it over to Spencer.

"The illustrious King Robert the First always keeps his promises."

Spencer unsheathed his sword and inspected the blade with an unbiased eye. When he was satisfied, he sheathed his sword and slung it over his shoulder where it sat comfortably centered on his back. Rose saw Spencer anew. The sword looked natural as it sat on his back like it was a part of him. Rose could hardly remember how he looked before, without it. He was no longer Spence, the Storyteller; this man was a warrior.

"What is so special about that sword anyway, huh?" Peter asked coolly.

Spencer looked back at Peter as if he were an insect that needed to be crushed.

"You mean, aside from it being mine?" Darien looked up abruptly at Spencer hopefully, but it was quickly snuffed out when Spencer took his place alongside Peter with ease.

"So, we both have what we wanted. Does this make us square? Are we done?" Spencer's voice was unyielding.

"Yes, yes," the man waved his hand carelessly to dismiss him. "You are free, as we have no further use for you."

"Then I will take my leave." He turned toward the prisoners and bowed to each in mock respect. "Your Highness… My lady." His easy smile beamed at Rose, and she could have sworn she saw him wink before he turned to leave.

Chapter 17

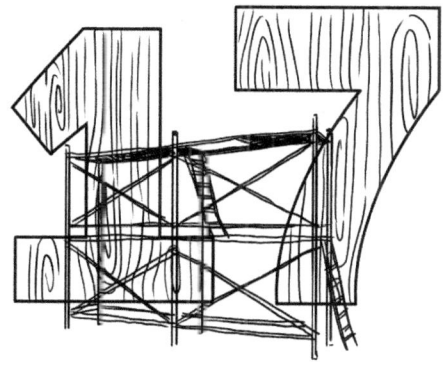

The older, bearded man finally directed his attention towards Rose. She wished he hadn't. His stare made her stomach turn, especially when he stroked his long pointy beard. Rose couldn't bear the sight of Peter, so she looked away, absolutely disgusted.

"Now this is a quandary," Peter continued to watch Rose with his shifty gaze. "King Robert has special plans for our honorable prince, but what shall become of you?"

"If you know what's best, you won't do anything to her," Darien spoke up confidently. Rose was surprised, to say the least.

Peter tore his eyes away from Rose and bent down in front of Darien so they were nose to nose. "And why would I do that?"

"Because this is Egeiro Red. She is one of the greatest traveling performers that have ever lived. Her face is known throughout our entire kingdom and several others. If something terrible were to happen to her, people would notice."

"Why would I care if some measly peasants don't see her perform anymore?"

"Because, it's not just some peasants, it's a whole crowd of peasants! Possibly a few dignitaries too, but we'll ignore that for now. Imagine a small army of angry, vengeful peasants who will storm the castle demanding justice from our oh so just King Robert. From what I know about my uncle, he will deny he had anything to do with her fate. He'll put the blame on you, since it was you who decided not to let her go."

Peter paused to consider the prince for a moment, then he shook his head. "She can't possibly be that important. Sure, people might miss her, who wouldn't," Peter leered at Rose's figure openly. "But after some time they will move on."

"Don't be too sure about that," Darien warned.

"I am sure of it. I'm not going to second guess myself because a sniveling prince says I need to."

Peter was already second-guessing himself. Rose could see the doubt plain as day in every hesitation, every flick of the eye, and shuffle of his feet. Rose couldn't believe how much control Darien had over this man. Furthermore, he was talking her up as if they were close friends with a strong, reliable past. Whether he was sincere or just trying to string Peter along remained to be seen. Either way, Rose was impressed.

"I wouldn't second guess myself because of a pathetic prince either," Darien continued his argument with ease. He was in control, and he knew it. "But your intelligence reports might give you pause."

"Intelligence reports?" Peter encouraged Darien to continue.

"Intelligence on traveling performers. Assuming you are current on your information, can you honestly say to me no person of interest would have this kind of a following?" Rose's heart skipped a beat as she held her breath. She remembered instantly why she didn't like Darien. He didn't care about her at all. He was trying to save his skin by selling her out! If not her, then he was talking about Zoe. That scoundrel!

Peter stood up and stepped over to Rose. The smell that emanated from the man-made Rose nauseous.

"I wonder," he spoke. Rose could see Peter's brain was working excessively hard to form an intelligent thought. "Could you be the gypsy who can see the future? I've heard a rumor about the prince over here. A rumor that some believe to be prophetic."

Rose would have started to sweat were it not for the man's revolting breath that managed to distract her from the serious trouble she was in.

"If I could see the future, they why would I allow myself to be taken prisoner by a smelly, disturbing man, such as you?" Rose wished Peter would step away, so she could breathe again. She heard Darien choke back a laugh then cough to cover it up.

"You are trying to trick me!" Peter roared at Darien. "She's nobody! No one will miss her."

Darien simply stared back as self-assured as ever. "If you say so."

Rose sat straight-backed and still, for fear of igniting the sparks of tension that flew through the room. From the corner of her eye, she saw Peter's confidence start to crumble. His feet were shifting, and the round man repeatedly glanced over at her, measuring her up.

"Fine!" Peter threw up his hands, "The woman will go to the castle as well. King Robert will decide what will become of both of you."

Rose smiled, glad that Peter no longer had authority over her. Peter noticed her reaction and sneered, "Don't look too pleased, my dear. The King will most likely save a pretty woman, like you, to be one of his personal servants — not something I would want for even my worst enemy." Peter turned to walk away, but Darien shouted after him.

"What about me? Do I get to be one of the King's personal servants too?" Rose's eyes went wide in shock as Darien taunted their captor. At least the prince had gumption.

Peter faced Darien menacingly. "The King has a special room waiting just for you. I wouldn't worry. You will remain his guest only for a short while, just until the summer is over."

"Autumn?" Rose accidentally spoke out loud.

"Yes, autumn, my dear." Peter grinned. "By then, the timeline for this so-called prophecy will be debunked, and everyone will see those who started this rumor as the frauds that they are. As for you, the heroic prince, you will be allowed to leave the castle to hear firsthand how you let your entire kingdom down again."

Peter left the room with two henchmen trailing close behind. The door slammed shut followed by a series of thuds Rose presumed were locks.

Chapter

"our life is quite the drama, Prince Darien." Rose tested the word out and, as she expected, it felt odd connecting the stranger who had knocked on her door at the beginning of winter to royalty. But an undeniable feeling confirmed the truth of Prince Darien. The name felt right on her tongue, and she agreed it suited him far better than the name 'Lee'.

"Tell me something I don't know," the prince sighed. "I've made one too many bad decisions, and they all come back to bite me at the same time."

"Now I'm tangled up in the middle of all of it," Rose shook her head. "Thank you so much."

Her sarcasm was not missed by Darien. "I didn't mean for you to fall into this mess."

"Oh, but you're perfectly comfortable dragging my sister into all of it."

"What? No, I would never put Brizo in danger," Darien promised.

"That smelly old man is looking for the person who prophesied the downfall of King Robert. Sound like anyone you know?"

"You cannot blame me for that. A story that intriguing would raise suspicions from any monarchy. I only assumed my uncle would be taking the same precautions I would have. It is not my fault I was right, nor do I take pleasure in it."

Rose swallowed hard as fear tried to overtake her. "So, they have been looking for her for a while now. Zoe is…" Rose couldn't finish her sentence.

"Brizo is in more danger than we thought, yes." Darien sighed. "But don't worry, she is a strong woman. If the king's men ever found her, she would know what to do."

"That's the problem, Darien." Rose shook her head at his stupidity. "You two love each other. You have her swooning over you, ready to do anything you asked. She would follow you into Hell and back if you asked her to."

Darien was silent for a moment, "She does? I mean, really? She swoons?"

Rose was glad her back was to the prince. She just knew he had a foolish smile on his face. The prince had jumped headfirst into being love-struck and missed the point entirely.

"You sicken me," Rose stated.

"Since when is falling for a guy like me a death sentence."

"It is, for Zoe." Rose snapped. "It may have escaped your idiotic mind, but my sister is frail. She could die if pushed too hard. Now, thanks to your love, you're willing to pull her into all of this without a second thought. This could be too much for her."

"She's lasted this long. Brizo is not as weak as you think she is."

"Because I take care of her. She is alive because she has me, and I'll do anything to protect her." Rose spoke defensively.

"I'll protect her," Darien responded.

"Please, you can barely protect yourself."

Darien paused, but refused to back down. "You know what I think?"

"No one wants to know what you think." Rose was beyond upset with Darien now.

Darien ignored her, "I think you're worried about what would happen to you if you didn't have to take care of Brizo anymore. If we ever decided to have a life together, just the two of us, what will become of you? It has always been about Brizo, to the point where you don't even allow yourself to be happy. You're scared that..."

Rose stopped listening to the prince. She had no interest in what the prince wanted to say about her. Instead, she started wiggling around in the ropes that tied her down. Something seemed oddly familiar about them. She kept hearing Spencer's voice in her ear: *nothing easy for this beautiful flower*, as if he was performing for an audience that wasn't there.

Unless… She concentrated on the knot that bound her hands. A few quick maneuvers and the ropes slid easily from her wrists. She moved onto the other knots around her ankles then located her knives, conveniently left on a table a few paces away.

Darien was still talking without even realizing what Rose was up to. "… You may be prolonging her life, but you aren't allowing her to live. Believe it or not, she does dream of something more than being waited on by her sister for the rest of her life."

Darien's jaw dropped when Rose stood in front of him, feet planted, arms crossed, lips tight and completely free.

"Look," Now that Rose had his full attention, she had no patience left on this subject. "Any man who pursues my sister knowing it is only a matter of time before she passes on, and is alright with it, is not alright with me."

The room was silent for a moment before the prince spoke softly. "All I know is, I am better when she is around. She makes the world seem not so dark, and I feel more like myself. And for reasons I cannot explain, she is happier when she is with me. I could never give that up. Not for me and certainly not for her. Especially if her days are already numbered."

Rose focused on him with a cool, calculated look. Then she sighed as a knife appeared in her fingertips. She leaned over to cut the prince loose.

"Does this mean you no longer hate me?" Darien rubbed his wrists to soothe them.

"It means my sister will be furious if she learned I left you here to rot. Don't make the mistake of thinking you know Zoe better than I do."

Darien watched Rose warily while she looked around the room, "Yes, my lady."

Rose scanned the room for a way out, with no success. Then she looked upward into the wooden rafters. She laughed to herself as if recalling a secret joke.

"Are you up to the challenge, Your Highness?" asked Rose.

Darien looked up at the interlocking beams which formed a precarious network of pathways that could lead them to the roof.

"Do I have a choice?" He swallowed hard.

"Not really. I'll need you to crouch down a bit, so I can hop on your shoulders." Darien looked confused but obediently lowered himself closer to the ground. Before he had a chance to think, Rose had stepped from his bent knee to his shoulders and sprang up to the lowest cross beam with ease.

The added flair did not go unnoticed by Darien. "Impressive, now how am I supposed to get up there?"

Rose had hooked her legs around a post and beam intersection, then dangled her head and outstretched arms to him like a trapeze artist. "Grab hold and I will swing you up."

Darien blinked then eyed the network of beams above them. He started to shake his head and step back as he started to wave his arms.

"Oh no, I'm not...!"

"Do it, or stay here and be the damsel in distress. It's your choice," she mocked.

He glared at her just for a moment before he leaped up to her. He held his breath as Rose took hold of his arm firmly and flung the prince upward.

He caught hold of the beam just in time with his other hand, pulling himself upright.

"Please keep in mind that I don't do this as often as you," the prince heaved as he tried to catch his breath.

"If you want to escape, then you need to learn fast," she shrugged as she daintily walked over to him while balancing on the balls of her feet. "Look, this is the path we are going to take."

Rose traced a complicated zig-zag toward a window that opened out to the roof. "If we keep quiet, and work quickly, they won't even notice us escaping out of that window."

"And then what? How do we get back down, and safely away?" Darien asked.

"I have a hunch. We will be fine, but we need to get to the roof first, understand?" Rose easily dismissed his questions.

It must have been a good enough answer because all the prince said next was, "Lead the way, my lady."

Chapter 12

ose had to help Darien up, so he could reach the window that led to the roof. "Wow, I didn't think I would make it to the roof without falling," Darien mused.

"You are so clumsy. I'm surprised we weren't caught over all the noise you were making." She shook her head with annoyance.

"Is it so hard to be nice to me, even once?" He chided.

"I'll say something nice when you actually do something noteworthy," she snapped.

When he was clear, she backed up a few paces on the beam, paused, and started a series of hops off of various beams before leaping easily through the window. She landed on the roof with a smooth tumble that ended with her on her feet, standing straight like it was one of her acrobatic tricks.

"You *are* showing off!" Darien whispered, taken aback.

Rose didn't bother denying it, "A little."

Darien swayed uneasily from foot to foot. "Look Rosie, You're a nice woman, but I'm in love with Brizo. She's the…"

"Oh do shut up before you embarrass yourself." Rose stormed over to the confused prince and grabbed him by the collar. Her hushed voice didn't diminish the seriousness of her words.

"There are two things you need to know. First, don't you ever… *ever*, call me 'Rosie' again, understand?"

The prince was so startled all he could do was nod his head.

"Second," Rose continued, "I wasn't showing off for you." She let go of the prince to take a few steps back.

Darien regained his courage. "Who then?"

The sound of footsteps caught their attention. Two knives appeared in Rose's hands and Darien clenched his fists, ready for a fight. A man appeared out of the shadows. He was tall, slender, and carried a large sword down the middle of his back. Rose relaxed.

"Spencer," she breathed while offering him a genuine smile.

"Took you long enough," he responded quietly. "But, I'll admit, it was a nice show to watch." Spencer gave a small bow in admiration. Rose relished the compliment as she tucked her knives away.

"Well, the prince slowed me down a bit," she claimed.

Darien was still on guard, trying not to yell. "What are you doing? Spencer's the one who captured us."

"And now, he's the one who's rescuing us," Rose answered calmly.

"Just like that?" Darien wasn't ready to ease up. "What was the point of capturing us in the first place?"

"The King had my sword," Spencer explained while fingering the hilt that hung behind his neck. "The deal was; he would give it back to me if I brought him you. I held up my end, got my sword, and the deal is all done. It's not my fault he doesn't know how to contain what I catch for him." He looked at Rose with a proud smirk.

Darien relaxed a little, "You had to have that sword specifically?"

"I like this sword," Spencer answered turning all his attention on the prince. "It reminds me of simpler times."

"Ironic, coming from you," Rose added.

"Not when you know the whole story, Rosie." He winked at her, and she grinned mysteriously back at him. It was a look that warned Spencer she would have her answers one way or another.

Darien broke the quiet tension between them. "Why does he get to call you 'Rosie'?"

Rose fought back the urge to slap Darien again, but the sound of men arguing about their disappearance gave her pause.

At first, the three could hear shouts from their previous captors from the streets below, yelling at each other to find the prince. Minutes later, there were more shouts of threats and curses when the men were unsuccessful with their search. The noise started to die down until there was only quiet.

Rose broke the silence with a low whisper, "Now's our chance. We should get going or this won't be much of an escape."

The three of them snuck across several rooftops before they made their way down to the streets and into the dark forest. Spencer and Rose were used to foraging in the forest by the cover of night, and they stepped easily around all the hidden obstacles in their way. Prince Darien was struggling terribly with every root, stump, branch, rock, hole, a patch of moss, and any other burden of the forest.

After falling countless times, Spencer pulled the prince up by grabbing a fistful of his shirt.

"You've gotten rusty, Highness," Spencer whispered. He dragged Darien along with Rose following close behind.

Spencer slowed down the pace to a steady hike, so they could continue to cover more ground. The moon was at its full height, allowing the prince to see much easier. Spencer let Darien take the lead, now that he was more comfortable tracking in the woods. Then he slowed down his pace to check on Rose. Their interaction was brief as a tense silence settled over the two of them. Rose was trying to make sense of the events of the night. It scared her to see Spencer in such a treacherous light, even if it was part of an elaborate ruse. What terrified her, even more, was how easily she dismissed his trickery when he was back on her side. Rose seemed so eager to dismiss his faults, she didn't stop to think if she should.

Rose broke the silence first. "Spencer, it's alright that you have secrets. You already know I have my own. But, you could have warned me beforehand."

Spencer suppressed a laugh. "What fun would that be?"

Rose shook her head at him. "I think you play these games just to watch me squirm."

"Of course, I enjoy watching you squirm. It's one of those few moments you remind me you are human beneath that hard exterior shell of yours," Spencer answered truthfully.

Rose contemplated his words in silence as they walked on. He was always on her side, even when she did not see it. He never forced her to do anything she didn't want to, but somehow he still challenged her. She would have never discovered half the things she knew about herself without Spencer by her side. He always saw the best in her, no matter the circumstance. Somehow, Spencer had become a true friend of hers, someone she could trust.

"Zoe is dying," Rose whispered so only Spencer could hear.

"Zoe has been dying for years, Rosie," was his response.

"Spence, I mean it. She does not have much time left," Rose was solemn.

Spencer's face yielded no emotion as he allowed her words to sink in. "Do you have any idea what's harming her?"

Rose took a deep breath to gather her courage.

"Her gift is killing her," she stated. Spencer couldn't hide his surprise. Although, Rose wasn't sure if he was surprised that magic was killing Zoe, or that she was finally being honest with him about it.

"Zoe can do more than just read cards to tell fortunes." Rose continued, feeling more and more relieved that she was finally telling Spencer. It was one less secret to keep and one more person to trust.

"She sees real prophecies about the people she meets. That's why everyone loves our stories, they stem from her prophecies. My mother had the same gift and passed it onto us. Only, for some reason, the gift has been slowly eating away at Zoe since it manifested in her. She has always been weak and tired, but lately, the small pains she has always felt have become almost crippling. Every time Zoe sees a vision, it's as if she is being stabbed by an invisible blade."

Rose stopped talking to collect herself. She was getting emotional and didn't want to. It was her responsibility to be strong for her sister.

Spencer changed the subject. "You said the gift passed to both of you. I've seen you read your cards, and tell your fortunes just as well as your sister. Why isn't this gift hurting you?"

Rose was completely honest with him. "I do what every fortune teller does; I trick them. I read the cards, and tell people what they already know or want to hear. I inherited a gift of prophecy, but I do not know how to use it. That's what our lessons are for: to try to trigger that gift inside of me. Someone needs to be able to take over after Zoe...."

"Why would you want to learn magic if it's just going to kill you too?" He asked dumbfounded.

"That's the thing. Mom had the gift and she never had this sickness. Regardless, I need to figure it out. Our troupe has a reputation to uphold."

"Hold on a minute. It's late, and you are being uncharacteristically forthcoming." Spencer rubbed his face with his hands. "Instead of trying to figure out how to stop this gift from killing your sister, the two of you have accepted that she is going to die? And you are working to activate that same gift in you, risking your own life, all for the sake of the show?"

"You don't understand, the show is our life." Rose tried to explain, but Spencer cut her off abruptly.

"Your life… is your life, Rosie! The show will go on just fine without you two sacrificing yourselves for it." He shook his head. "I thought matriarchs were supposed to be smart."

"Now you sound like, Darien," Rose sighed.

"Do not change the subject," Spencer said. "There has to be something else you can do."

"Even if there was, Zoe has foreseen it, and everything Zoe foresees happens."

"And you are not bothered by that at all?"

Rose hesitated, "No, I'm not."

Spencer eyed her carefully, "Nope, not buying it. I know you. There is no way you would be comfortable with a plan that ended in anyone's death – let alone your sister's."

"You're just upset because you don't like the plan. I'm the one who has to make the hard decisions, and you're angry because you don't want to see me hurt." She argued.

"Of course I don't, woman! I don't want to comprehend a world that you are not a part of."

Rose closed her eyes in annoyance. "Our future is already set; this is going to happen one way or another. Getting angry and upset about it won't change it. Imagine how Zoe is feeling right now. She's never foreseen anyone's death before, and the first time she does, it is her own. That alone must be terrifying for her. Right now Zoe needs our support more than ever. My sister and I made a promise to always watch out for each other. I can't be selfish now." Rose glared at Spencer in defense.

"And you think the best way to watch out for your only sister is to allow her to die?" Spencer scratched his head.

"Like I said it's not about what I think. Our future is set. You cannot change a prophecy," Rose answered obviously.

"I don't like it when you talk about prophecies as absolutes. It makes me feel uneasy." Spencer was relentless. "And I don't think you realize how this prophecy will affect you. If you do this, then you will wrestle with her death for the remainder of your life. Guilt will overwhelm you like poison. Guilt that you are alive, and she is not. Guilt that you didn't do more to try to stop it. It is a life of pain that even the strongest of men struggle to endure. And all this will be in addition to the physical pain your newly developed gift will inflict on you."

Rose flinched. Spencer's words sounded a bit too real to her. She wondered where this insight was coming from. She spoke her next words slowly.

"What I want doesn't matter. I'll just have to figure it out, I'm stronger than you think."

"So you keep reminding me," Spencer answered her flatly. "Everyone has a breaking point, and you are dangerously close to yours. Don't you understand? You can't handle this on your own."

Spencer sounded almost desperate as he spoke, and Rose felt sorry for him. "I can take care of myself."

"Oh, you can? Really, how's that working out for you?" Spencer already knew the truth, and it upset Rose that she knew it. She rather enjoyed having a friend that knew her so well, but when it came to matters such as this, she wished they weren't so friendly. Then she wouldn't have to answer his hard, prying questions.

Lights started to flicker in the distance. It was their caravan. The softly glowing lanterns that hung beside each wagon door were inviting to any stray traveler. Even Darien picked up his step, recognizing that he was almost back home… with Zoe. Rose flinched when she saw the lights, and her steps slowed. A motion not missed by Spencer either.

"Problem?" He asked.

"I'm fine," was all she could say.

Rose put on her hard, strong face. She wasn't fine. She thought about all the people who relied on her. The members of her troupe always looked to her for help—the people who trusted her with their livelihood every time they performed a show, everyone who relied on her for their safety. She thought about Zoe, and all the special attention she required as of late. More and more, Rose's identity drifted further away from her joys and desires and was defined by the success of everyone else. She had sacrificed so much for her troupe and now she was asked to sacrifice her sister to the demands of fate as well.

Spencer scowled, "Right, because not wanting to rush to be with your friends and family is a perfectly *fine* reaction, after you have been held captive."

Rose remained still, eyes fixed on the lights ahead of her, her lips closed tight… wordless.

"Are you even happy, Rose?" Spencer's voice softened.

"Of course I am," She answered back too quickly.

"Rosie, I see you. When you think no one is watching, when you don't have your brave face, I see you. You're not happy." He reached for her hand, but she quickly shoved them in her pockets. "You need someone to help you through all this. Someone watching out for you."

Rose was instantly annoyed that Spencer had turned the conversation onto him again. She was even more upset by the image of his death permanently burned inside her eyelids.

"Are you implying I'm supposed to let *you* take care of me?"

"Yes Rose, me. I want to take care of you. That's a normal thing that people who love each other do."

Rose walked closer to the lights, away from Spencer, but turned back to face him.

"Every time you talk like this, you make me wish I had left you to the wolves all those years ago."

"Oh, come on. That's not fair. I was lost!"

Rose regained control of her face as she recalled the night Spencer met the great Egeiro Red for the first time

"Yes, lost in the middle of the forest, at the edge of a cliff, and screaming like a little old lady."

"Well," Spencer said and flashed her another smile. "It got your attention, didn't it?"

"You were lucky. I wasn't supposed to be out so late that night," she retorted.

He let out an amused laugh as he grinned at her. "Lucky? I thought you were some sort of monster. I couldn't tell what in the world was swooping down on the wolves with sparks and sulfur swirling around you like some... demon or something."

Rose flushed and looked at him indignantly, her anger from earlier temporarily forgotten. "Now you're exaggerating."

"No, not really." Spencer watched her with a twinkle in his eye. "The way you were howling, made me more scared of you than the wolves. It wasn't until after the smoke cleared, that I realized it was just some little girl being clever with a cloak. Then you decided to let me stay with your troupe."

"Only until you found a better place to call home. Remember, I thought it was going to be temporary." Rose sighed and crossed her arms tightly as she looked out and watched her people as they moved about in the firelight.

"It was, originally," Spencer murmured and turned his attention to the caravan as well. "But it had been a while since I had felt that welcome and wanted. It made me happy."

"Now you're getting sappy."

"Of course I am," Spencer grinned and looked at her. "I'm around you."

Rose let out an annoyed sigh and started walking down the hill again. "I don't know why I let you stick around."

"It's because you're soft," Spencer announced loudly with confidence to answer Rose's question.

Rose quickly scanned the surrounding area for any passersby who might have gotten the wrong idea about her. She knew she looked ridiculous as they still were well beyond earshot from anyone in the troupe. She stalked back and jabbed him with her finger.

"I am many things, Spencer, but *soft* is not one of them.' She insisted.

Spencer folded his arms, still as confident as ever. "Your actions tell a different story."

"That was one kiss, Spencer. I couldn't breathe, and I almost died. I wasn't being soft, I was being grateful," she defied him with every word, furious that he would use her moment of weakness against her.

Spencer's grin only grew wider as he tried not to laugh.

"What's so funny?" She asked.

"You are!" Spencer took a deep breath to calm himself. "I was merely talking about what you told me when we first met. Funny how you immediately think of our kiss."

Rose looked away, relieved by the red sunrise that hid her blush, which was true to her name.

Spencer continued, "Ten years ago, you told me you could never allow an innocent man to be hurt, especially if there was something you could do to help."

"I call that honor. A quality you should be thankful for, or you would not be here now." Rose snapped at him.

Spencer didn't allow her tone to have any effect on him. "Yes, yes, honor and all that. Truthfully, I see compassion, empathy, and above all love. You may be the toughest woman I know, but underneath all of that, you are soft. They are the most precious qualities that define you, and they need to be protected."

He reached for her hand again, this time she allowed him to take it. Rose looked up in his eyes, longingly, unable to speak.

"You don't have to be afraid of being so vulnerable with me," Spencer whispered.

His death flashed in Rose's mind again, and she quickly shook it out of her mind. "Even if I wanted to, it will never work out. Our destinies simply won't allow it."

He tightened his grip on her hand when she turned to leave. "I'm wearing you down," Spencer whispered.

"What?" Rose looked confused.

"You usually conjure shallow excuses to push me away; now you are blaming it on our destinies?" There was a familiar glint in his eye. "I'm wearing you down."

Rose mustered all the courage she could to sound confident. "You have got to stop. Our future is risky."

Spencer smiled at yet another excuse from her. "I'll never stop, so long as you keep giving me hope."

Rose allowed a corner of her mouth to turn up into a hint of a smile before finally leaving him alone in the night.

Chapter 20

Several months later, memories of the cold, unforgiving winter were talked about with fondness as the merciless heat beat down on the land. Summer had come to Marconia and not in a playful happy sort of way. What should have been green and flowered meadows were simply brown, dry slopes, devoid of life. Lush farmland that the troupe's wagons would pass by were replaced with whithered, yellow stems of what might have been a plentiful crop. The People of Marconia were only annoyed by the heat at first. If there is one thing Marconians are known for, it is their unfailing ability to look misfortune in the eye and push back. In every field, he would see persistent workers busy with every trick up their sleeve to salvage whatever they could from their crop.

This was not the first time Marconia was in a drought, and the people had handled themselves well in the past. Hard times like these was when the best nature of Marconians seemed to shine the brightest. Communities would band together to ensure everyone was taken care of. Droughts were nothing to sneer at, but at the same time, everyone knew if they worked hard they would get through it; they always did.

However, this time King Robert was in charge of things. And his way of helping out during troubling times such as these was to tax the people more and take a hefty portion of what little food each family had. While the troop was performing in one of the towns, Darien resisted the urge to start a brawl when men in armor had entered a nearby city demanding more food from the townspeople. It was obvious that his uncle was taking far too much, leaving much too little for these communities to survive with. The kingdom was starving, just so King Robert could continue to sit in the lap of luxury without a care in the world. The hot days only flared his temper more when the soldiers wouldn't take no for an answer, and proceeded to ransack the people's own homes for items of value. Those were the days that the White and Red Troupe's performance of the Prince's Prophecy was received with tears of joy, grown men falling on their knees in prayer, and shouts of praise for the hope of what could be. Those were also the days when Darien felt the absolute worst.

It's true, Zoe's prophecy was very convincing and inspiring to all. But, it put all the responsibility for saving the kingdom entirely in Darien's hands. And the hotter the days grew, the heavier the prophecy weighed on his shoulders.

> *There will come a time when the*
> *heat of the sun will be too great...*
> *And, in the summer of that year,*
> *the Red Bear of Marconia will awaken...*
> *He will find strength from his misery*
> *and remember his courage.*

Darien knew the time of the prophecy had come, and he was not ready. He wanted to help his people, but he didn't feel strong or courageous. These people would be much happier to have a prince, long forgotten, to remain forgotten, rather than have him show up to save the day, only to fail them once again. His past failures loomed over him like a dark cloud. He would not allow himself to ruin his kingdom again, so Darien chose to stay hidden.

Darien sat on a stump just outside of Zoe's wagon. Rose had asked him to keep an eye on her sister since she could no longer put off her usual troupe business. They had agreed to keep their adventure with the king's guards a secret from Zoe to spare her any unnecessary stress or unsolicited prophecies. Practices had to be done and scripts to be written to keep life running as normal as possible for the troupe, as opposed to the actuality that their life had been turned upside down with a disgraced prince living amongst them while the country's former general had been posing as their head storyteller for the past ten years. Oh, and now both of them were on the top of the king's most wanted list. Darien had to admit he unknowingly brought this chaos onto the White and Red Troupe. He also understood Rose's insistence on the illusion of normality until they knew exactly what was going on and how they would handle it.

In all honesty, this was the last thing that Darien expected to happen when he began his search for Brizo White. He had searched far and wide for the seer in the hopes she could give him more answers about her latest prophecy. His prophecy promised everyone in his kingdom he would bring his evil Uncle Robert to ruin, and take his rightful place on the throne, thus, restoring peace and balance to the kingdom again. It was a beautiful vision but lacked a few valuable pieces of information. Important things, along the lines of how, prevented him from fulfilling his destiny.

When he finally found Zoe, Darien was enchanted. She had been sitting in the forest with her sister before the first snowstorm of winter. They sat next to a cliff face where the sun's rays shined brightly on them, offering the illusion of summer while still on the doorstep of winter. Zoe's fair skin and white, blonde hair managed to glow under the sun's rays. Zoe appeared almost ethereal, and yet she was as real as he was. When he was found, and taken in by their kindness, she spoke to him with such eloquence. Zoe was far more knowledgeable about certain subjects than he was. Her voice was soft and airy, like a summer breeze, yet emanated all the force and authority of a raging river. That's all it took. One look and one word, and he was officially smitten. He no longer cared about the prophecy or the questions that gnawed at him concerning it. He no longer cared about his uncle or even himself. All that mattered was her.

Darien sprang to his feet when he heard the wagon door creak open behind him. He smiled affectionately at Zoe, offering his hand to help her down the steps. She chuckled at his eagerness and accepted his help.

"Where is Rose?" she asked.

Darien's heart sank when Zoe's first words were about her sister, "She's working with Spencer. Something about performance notes?"

"Is she?" Zoe breathed excitedly. "And she asked you to keep an eye on me while she was working?"

"She did." It's true she asked him to keep an eye on her, but he would never agree to a favor from Rose willingly. She had to send Spencer around a few minutes later asking for the same thing as a personal favor to him. It was a childish game to play, but he was not ready to grant Rose the satisfaction of ordering him around. Darien's spirits started to lift when he saw Zoe's sweet smile growing bigger.

"Well, then we should do something fun before she changes her mind," Zoe said.

"Like what?" Darien asked.

"I don't know about you, but I feel like venturing into the woods. You're welcome to join…" Zoe laughed when Darien almost tripped over his feet to join her.

Darien could see Zoe had more energy than usual, so he didn't think a hike in the woods would do any harm. Besides, the chance to be alone with Zoe, without the looming eyes of Rose or Spencer, lifted Darien's usual dark mood. Deeper and deeper into the woods they carried on without a care in the world, discovering new, beautiful sights, and laughing with each other throughout the day. It wasn't until later in the afternoon that they decided to settle down for some lunch in a lovely meadow by a nearby stream. The sun was warm and glistened off of the cool waters rushing nearby. The bright light gave Zoe an ethereal hue again, which made Darien's heart skip a beat.

He cleared his throat to settle his nerves, "So, how does this compare to your usual resting spots?"

Zoe blinked at him, "You mean, compared to the inside of my wagon?"

Darien shook his head, "No, I mean when you usually go out exploring."

Zoe smiled, "It is a lovely spot you've found, but I haven't gone exploring in the woods for several years now. I usually keep close to the camp because... you know."

"It hurts that much?" He asked. Zoe nodded, reluctantly. "I've always imagined having a special gift, but I've never thought there would be repercussions along with it."

"It isn't that big of a deal," Zoe smiled to herself. "It didn't always hurt this much, just lately. I suppose it was a price I didn't mind paying, until now."

Darien took her hand sympathetically, "You seriously have never been this far from your camp before?"

Zoe smiled confidently, "I'm out here with you now."

His golden eyes brightened when the meaning of her words struck him. Before, all that mattered to her was the troupe and telling fortunes. That was her life, and although it was a nice life, she never thought it would ever change, until now. She had fallen in love with him, and Darien had fallen hard for her. Her life had changed, but now she didn't think she had much time left to enjoy it. The thing was, he didn't care how much time he had left with her. All that mattered is they were together, and he loved being with her. Whenever Zoe was around he felt welcome. It was a feeling he hadn't felt in a long time.

"Why do you do that?" he looked away, embarrassed.

"Do what?" She answered innocently.

"Every time you look at me, it feels like you're staring straight to my soul. And you smile as if I'm the greatest person you have ever had the pleasure of knowing."

Zoe's brow furrowed, "Who says you are not?"

"I do," Darien blushed again. "I'm not as remarkable as you think I am. I'm not even very good. Anyone who I allow to get close to me gets hurt, or worse. I'm destined to be miserable."

Zoe offered a soft giggle, "Lee, if there is one thing I know for sure about you, it is that your destiny is not set in stone."

Darien winced when she spoke his false name. He wondered if she would still be saying such things about him if Zoe knew who he really was. "How could you possibly know that?"

"Because all the visions I have are final. They will happen no matter what. However, when I look at you, all I see is a blurry haze." She spoke as if she had just explained everything clearly.

Darien still didn't understand. "That isn't very cheerful, Brizo."

Zoe smiled, "Actually it is! Don't you see? If I can't see any absolutes that means your future is whatever you want it to be. Nothing is set, unless you decide it is so." She was getting more and more excited with her explanation that Darien couldn't help smiling back at her in amusement.

"I wish I had your enthusiasm," Darien sighed. "I just don't see the merit in a life so uncertain."

"Oh, but I do!" Her eyes were wild with life as she continued, "Everyone I have read has a definite future."

"Everyone?"

"Yes, they may have control of their choices or desires, likes, and dislikes, but it is their heart that sets their fate. Now, I know people change all the time, but their heart always remains steadfast to the person they truly are."

"Are you saying my heart is broken?" Darien was trying to understand a lifetime of magic in a small amount of time.

Zoe just smiled patiently, "I'm saying, your heart is unsure, thus your destiny is unsure. Only when your heart settles on its truest desires can I be able to read…" Zoe's eyes focused on something over Darien's shoulder then she quickly turned away blushing.

"What is going on?" Darien watched her curiously as Zoe simply blushed redder. "Did, did you see something?"

"Only a glimmer, and then it blurred," she admitted.

"What was it?"

"It is probably nothing," she dismissed, "It didn't stay very long."

"Come on, now I'm curious. You have to tell me," he urged.

Zoe smoothed her hair nervously, "I don't know."

Darien's voice turned soft and gentle which caught her attention. "Brizo, please tell me."

His tone sounded almost desperate. Desperate to know that his life had some direction, and desperate to know if it was for the good or bad.

"I saw a face," Zoe answered.

Darien's muscles tensed as he predicted whose face she might have seen. A silver-haired, thin man with a long pointed beard, and eyes like emeralds—the face that haunts his dreams at night and is spoken by everyone around him during the day. The looming face of his uncle, King Robert. It was a face he never wished for Zoe to see, in reality, nor visions. He would never want such a terrifying image to cast a shadow on her innocent eyes.

"Whose face did you see?" he asked hesitantly.

"Mine," Zoe answered timidly, but her bright smile warmed Darien to his core. Zoe promptly turned away again, embarrassed.

Darien was surprised by her answer. Thrilled, of course, but not what he expected. He never expected something so lovely and genuinely virtuous to be in his future. Then again, he never expected to be sitting with, or having a conversation with someone of that nature either. Her answer delighted him, and he was able to relax.

"Perhaps my heart isn't as directionless as you thought," Darien smiled.

Zoe drank in his attention like the sweetest nectar in the world.

"It's just as I said, Lee. Your destiny is whatever you want it to be," she reminded him.

Darien's heart sank at the sound of that name again. If he couldn't trust Zoe to know his true identity then did he deserve to have her in his future?

"Brizo, there is something you need to know about me. Who I really am."

All that Darien wanted to say was left on the tip of his tongue as a burlap sack was thrown over Zoe's head; and her hands were bound with coarse, scratchy ropes. Darien immediately tried to protect Zoe from her captor. Instead, all he could do was shout and struggle as another burlap sack and more ropes rendered him useless as well. Regardless, he continued to holler in the hopes of saving Zoe from whatever fate awaited her.

"Let her go! It's me you want!" was all he could say before his voice was muffled and the world went black.

Chapter 21

Darien and Zoe were tied up together beside the bank of a rushing river. A guard who was even taller than Spencer paced back and forth, nervously. Closer to the trees, two more guards were tending to their horses and casting several glances in their direction. A stout, little man sauntered over to the captives; fingering his mustache with a wide grin. Prince Darien was annoyed to see the all too familiar face of Peter again.

"You found him!" Peter clapped his hands with delight. "Excellent work."

"Yes Peter, and now he's all yours. So if he slips away again it will be your fault, not mine," the guard said.

"If? You can't possibly believe he will be that lucky again," The guard looked down at Peter, unimpressed.

"Darien never needs luck, he's as slippery as an eel, he is," the man grumbled while he walked off to join his men by the horses. Peter dismissed the guard's warning with a wave of his hand and bent down to speak to the Prince.

"Back in my clutches again, your highness. This time I will collect on the reward your uncle has promised me. I may even become an overlord to part of your kingdom" he sneered.

"I'm just passing through, Peter," admitted Darien, "only because I miss these talks of ours."

Peter snarled at Darien's ease and his eyes flickered over to Zoe. "This one is new, what happened to the brunette? Did you get tired of her already?"

"Brunette?" Zoe whispered to Darien.

Before Darien had a chance to answer, Peter butted in, "That's right darling, a couple of months ago I found him with a long-haired brunette dressed in red. She was lovely with the most beautiful rosy cheeks I've ever seen. Not at all like you. Why, you look as pale as a ghost."

Zoe's eyes kept darting over to Darien for more information, a move that Peter spotted instantly. "Oh, you didn't know, darling? Well, I hate to be the one to tell you, but Prince Darien here is dripping with all sorts of secrets and lies. Quite frankly, he'll say anything to impress a pretty girl."

"Apparently," Zoe mumbled to herself. Darien's heart sank when he heard her, wishing he had the time to explain everything.

Zoe's saddened face seemed to invigorate Peter, "Oh, don't you worry, darling. If you are unhappy with how our little prince has treated you, then you can always turn to me. I have a soft spot for blondes, you know."

"I had no idea you were allowing women a choice, these days," Darien feigned being impressed with Peter.

"I see what you mean, highness," Peter snarled maliciously as he grabbed a fistful of Zoe's hair, pulling her close.

"Let go of her!" Darien shouted. He struggled to free himself from his ropes.

Peter simply faced Darien with pure delight.

"Oh, so this one is important to you." Darien's eyes seethed with rage. "Don't worry, I would never spoil this harmless little beauty. Not when she can be so useful to me."

"You will never use her to play me. She is too smart for you," Darien warned.

"We will see," Peter responded.

"Actually," Zoe's soft voice sliced through the two men's low gravely tones, "you're right. I can be quite useful." Darien's mouth fell open, aghast while Peter laughed triumphantly.

"See Darien, ladies always find themselves running to me in the end."

"Only because you get in their way," Darien taunted.

Peter gritted his teeth, pulling Zoe closer to him. "Now, darling, what is it you were going to say?"

Zoe looked frail and harmless next to Peter, but her eyes were set and resolute.

"I can tell you things," she offered politely.

"No!" Darien pleaded.

"What kind of things?" Peter asked.

"Hidden things about you, and your future."

"My future?" Peter was bursting with intrigue.

"No, she cannot," Darien insisted.

"Yes, I can see all that you will have, and what you will become," Zoe promised.

Peter's eyes narrowed, "Why should I believe you?"

"Sir, I am the beloved Brizo White, seer of all that is good. Just ask Darien, he will tell you."

Immediately Darien denied everything when Peter looked at him expectantly. "She's lying! She doesn't know any more about the future than I do. She is a harmless gypsy trying to trick you."

Zoe cast a dark look down on the prince, "I suppose he just wants to keep my skills all for himself. You can't blame him for trying. Would *you* announce to everyone that you had a personal fortune teller in your employment?"

"So you're the notorious Brizo White we have been looking for?" Peter took in her appearance as if seeing her for the first time. Then he turned his attention back on Darien, "Thought you could hide such a treasure from me?"

Darien glared at Zoe, "I was doing alright, until just now."

"Well, obviously you failed, just like you fail in everything you do." Peter looked at Zoe, "Now, darling, will you be so kind as to give me a taste of your powers? Just a technicality to prove you are who you claim to be. Come on, tell me what you see?"

Peter tried hard to sound uninterested, but the drippings of intrigue was not lost on the fortune teller. He was hooked and she had him right where she wanted.

Zoe gave Darien a long, sideways glance, then smiled knowingly at Peter. Her usual soft voice took on a firm, bold quality that startled the two men. The wind suddenly kicked up and swirled heavy, grey clouds into the sky above them, as the grass and weeds twirled in a torrent of movement down by the river. Her stare had locked onto Peter's gaze who now stood motionless, unable to speak. All he could do was shift his eyes back and forth in terror.

"I know your fate, Peter, son of a cobbler. Your days are marked with safety and security in the life you have established for yourself. I see great riches in your future, piles of precious gems, towers of gold, and the finest silks to be made into luxurious robes; that will never be yours. Indeed King Robert will recognize all that you have done in your service to him, but the credit will be given to another, less deserving servant of his. Rest assured you will have the chance to oversee a small part of the kingdom, but only through occasional peeks and glances over your master's shoulder. But fear not, for not all riches glimmer like gold. You will meet an acceptable woman who will find you genuinely acceptable and will bear you rather acceptable children who will grow up to accept the mediocrity of their father. All of which will live average lives, doing average things with their own average families, far away so they never will burden you with anything of worth. You will live your life free of sorrows and joy, misery, and excitement. You, Peter, will be forever stuck in the mundane void of anything noteworthy, lacking the intense motivation needed to run from it. In the end, you will be content right where you are."

The bearded man remained frozen in time, eyes still wide as saucers and mouth hanging open. His face was locked in a perpetual state of fear and pain, unable to move. Zoe wasted no time freeing herself from Peter's grip and then her ropes. Next, she promptly rushed over to help Darien out of his bounds.

"Seriously?" Darien couldn't believe that Zoe was out of her knots before he was, the same way Rose had been when they were captured. "How in the blazes were you able to get out of your ropes?"

"Oh please, it's not that hard to untie a knot," Zoe answered as she effortlessly pulled the ropes off him. "We need to get away fast! He won't stay frozen like this for long."

As much as Darien wanted to sit in amazement by all Zoe had just done, he knew he didn't have the time for it. He scanned his surroundings to assess his options. The three guards by the horses were no longer distracted by the wind and began to charge. If the two of them ran, the men would catch them in no time. Neither were there any good places to hide or get lost in from their captors. The only thing nearby was the river, which roared even louder than the wind.

"Hold on to me," he shouted so Zoe could hear, "and don't let go!" Zoe nodded as he swept her into his arms, and jumped into the rushing waters.

Chapter 22

The only thing Zoe could see was the color of white being smashed in her face along with occasional bouts of blue when she was submerged in the water. She managed a few labored breaths that sustained her, as they continued to swirl downstream. If the guards were nearby, she couldn't hear them. All that existed was the deafening roar of the waves. The next thing Zoe knew, her arm was being pulled into the opposite direction of the water's flow. Her hand slapped against a dry rock that felt warm to the touch. Her fingers clutched tightly around the handhold, and she pulled herself free from the rushing waters. Darien was helping her to the top of the rock with his hand fixed in a tight grip around her. She gulped in the fresh air greedily, thankful the watery ride was over.

"How far away are they?" Zoe gasped and choked water from her lungs.

"Nowhere nearby, but we need to keep some distance between us." Zoe looked up at him confused. "Distance between us and them, I mean. But we need to get our bearings, and I'm not sure where we are."

Zoe breathed in deeply while taking in her new surroundings. All she could see was the river and more trees. She closed her eyes and thought about her sister. She focused on every detail, from the color of Rose's hair to the folds of her skirt. Zoe saw her as plain as day. Next, Rose's surroundings materialized around her in Zoe's mind. She and Spencer were competing to get their hands on a sword before the other person. As unexpected as that scene was for Zoe she knew she didn't have time to figure out what that was all about. Instead, she pulled her vision back as if stepping away from them, further and faster. The clouds blurred overhead and the trees blended into a continual shade of green until the path drew closer and closer to a clear vision of herself standing with Darien next to the raging stream. Zoe opened her eyes and pointed west, in the direction she saw herself appear in the woods. Then grabbed her right side with a minor wince.

"Our troupe is that way. Let's go," she said confidently, but still strained with pain. Darien didn't feel the need to question her, but instead hurried west with Zoe's hand in his without hesitation. When they were deep into the forest, well away from the river, his curiosity got the better of him.

"What was that, back there by the river. How did you know which way to go?" He asked.

"It's an old trick I learned when I was young. Rose and I would play hide and seek in the forest sometimes. Rose always won. She has always been more adventuresome than me. One day, I got so tired of losing that I tried to use my gift to find her. It worked every time. So, hide and seek became our new favorite game. She would try to find even better places to hide from me, and I was able to hone my skills to see her no matter where she was."

"Can she see you?"

"If she ever figures out how to use her gift she can," Zoe sighed.

"And our escape?" Darien added, still astonished by what she had done. "How were you able to immobilize Peter with only his fortune?"

"Most people are dumb, and easily manipulated." She spoke as is if it was the most obvious statement. "People who have never learned to think for themselves will believe whatever they want to believe or are told to believe. I told him an unimpressive fortune, which promised him an unimpressive life. He believed it to be true because he believed I had power over him. He merely assumed I was able to subdue him with only a word from me. We were able to escape because of his stupidity. The truth is, he was immobilized by his own belief in his own lie."

"Lie, you mean that prophecy was a fake?" Darien asked, stunned.

"Of course it was a fake; didn't you notice?" Her blue eyes gave him an expectant look, waiting for him to answer his question.

One corner of Darien's mouth lifted into a half-smile, "You weren't in pain afterward. All of that was a trick."

"I am a gypsy, after all," she reminded him.

"How did you know his father was a cobbler?"

Zoe motioned to her waist, "He had a pair of shoe pliers hanging from his belt, and I saw some curved knives in his jacket that cobblers use. I guessed he grew up in the home of one." Darien looked at her in pure adoration. He hadn't even noticed the tools, yet now that he thought about it, Peter always had them with him.

"What about the weather? The winds and the dark clouds suddenly picking up. Was that in our minds too?"

"Nope," she smiled proudly, "that was luck."

"LUCK?"

"I have no control over the weather; it all happened on its own. It's not my fault everyone credited me for a possible storm."

Darien stared at her in wonder, "Amazing! That's brilliant. It all makes perfect sense now."

Zoe nodded, "It usually does make sense, when you know all the secrets."

Guilt immediately overcame Darien, "Look, I wanted to tell you everything that happened, but then Rose told me not to, so…"

"Rose? You mean, Rose knows you are Prince Darien? When did this happen?" Zoe thought for a second, "Wait a minute; is *she* the brunette with the red skirts Peter mentioned?"

"Well, yes…" Zoe didn't let Darien get any more words in.

"She knew all of this and still didn't tell me? Wait, Rose is as clever as they come, how did she manage to be captured by someone as oblivious as that guy?" Zoe waved her hand vaguely in the direction Peter could be.

"It wasn't that big of a deal. Peter didn't capture us at all, it was Spencer who…"

"Spencer was there too? And what would he need to capture you for?"

"This all sounds much worse than what happened.' Darien kept trying to underplay the event but Zoe wouldn't allow it.

"Yeah, it does! It sounds like all three of you have been keeping a story from me! And you are never supposed to keep stories from me. I am the Record Keeper in my troupe! I need to know what's going on to be an effective Matriarch of my troupe. That includes you. But if you insist on keeping me in the dark I am no good to anyone. And I refuse to be the helpless sage that everyone feels the need to protect and watch over so I can live a long, boring life of solitude! There's more to me than that; there's always been more to me than that kind of life. And just because my body insists on failing me more each day doesn't mean everything I am is lost too. I am stronger than you think, and I thought you knew that. I thought…" Her words caught in her throat. "I thought you were different."

Darien felt as if the ground had disappeared from underneath him. He felt horrible mainly because he had been keeping several secrets from Zoe — secrets she deserved to know, and probably needed to know. He didn't want there to be any secrets between them, and Zoe was always straightforward and honest with him.

"Brizo, I'm so sorry. You're right, you are different. I have never known anyone as intriguing as you. You may be small and frail, but you are the strongest person I know. Every day you fight through the pain of your gift, to help those around you. Serving your troupe is all you ever think about. Just like a true Matriarch would. You are a remarkable woman; anyone can see that."

He was glad to see her look up at him. He wanted to make sure she knew he was speaking what was in his heart, and not just what she wanted to hear.

"I should have told you who I was at the beginning. The truth is, I've been looking for you for a long time. Ever since I first heard your prophecy about me, I wanted to find you. I wanted to see if there was any more information you may have left out of your performance that could tell me how I'm supposed to take back my kingdom. I wanted to know how to fulfill your prophecy."

Zoe's face offered no clue as to what she was thinking. It was a mask of contemplation as she listened to his story. "A warrior as smart and resilient as you should already know."

"I'm not as resilient as you think, and I doubt myself all the time." He sighed deeply rubbing his neck nervously. "I'm not sure I can command my troops, or lead my kingdom the way everyone expects me to."

"Why do you say that?" She asked, with a hint of sharpness. Even though she was making conversation with him, Darien knew Zoe was still upset with him.

"You know the story. Ten years ago both my parents died, and Marconia was invaded," he said coldly. Then he reminded himself that was not the entire story, and he wanted to be completely honest with

Zoe. "I was heartbroken for my parents. I also wasn't allowed the chance to mourn them properly, thanks to the invasion. Besides, I could hear my father's voice in my head telling me there were more important things to deal with. Thanks to Robert, I was able to lead my army on the battleground instead of giving orders behind a desk. I never told anyone that the rush of the battle and the swing of my blade felt good to me. It made the pain go away. It wasn't long until I stopped seeing my enemy as a person and just saw them as something to destroy. There was so much death, and mostly by my hand. Looking back, I realize how crazy scary I was. My bloodlust to chase away the pain had consumed me. And yet, these men, my brothers continued to follow me.

"Every time I close my eyes I see my three hundred men marching through the valley, for the final battle. All I can wonder is why. Why did they agree to follow me? I wouldn't have followed me. I was a mess, and yet there they were, believing in me. Next thing I knew an arrow scratched me, the world went dark, and when I woke up all my men were dead." He rubbed his eyes then Zoe took his hand in a tight squeeze for support.

"I see their faces in my dreams, and I hear their voices throughout the day. I'm haunted by them— every one. I wish I were the one who died and they all lived. Life is a torment for me because I'm the lucky one who was spared. I can't even remember what happened. I can't even say that they fought bravely because I just cannot remember. The entire thing is unfair, unfair to them, unfair to their families, their friends…

"I am their king, I was their leader, and I have nothing to tell. I have no words of comfort, no answers to give, no explanation; I have nothing." Darien shook his head, "That's not the kind of person you want as a leader."

They walked for a while in silence. Darien noticed Zoe's pace slowing drastically; warning him her energy was fading quickly. She politely asked if they could rest for a moment. The woods showed no signs that they were being followed, so he helped her over to sit on the trunk of a large tree that had fallen.

"I'm sorry I didn't have a better story to tell you, Brizo," Darien admitted, slightly embarrassed.

Zoe tilted her head, "Your story is fine. Everything makes sense now."

"It does?"

Zoe looked at Darien gravely, "My gift allows me to see much more than anyone in this world, but I cannot see death. You have allowed yourself, your heart, and your mind, to be consumed by death every time you relive that battle. Because of this, your very existence is shrouded to me. I believe your heart cannot be sure of anything until you can accept what has happened. You need to untether yourself from all that loss."

Zoe pulled a long chain necklace off of her neck, and handed it solemnly to Darien. Hanging from the chain was a small metallic disk with a red and white symbol embedded in it. On it was a white tree with blossoming branches scrawled out of the top and down to create a border around the disc. There were roots, carved just as ornately branching from the bottom of the tree completing the other half of the circle. The exquisite tree was contrasted by the deep red background that created a beautiful balance of light and dark.

"What's this for?" Darien asked.

"For your dreams," Zoe struggled to speak, she was growing more and more out of breath by the second. "It is a charm our family has passed down over the years. It will help give balance to your dreams, so you are not overwhelmed by death all the time."

"I can get all that from this?" he mocked.

Zoe gave him a little smile before she continued. "This tree is the symbol for my family. The roots of the tree reach far into the ground as much as the branches extend into the sky. A tree must live in both realms of light and dark if it is to thrive. A tree without roots has no stability, and roots without a tree have no purpose."

"Okay," Darien shrugged. "But, what does this have to do with me?"

"Right now, you are hiding in the darkness. You refuse to extend into the light to fulfill a grand purpose with your life. You think that the darkness is all there is, but it is just the beginning. A tree's roots glean nourishment from the dark, rich soil in order to grow to its full potential. Thus, only when we find meaning in the darkness can we thrive in the light."

Darien placed the necklace in his pocket, "Thank you, but have you ever considered that this is my penance? That, as payment for my life, death must always be with me."

Zoe breathed deeply, "It has been ten years. You need to give these men the rest that they need. You need to give yourself the rest that you need so that you can progress away from death. I cannot tell you any more about your future if you continue to exist in your past."

Darien gave Zoe a pained look, "I don't know if I can do that."

Zoe looked exhausted but refused to allow sleep to overcome her. "You must find a way. Otherwise, you will be stuck in the darkness forever, and your heart will fail you."

Chapter 23

Spencer sat next to a small wooden desk that was buried with various piles of papers and notes. Each pile was for every act that was scripted down to the very last stitch on the costumes. He poured over the pages, following along with the performers, and making occasional notes to address later. Leaning against the side of his chair was the highly polished sword he had worked so hard to retrieve from King Robert. It glistened in the sunlight attracting his gaze causing him to frown in thought. Rose had been diligently practicing her knife routine while a group of dancers practiced on stage. Spencer had convinced her to do more knife routines instead of her traditional dancing. Something about making the show more exciting and showing the audience that she can do more than dance. She had crude targets set up that marked exactly where she needed to hit. It didn't look all that exciting but when more performers and effects are added, it will be an excellently nervous and exciting show for the audience. She ran through her routine over and over, fixating on the timing as well as her aim. By now Rose was working on her muscle memory. That way every performer would remain safe, so long as they remained on their mark. Unlike many of their other shows, there was no room for improvisation when it came to Rose with her knives. The day gradually became hotter as the clouds moved east away from the camp. The sunlight beat down harshly on the makeshift stage, roasting the dancers until Rose insisted everyone take a break to cool off. She flopped down in a chair set up on the other side of the desk, wiped her face with a rose-patterned handkerchief, and gulped down some water.

"More changes?" Rose asked, trying to strike up a conversation.

"A few here and there, but only minor tweaks," Spencer answered. He scribbled a couple more notes on the page he was reading.

Spencer noticed Rose looking intently at the sword that was by his side. Then she snatched up a stack of papers from his desk to read.

"Spencer, how come you don't have any notes for the battle sequence?"

"I usually leave the fighting scenes up to the performers."

Rose looked at him doubtfully, "Yes, you do, but I thought since you have some kind of past with that sword, you might want to share a few moves to make the scene more entertaining?"

"The battle is just fine the way it is," Spencer said flatly.

"Really?" Rose asked, baiting him. "You wouldn't change a thing?"

"Nope."

"Uh-huh," Rose smirked. "So, if I were to tell you that two of your men, who are supposed to be fighting for King Robert in the play, always end up fighting each other. You wouldn't have anything to say about that?"

Spencer just shrugged, "I would say: it sounds like a good laugh for the audience. I'm sure it will all go over just fine. It always does."

Rose crossed her arms, starting at Spencer in bewilderment. "Why work so hard to get your hands on your old sword if you still aren't going to use it, or at least use all that knowledge to help us out now?"

Spencer put his papers down and gave Rose his full attention.

"Because it's more about using it at the proper time. I don't need to use my past to help with entertainment purposes."

Rose blinked at the gravity of his answer. "You're being awfully serious today."

"I just have a lot on my mind, Rosie."

"Do you feel like sharing any of that with me?" Rose's face pleaded with Spencer when he looked at her with unforgiving eyes. "I just want to be helpful."

His face softened into a warm smile.

"Tell you what," Spencer took Rose's hand while standing, and walked several paces away from the desk. "We will have a game."

Rose was suspicious, "What kind of game?"

"A game of skill," Spencer pointed behind him where his sword was propped up. "Your goal is to reach the sword before I pin you down."

"What happens if I win?" Rose asked.

"If you win, I will tell you everything about that sword," Spencer's smug smile taunted Rose.

"And if I get pinned?"

Spencer's eyes sparkled, "Why, I get an outing alone with you, of course."

Rose laughed softly as she shook her head, "How about you get to keep your secrets instead?"

Spencer gave her a half-smile, "That works too."

Rose hesitated for a moment, weighing the odds in her head. Finally, she held her hand out to Spencer. He took it, and they shook firmly.

"Agreed," Rose stated. In an instant she had freed her hand from his and easily sank to the ground, sliding between his legs to get behind him. The move was quick and smooth. Spencer barely caught her hand with his ankles and then turned to grab her wrist. Spencer worked to maintain his grip to pull her back up to her feet. It was like trying to grab butter. She easily twirled around him, twisting her wrist free, and taking a few steps back from him. Every step he made toward her was matched with a perfectly synchronized step of hers away from him. Spencer admitted to himself he was either rusty, or he had greatly underestimated the determination of Rose. She changed tactics and spun quickly toward him to easily pass. Spencer caught up to Rose and snatched her around the waist lifting her off the ground causing her arms and legs to flail uselessly in front of her. She managed to hook her foot around the back of his knee causing him to fall to the ground with her. She crawled and clawed her way closer to the sword, but Spencer pulled her farther away by her foot. She rolled to the side, giving her a split second of freedom to sprint for the sword. Spencer leaped behind her causing him to crash down on top of Rose pinning her securely to the ground.

"There," Spencer breathed, catching his breath. "I win!"

Rose answered him with a wide smile, "Did you?"

She looked to her right to reveal her hand had a firm grasp on the hilt of the sword that had fallen next to her amongst their chaos. Spencer bowed his head in defeat, then released Rose by rolling off to one side. He watched her finger the hilt carefully, then sit up abruptly to inspect the engraving of the letter M more closely. Rose's face went pale. She gasped then dropped the sword as if it burned her. Spencer was on his feet, then bent over to pick up the sword, securing it easily on his back.

"Are you alright? Did you cut yourself?" Spencer offered his hand to help Rose up.

Rose took his hand eagerly, then busied herself with brushing dirt from her skirts to not have to look at Spencer. "No, I'm fine, it's nothing."

"You're sure?" Spencer was genuinely worried now. Rose just changed the subject.

"So, this means I get a story," Rose announced proudly, relishing her win.

"A deal's a deal," Spencer admitted. "I'll tell you all about the sword, but not right now."

"What?" Rose felt blindsided. "You said…"

"I said…" Spencer cut her off, "I would tell you about the sword. I never told you when."

Spencer laughed in triumph. Rose was trying to be upset with him but laughed with him instead.

"You tricked me!" She accused.

"I am a gypsy after all," he laughed at her, which only caused her to laugh harder.

"I'm going to make you regret that," she warned.

Spencer continued to laugh, "Oh, promises, promises!"

Rose punched his shoulder playfully, laughing even harder, bringing tears to her eyes. Spencer took Rose's handkerchief from the table and offered it to Rose. He was glad to laugh again. Ever since he regained his sword, the weight of his past hung heavily on his shoulders. Rose was right; he was much more somber lately. He had made a good life for himself here with the Red and White Troupe, a happy one. He had let go of the wrongs against him in the past, but now ghosts from his past were begging him to finish what he had started. Obligation and duty from another time wouldn't allow him to ignore it. He knew he had to set things right before he could move on to a simpler and better life.

"What on earth?" Rose shouted as she bolted away from him. Spencer was pulled from his thoughts as he looked to see Rose running over to Prince Darien and Zoe.

Darien was carrying Zoe who was half asleep, and more pale than usual. Both of their clothes were damp and they looked like drowned rats. Spencer ran to catch up with Rose.

"What happened?" she demanded. "You were supposed to be keeping an eye on Zoe."

"I was," Darien spoke up defensively. "We went for a hike in the forest when the king's men captured us again."

"You were in the forest?" Rose yelled.

"They found you on their own?" Spencer asked sternly.

"Yes, and yes," Darien exchanged a glance with Spencer dripping with dread. "We were able to escape by jumping into the river, but they are not going to stop looking for me."

"What's wrong with my sister?" Rose hissed at Darien like a snake ready to attack its prey.

"I'm fine," Zoe's soft voice answered before Darien could answer. "I'm just tired, is all. We needed to move fast, and I couldn't keep up."

"I told you to keep an eye on her, not go for a jaunt in the woods! Look at her! You're killing her, just as I said you would!" Rose snapped at Darien.

"She wanted to go into the woods, I was keeping my eye on her just like I promised."

Rose was ready to unleash a fury of anger onto Darien when Zoe's soft voice cut her off again.

"Darien is the reason why I am still alive. I was the one being reckless while he was watching out for me. All of this is my fault, not his."

"Were you followed?" Spencer asked.

"No," Darien answered. "But now Peter has a face for the name Brizo White."

"Will they come after her?" Spencer kept his tone calm although urgency swelled inside him.

"I don't know. For now, all they want is me, but all it takes is one report from Peter, and Robert's eyes may have a new target." Darien stated.

"What does King Robert want with Zoe?" Rose asked acidly.

Darien looked at Rose coldly, "What does King Robert want with the woman who is credited with prophesying his demise?"

Rose's glare darkened toward Darien, "You, you brought this on her!"

"I brought this on myself," Zoe interrupted. "I painted a target on my chest the moment we agreed to add the prophecy to our performance. And he knows my name only because I was the one who revealed it to Peter in our effort to escape."

Members of the camp began congregating around the four of them, as curiosity snatched at their imaginations. Upon realizing the scene, they were making, Spencer motioned toward the matriarch's wagon.

"I think we need to continue this conversation behind closed doors," he suggested.

Chapter

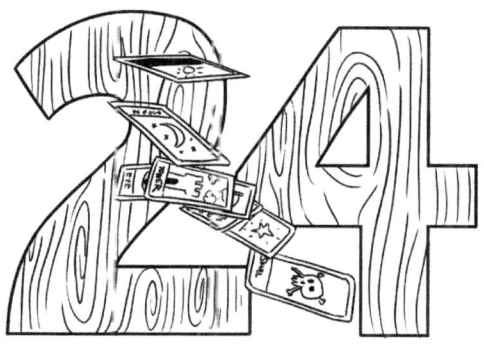

Spencer stood as if he were a statue in the corner of the room, watching everyone carefully, trying to sort out the facts from simple panic. He watched as Darien lovingly wrapped Zoe in a couple of heavy blankets before she settled comfortably into a chair to relax. Then he immediately went to work brewing that special calming tea she often relied on. Rose was fingering a deck of cards she had drawn out of her pocket. The action of dragging her thumbnail across the corner of the cards, again and again, seemed to help Rose to think, while the sound slowly annoyed everyone else. Spencer had seen that look on her face many times before. It was the look of a woman who wanted desperately to yell. Instead, she tried to remain composed, so she would be allowed to ask all her questions.

When Rose finally spoke she singled Darien out as the villain. "If Zoe had not gone into the woods, where palace guards have been on the lookout for you, she would not have needed to use her name. You realize she only divulged it so you could escape."

It was Zoe who spoke up in Darien's defense. "And if you had not kept your first capture of Peter hidden from me I would not have ventured off into the woods of my own volition."

"It doesn't matter how Robert's attention was drawn to us," Spencer gave a cautionary glare at Rose, "The fact is he knows about the prophecy, and he's coming for Darien to prevent it from coming true."

Rose twitched her lips as if she had tasted something sour. Her silence read loud and clear to Spencer as reluctant agreement. She then proceeded to deal her cards out on the table. Spencer watched her study the cards for a minute, furrow her brow, and then swoop them back up in her hands to deal again. Her reaction after every deal grew more and more bothered, yet Rose continued to keep dealing as if she might see something new. Spencer eyed her curiously then turned his attention back to Darien.

"Well, the heat of summer is upon us. And, people everywhere are struggling. It won't be long until the chill of autumn is back." Darien shrugged his shoulders, "Maybe it's time for me to fulfill the prophecy and save the day."

Darien pointed out the facts like he was checking things off a list.

Spencer called him out disapprovingly, "Do you even *want* to take back the kingdom?"

Darien glared at his old friend, "I do!" Everyone simply looked back at him unconvinced.

"Of course I do." Darien continued honestly. "However, the last time I was in charge, it was a disaster. Many men... *too many* men died because of me. I don't even know what I did or how it happened, but I was their leader, and I failed them."

Darien looked up at Spencer. "I want to help, but surely there is someone better qualified than me. I may have survived that slaughter, but death haunts me every moment of my life. It is all I can think of. I do not know how I could convince my troops to follow me again. Even if I could, I don't trust myself to lead a battle. I've killed too many people already. Who's to say I won't snap and become that monster again?"

He looked up at Zoe, hopefully, "Unless there's more you can tell me?"

Zoe's eyes grew wide with panic when the men turned to her for answers. "I can only tell you what you already know. You need to rally your friends, regain their trust, and lead them into battle to restore their freedom."

"Well that is unspecific," Darien sighed.

"Most prophecies are." Spencer shrugged while continuing to watch Rose out of the side of his eye. Frustration had escalated into an angry form of concentration.

"You must be the one to lead them. Otherwise, things will be much worse than they are now." Zoe spoke softly.

"Thank you, Brizo, but it is hard to imagine myself as a leader again." Darien didn't want to dispute Zoe, but he couldn't stop his doubts from getting the best of him.

"Then don't do anything," Rose snapped at the prince.

Surprise and sympathy could be read in Spencer's and Zoe's eyes, but Darien glared only hatred at her. Rose looked back at the prince defiantly.

"Don't listen to my sister who has far more experience with prophecies than you do. Don't believe the gravest of warnings that she is trying to impress on you. Don't do anything. But you will believe her when everything falls apart exactly as she said it would." Rose leaned in closer to Darien, "Only then, it will be too late."

The harsh reality of Rose's words weighed heavily on Darien. "Either way I choose, more people will die because of me. I can't bear the thought of more death, all for my sake."

"Not to put a damper on your narcissistic perspective, but warriors don't fight for one person. If they die, they aren't dying for you. They fight for a cause, a righteous one that promotes a better life. If they die, which is a possibility for any warrior, they die for their belief. That's something far more important than you." Darien didn't enjoy Rose's comments m ainly because she was right, and he hated it when she was right.

"A warrior still needs to trust the person who leads them." He gritted his teeth, knowing it was a weak rebuttal. He still stood by his argument, refusing to allow Rose to get the best of him. "My people hate me. They see me as a bloodthirsty murderer—a loose cannon they could not rely on when they need me most. They will not follow me into battle again."

Spencer scratched his neck. "No, your subjects don't hate you."

"What?" Now it was Darien's turn to be shocked.

"I can't believe I'm saying this, but I agree with the prince," Rose commented. "I'm one of his subjects, and I have a deep loathing towards him."

Spencer smirked at Rose, then continued. "Think about it. In every place we have performed, the people love the King's Play. Yes, they all boo when Darien failed them and lost the kingdom. However, ever since we added the prophecy, they started to cheer. They love it because they want it to be true. Darien, your people have been hurt, and have lost faith in many things. But they want things to get better, too. They want someone to fight for them. And if you can convince them that someone is you, they will follow."

"That is easier said than done," Darien pointed out.

"No, it isn't," Rose dismissed the prince's negativity. "We do it all the time when we perform. With Spencer's flair and Zoe's eloquence, we can make any fool sound convincing."

"Then go and get one of your fools to do it," Darien mumbled.

Rose's temper flared, "Why should I when we have the perfect fool sitting in front of me!"

The two of them looked as if they were about to throw a few punches when Zoe stood up, stilling them both. Darien looked up tenderly at Zoe, while Rose shrank meekly in her seat to fiddle with her cards again.

"Darien," Zoe put a gentle hand on his shoulder. "Why won't you let us help you?"

"I have already put you in danger." He spoke directly to Zoe as if she were the only one in the wagon. "If I allow you to get involved, it could put your entire troupe in jeopardy. My uncle will not only come after me, he will come after you all—for treason."

"But, Darien…" Zoe started.

"No, I've hurt you too much already. Please don't ask me again." He kissed her hand gently and left the wagon, leaving the three others awash with uncertainty.

Chapter 25

Zoe jumped when Rose flung her cards on the table, letting out a cry of frustration. "What is going on here?"

Spencer answered her sympathetically, "He was a young man who lost too much too fast. Now he's realizing that there are always casualties, usually the people you care the most about. He still hasn't come to terms with that... loss yet."

Rose looked up from her cards, "What?"

"Weren't you just listening?" Spencer asked.

"What are you talking about?" Rose replied, still confused.

"I'm talking about Darien, what are you talking about?"

"Not Darien. I'm talking about the cards, Spence, something's wrong."

Spencer blinked with confusion, "You're not making any sense."

"The cards, they're... they're wrong," Rose insisted. Zoe listened intently, growing more anxious.

Spencer sat down across from Rose and snatched up her hand, forcing her to leave the cards alone. "Rosie, start at the beginning."

"Ever since Darien showed up, and was being all secretive with us, I started consulting my cards to learn more about him. All I could get were glimpses of him wandering the kingdom, but never his future. Once I learned his true identity, I started consulting the cards about Zoe's prophecy specifically. I wanted to know it first hand to see if I could find something that was missed, that could help him out. But they keep telling me rubbish, as if there is no prophecy at all." She turned to Zoe, "What am I doing wrong? I should be able to see something, shouldn't I?"

Zoe glanced at the door making sure it was shut tight. "You're not doing anything wrong."

"Are you sure you're asking the right questions?" Spencer asked gently.

Rose glared at him, clearly perturbed. "Seriously, tell me how long have you been reading fortunes?"

"Hey, I'm just trying to help. Why are you snapping at me?" Spencer sat back a little.

"Why do you keep implying you know more than me?" Rose mumbled.

"I never..."

"I have a brain, too!" Rose's anger boiled. "I know what I am doing."

Spencer flung up his hands, "Yes, you always know what you are doing because you always have all the answers, don't you? No one else could ever know a better way than you."

"That's because my way is usually right."

"No, you *think* your way is right; in reality, it's much more complicated than it should be." Spencer insisted.

"That's absurd! Name one time I over complicate things!"

"Um, how about right now with how you and your sister are handling her prophecy?"

"If you know a better way to get through to Darien then, by all means, we are listening," Rose offered.

"I was referring to the one about you and your sister!" Spencer gritted his teeth. Zoe uttered an audible gasp of shock.

"This has nothing to do with that. This is about you telling me how to do my job. I don't go around telling you how to direct."

"You do all the time, woman!" Spencer shouted.

"Oh, I don't!"

"You do!"

"Enough!" shouted Zoe. Spencer didn't realize how weak Zoe was until she paused for a moment to hold her head in her hands. He immediately felt guilty for goading Rose into an argument in front of her. Zoe gave Rose a guilty look as well. "You're not doing anything wrong."

"What makes you so sure?" Rose asked as gently as she could.

"Because there isn't anything to see," Zoe admitted. Rose and Spencer looked at each other equally confused. "I made it up."

"You what?" Spencer lashed out sharply.

"Why would you do that?" Rose's mouth gaped open as she insisted on answers.

"The story was old. It needed something new—a better ending. Since there wasn't any new news to tell, I invented a prophecy."

"You told me he was someone important." Rose had trouble staying calm for her sister's sake.

"He is," Zoe answered.

"You said he had the potential to be a great leader," Rose continued.

"He does. I can use the word 'potential' without talking about a prophecy." Zoe stated.

"Not when you have already made up a prophecy about him," Rose was having trouble containing her emotions.

Zoe hung her head in shame. "I'm sorry."

"This is why I never like it when you read my fortune," Spencer mumbled. "You lie too easily. And when you do tell the truth, it is so cryptic that everyone second-guesses what you say."

The two women turned to frown at him.

"Glower at me all you want. You know it's all true." Spencer folded his arms daring either of them to correct him.

"Spencer's right, Zoe. You lied to me… me! I'm your twin sister; we never keep secrets from each other."

Rose sounded hurt, and Spencer felt uncomfortable when he realized the direction the conversation was headed.

"Well, I can see you two have a lot to talk about, so I'll just be going." He turned toward the door.

"Don't you dare," Zoe's face was tense but firm. "You are not leaving this wagon until you promise you won't tell Darien."

"Has your sickness reached your mind?" Spencer's patience had worn out. "Of course I'm going to tell Darien."

"No, you cannot," Zoe begged. "If you do, then all hope of the kingdom being restored to its original glory will be lost."

"All hope? You said the prophecy was fake." He wasn't sure how much more he could hear before his anger would take over.

"It is, but that doesn't mean we can't have hope. There's still the hope that Darien can do what he needs to make the story a reality."

Spencer heaved a heavy sigh. Zoe always saw people for more than what they were. She saw them as who they could be if given the chance.

This only made things so much harder when some refused that chance, and let her down.

"Zoe," Rose shook her head with disbelief. "No offense to your feelings towards Darien, but he's not a king anymore. From what I gather, he doesn't want to be a king."

"Rose is right," Spencer added. "If he cares so much he would have found a way to restore the kingdom by now. Or, at least, be more excited when you offered him help. I honestly think the only person he cares about now is… you."

Zoe blushed, and Spencer realized she didn't care about what they were saying until the last sentence. She looked up at him pleadingly, "Darien can be better. There is always a chance he will do the right thing. He can still succeed."

Rose responded, "You're hoping for an awful lot of change from one man. Especially when your timeline is getting short. A *made-up* timeline, I should add."

"He once was the man we need him to be. We just need to remind him of that. He will come through, and do the right thing; I know he will. You just need to show a little faith," Zoe promised.

"You are asking an awful lot, Zoe," Spencer whispered. "The last time I had faith in this guy I was banished from the castle. I lost everything: my command, my friend, my life."

"And what is wrong with your life now?" Zoe asked.

Spencer gave a stuttered answer, "Nothing, it's just…. I…"

"I know you have lost much, but look at all you have gained since then." Spencer glanced over at Rose to see she was already watching him. She quickly turned away to hide her embarrassment.

"Please do this for me," Zoe continued, "as a personal favor."

Spencer glared back at Zoe, considering her. She was always so nice to him. He also had to admit, all her talk about faith and hope always seemed to come through in the end.

"I'll keep this quiet for you." He emphasized the last words so he was clear. "But, this is Darien's life we're playing with. He deserves to know the truth."

Zoe nodded in appreciation as Spencer left, leaving the women alone.

Chapter

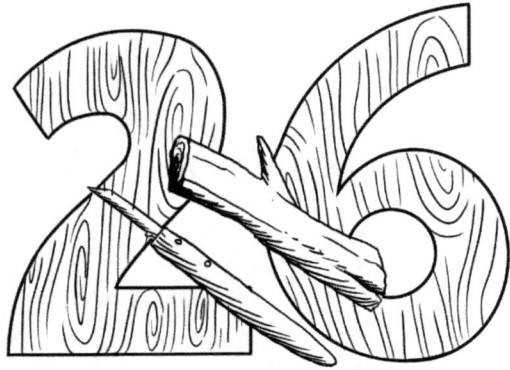

Spencer spotted Darien sitting by a fire, brooding with his thoughts. He took a calming breath before joining his old friend. The former general sat down next to the disgraced prince and took out a small piece of wood from his pocket to whittle with his knife.

Darien was the first to speak. "I know they sent you here to talk to me. I promise, there is nothing you can say that will change how I feel."

"They didn't and I won't," was all Spencer said. He continued to whittle the wood without any further acknowledgment for Darien. Darien looked at Spencer suspiciously.

"I have already put too many people in danger as it is."

Spencer continued with his whittling, still silent. Darien squirmed a little in his seat.

"Even if I did allow Brizo to help, I don't think anyone would want to follow me. I'd just let them down again. Everyone's eyes will be on me, expecting me to solve all their problems. Even if I succeeded, and I was king again, any slip-up I make has massive consequences. Innocent people could be hurt because of one accidental wave of my hand."

Spencer remained silent.

"I don't think I could accept that responsibility."

More silence.

"It's too much for me to handle,"

More whittling.

"For heaven's sake man, say something!"

Spencer shrugged. "What do you want me to say? I thought I couldn't change your mind."

"Well, say something instead of sitting there wasting space," Darien ordered.

"Something, like what?" Spencer asked.

"Anything," Darien said.

"Anything?" Spencer clarified.

"Yes!" Darien demanded.

Spencer gave Darien a sideways look from under his brow.

"Are you in love with Zoe?" Spencer asked calmly.

Darien blinked in surprise at the question.

"Well... I... she's very..." he stumbled over his words, unable to form a thought.

Spencer sighed, "This is not a trick question."

Darien gave Spencer an irritated stare before he softly answered, "Yes, I love her."

Darien bowed his head and pulled his hair in frustration while Spencer slapped the prince on his back.

"Don't take it so hard, man. You're not the first person in the world who fell in love with someone far better than they ever could be."

Darien looked up, "Just like you and Rose?"

"Ah," Spencer stuttered which led to a small exchange of laughter between the two men. Spencer shook his head, "Don't make this about me."

Darien simply stared back with a smug smile.

"The answer is simple," Spencer continued, "you're thinking too big."

"I thought I was *supposed* to consider the big picture," Darien stated plainly.

"Yes, but you're terrible at it," Spencer shook his head in amusement. "All you see is the pain and suffering, and none of the good."

"That's because, when I try to fix everything it all turns out badly."

"There you go again, thinking you have to fix everything. You are still thinking too big. You need to rein in your thoughts, and focus on what you care about."

"Brizo?" Darien whispered, unsure.

"Mm-hm. You love her, and for reasons I cannot fathom, she loves you, too." Spencer saw Darien blush, doing a terrible job of hiding the joy on his face.

"Hey, focus," Spencer reminded. "The facts are this: King Robert has heard of Zoe's prophecy concerning you, and we both know he has been trying to pin down the person who started it all."

"So, it's only a matter of time before Robert turns his eye entirely on Brizo," Darien whispered. His shoulders sank as the facts weighed heavily on him.

Spencer broke the silence, "So, how do you save her?"

"We need to hide her somewhere safe. She needs to be as far away from me as possible." Darien was resolute.

"It is a good plan, but a temporary one. She cannot stay hidden forever. Whether you are with her or not, Robert will find her, and she will be in danger again."

"Then we need to eliminate the possibility of Robert hurting her," Darien thought some more. "We need to remove Robert's power, so he cannot keep sending people with orders to find her. He would have to seek her out on his own." Darien stared into the flames, "I know what I must do, but I'm still scared."

"Scared of what?" asked Spencer.

"That I'm not the man she believes I can be," Darien admitted.

Spencer stopped his work and looked up at the stars. "Well, let me put it this way. Zoe loves you, whether you live up to this prophecy or not. She believes wholeheartedly in the best part of you. Women like that rarely exist nowadays. And if you feel that same love towards her, then the absolute least you can do is try to be that man. Who knows, you may prove her right."

They looked at each other in awkward silence.

"Are you saying you believe in me, too?" Darien asked uncomfortably.

"Oh, no, no! I don't think you can pull this off." Spencer coughed, and Darien's shoulders sank a little. "But, Zoe does, and I've learned to trust in her."

Darien smiled to himself. After all these years hiding and wandering from place to place, he was no longer alone. "Thank you, General."

Spencer's back straightened when he realized Darien was referring to him.

"I better turn in for the night," Darien said. Then he left Spencer alone with the fire.

Spencer threw the wood he was whittling into the fire then returned his dagger to his belt. He continued to sit, stone still, lost in thought. He thought about his men, now that they were disbanded. He wondered if any of them were happier with their new life, like him. How many of them crumbled in the civilian world without order or absolutes? The weight of his sword felt like the weight of the world bearing down on him. He was their general, and for several years, they had no one. The former general started to wonder if his men, his brothers, hated him just as much as they hated their prince.

Chapter 27

"Please don't hate me for lying to you," Zoe pleaded.

"I don't hate you for lying to me," Rose stood, crossing her arms over her chest. "I've been lying to you about Darien, so I can't say much."

"I suppose you're right," Zoe agreed.

"Please, just answer me one thing, Zoe," Rose rubbed her head in pain. "Why him?"

"I beg your pardon?" Zoe asked.

Rose pointed a hard stare at her sister. "Why did you choose to fall in love with him? There are so many better people you could be happy with. Why must you choose him?"

"Why do you hate Darien so much?" Zoe asked innocently.

"I don't hate him," Rose admitted. "He's not so bad. He has a lot of issues, and is trying to be better."

"Then what is the problem?"

"The problem is that he is not just some guy trying to make a decent life for himself," Rose's anger flared. "This is the disgraced prince of Marconia. Do I need to remind you how much blood is on this man's hands, how many families broken, and lives lost because of his rampage?"

"In defense of his kingdom, Rose, It isn't his fault someone wanted to wage war on us," answered Zoe.

"There is a big difference between an honorable war in defense of what's right, and mercilessly slaughtering every man in sight. This man has no honor, and surely holds no remorse for the men he killed—not even the innocent ones who were just following orders, or the ones who tried to retreat for their lives."

"How could you possibly know this? You weren't there." Zoe shouted back at her.

Rose paused for a moment. How did she know that? She knew what she had said was the truth. But no one had told her these facts, nor was she there to witness it. But she did indeed know it to be true. She could hear the screams for mercy, the cries of pain I n the wind, accompanied by a fearsome image of Darien dripping with blood. The soft, skeletal laugh returned to her thoughts.

"That's not important. It's all true, and you know it, too. And yet you still find yourself capable of loving this monster. This is not the kind of person with whom you should be spending your life." Rose wished her sister would see reason.

"Of course I know this to be true," Zoe softly answered, but still with a firm dominance that held Rose's attention. "He confessed everything to me concerning what he had done. You know as well as I, Darien is not the same man he was back then. He was a young man who had just lost his parents. Can you blame him for lashing out? He feels remorse for his sins, he feels the pain he has inflicted, he sees the darkness that has overtaken him, and he wants to be rid of it."

Zoe was breathing heavily from the exertion of their argument and was having a hard time standing up.

"Does he?" Rose asked. Her sister hesitated, unsure "Perhaps he doesn't deserve to be rid of it. How does the death of two justify the death of hundreds or thousands?"

"Not just the death of two, Rose, the death of his parents," Zoe's face twisted in sadness. "Would you allow me to be this callused towards your suffering about Mother's death?"

Dizziness overcame Zoe and she started to wobble. Rose caught her shoulders before she fell, and helped her to bed. When Rose saw her sister start to shiver she snatched up an extra blanket to swaddle Zoe with.

"Can you handle tea right now?" Rose's voice was gentle and loving, a stark contrast from a moment ago. Zoe could only nod in affirmation in between shivers, her teeth chattering too hard to speak.

"Let me fetch some," Rose said. She quickly grabbed a mug and a jar of herbs simultaneously before turning to the kettle of water which was always warming on the stove. Zoe forced herself to take deeper breaths while rubbing her arms to warm up. It was something Rose saw her sister do often but knew the shivering wouldn't stop until she had a warm mug of tea for her to hold. She handed the mug to her sister, who immediately took a few calming sips. It was too soon for the water to be infused with flavor from the herbs, but at least her sister was no longer shivering.

"I miss Mom," Rose whispered under her breath.

Zoe glanced up from her mug with a kind smile, "I miss her too. Especially when we fight."

"Right," Rose agreed solemnly. "She always knew just the right thing to say to make us both feel better."

Zoe laughed to herself, "And then she would make sure to remind us: *What one has the other must also.*"

Rose laughed with her sister, "I remember. She honestly believed that was the say all, end-all, to every problem we could ever have."

The women smiled at each other as they recalled their childhood memories, then saddened at the thought of their mother.

"Do you remember our promise after she died?" Rose asked her sister.

"Of course I do," Zoe took another sip of tea. Then she spoke to her sister as if reciting from one of their scripts. "We will never leave each other. You will never be alone,"

Rose smiled and recited her promise as well. "Never, as long as we live, I will be there for you."

The two sat in silence for a moment, allowing their promise to loom in the wagon with them.

Rose pleaded with her sister. "No matter what, you know I'm on your side and will support anything you say. But you cannot keep doing this. You cannot keep expecting everyone to be wonderful and perfect. The world is messy, people are messy. Sometimes a person is just bad, or they just can't do the right thing all the time. It's not fair for you to hold everyone to this standard that for most is simply unattainable. It's not fair to them, and it's hurting you."

Zoe took Rose's hand in hers and stared back at her sister. "And you cannot keep expecting the worst from everyone. All you see is darkness. You push everyone away and insist on being alone. You are denying yourself the chance to be happy, and hurting those who love you most."

"I'm perfectly happy as I am, Zoe," Rose corrected. "And, last I checked, I'm not hurting anyone."

"Really?" Zoe took a long blink. "Why aren't you with Spencer?"

"This again, Zoe?"

"Yes, why haven't you allowed yourself to be with Spencer? We all know you have feelings for him. You have since the first moment you laid eyes on him. You've been holding back everything. Why?"

An image of Spencer's pained face of death crossed Rose's mind.

The laughter rattled inside her head, louder this time.

"Because he deserves to be with someone better," Rose answered with complete honesty.

"Did it ever occur to you that he doesn't want anyone better than you?" Zoe asked.

"Then he's a fool," Rose stated.

"A fool for you, maybe," Zoe laughed. "And you're a fool for letting your fears get in the way of your happiness. I love you very much, sister, but I am not the end of your story."

Rose blushed, "You need to get some rest, Zoe. Nothing is going on between Spencer and me. We are perfectly happy just as friends."

The obnoxious laughter of death grew louder in the back of Rose's mind then started to chant in a hollow echo. *Rose Red, Rose Red, will you beat your lover dead?*

"Rose? Rose, what are you staring at?" Zoe asked. Rose blinked, not realizing she was staring at nothing in particular. She turned her head to see her sister was watching her curiously.

"Nothing," she lied. "It's nothing. I suppose all this information at one time is tiring me out."

Zoe merely nodded as she continued to fight off her need for sleep.

"Still no answers on how to heal you?" Rose asked.

Zoe allowed a few long breaths before responding, "I keep getting the same answer. You need to learn how to use your gift."

"I'm trying Zoe, I am. But there has to be another way. I'm not ready for you to die." Rose clutched Zoe's hand, holding on tightly.

Zoe's eyes fluttered sleepily and tried to focus on Rose.

"It's the right thing to do, no matter the outcome. I believe it. And you need to believe it," Zoe whispered. "Forget everything else, and just believe."

Zoe dozed off into one of her much-needed rests. Rose took the mug from her sister's hand and set it on a table nearby. Zoe was not used to burning so much energy in one day. She had gone out with Darien, gotten captured, escaped, and now all this unnecessary drama about Darien and Spencer was too much. Rose cursed for allowing herself to yell at her sister, knowing it would only wear her out faster. She kissed Zoe gently on her forehead and tucked the blankets snugly around her sister before leaving her to rest.

Chapter 28

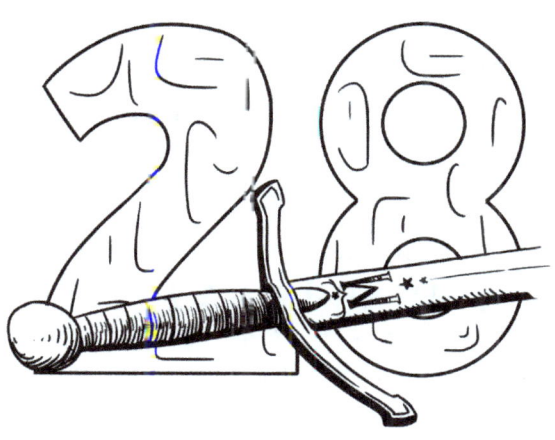

Spencer looked up to see Rose heading toward him, throwing a shawl around her shoulders. In an instant, his spirits didn't feel quite so heavy. He knew Rose couldn't return the same affection he had for her, thanks to her responsibilities she securely hid behind. But he still delighted in her company and her lovely face. She always made him smile, even if he didn't show it as obviously as Darien's goofy grin for Zoe. Her dark hair swirled in the cool breeze causing Rose to quicken her pace toward the warm fire… to get closer to *him* quicker. He rearranged the burning logs to appear busy, setting the flames higher for more heat. He breathed in the smell of burning coals deeply to squelch his emotions and was once again a figure of calm, cool control — a trick he had always used before going into battle in his youth. Nowadays, the battle raged within him.

"May I join you?" she asked politely. Spencer nodded to a spot next to him. She settled in comfortably, holding her hands out to warm by the fire. "I'm sorry for losing my cool in there. I do appreciate you, even though I keep pushing you away, as you say."

Spencer allowed a small smirk to touch his lips. "So, how is your other half?"

Rose looked back to the wagon as if she could see Zoe through the wooden boards. "Exhausted from the events of the day. I pushed her too far, so she..." Rose hesitated. "She is resting now, is all that matters."

Spencer noticed Rose's concern for her sister. "I've been thinking about Zoe, and everything you told me. Can I ask, did she see her actual death? Is there any way she can learn when or how?"

Rose pulled her warm shawl tighter around herself. "Mother always told us that the ability to see a person's death uses a dark form of the gift she was forbidden to use and we should never try. Not like that advice pertains to me since I'm gift-less." She sounded annoyed.

"If she's not supposed to be prophesying death, then how does Zoe know she is going to die?"

Rose clicked her tongue sharply, "She just knows, alright? I don't know how, but she seems pretty resolute about it."

"Alright, alright, I didn't mean to get you upset." Spencer tried to calm her back down. "I'm just trying to understand."

The problem was Spencer didn't understand. The facts weren't adding up, and Rose was still hiding something from him.

"Is there no chance of avoiding it?" He asked gently.

Rose sighed deeply, "Trying to change a vision only makes things worse."

"What could be worse than death?"

She looked at Spencer, debating exactly how to answer his question. She finally relented with the entire truth.

"Before you became a part of the troupe, Zoe had a vision that I would break my leg while hunting. She knew how important dancing, hunting, just being out and about was for me. And she knew just sitting around, doing nothing, while I healed would feel like torture. So, Zoe warned me what would happen, and begged me to do something else that day. Instead of going hunting, I spent the day practicing on our stage. I couldn't escape my fate. The stage collapsed and five other people, including myself, and our mother were hurt."

"So, your fate is projected on those around you?" Spencer asked.

"It is worse," Rose's eyes started to tear up. "We all broke something. I broke my leg. Mother broke her arm. Eventually, all of us began to feel better except for her. Her arm was infected; we were unable to fight it. After a time, the sickness spread to her heart, and she died." Spencer put his arm around Rose as she wiped tears from her cheeks. "The worst part is, I knew something bad was going to happen. I just knew someone was going to die. I just figured it was going to be me, since I was the one who tried to escape my fate. I should have paid the price, not her."

"And do you feel that way now? Do you feel that someone is going to die?" He asked carefully.

Rose wanted to shake her head at him, but she found herself smiling instead. "You're asking a lot of questions tonight, Spence."

"You seem to be speaking a lot of truth tonight, Rosie," he answered.

Rose sighed, "This needs to stay strictly between us, understand?"

Spencer nodded, "Of course."

"Do you promise?" insisted Rose.

"I promise," Spenser answered without hesitation.

Rose considered Spencer for another moment then continued with their conversation.

"I feel like a lot of people are going to die. Just between us, I have been seeing some things… dark things— things I have been warned to stay away from. Zoe has been teaching me how to harness my gift the way she uses hers, so I assumed I would start to see things the same way she does."

Rose took a breath before admitting the rest to Spencer. "I don't see the world the same as her. I see the opposite. I see the darkness and it scares me. I don't want to hone my gift if it is just going to turn me into someone I don't want to be, someone evil."

Rose put her head in her hands raking her fingers through her hair. "I also know that if I do nothing, Zoe will die. I can't let that happen either."

"And you still think this is the right thing to do, for the both of you?"

Rose closed her eyes, "We don't think it, Zoe has prophesied it. No matter how many times you ask, the answer is still the same. Zoe is going to die, and I need to use my gift."

Spencer's face grew hard. He didn't like it when she used the word prophesied. The word was always good for entertainment purposes, but in the real world, all it felt like was a trap to him.

"She still seems to think I can do it, which makes me feel even worse when I can't."

"Yeah? You're not the only one who feels that way," Spencer was amused by the faint case of deja vu he was experiencing.

Rose looked at him, confused. "You?"

Spencer tilted his head, "Actually, Darien."

Rose groaned, "Please don't tell me I have something in common with that man."

Spencer laughed, "You two have more in common than you think. That's why you have such a hard time getting along." Rose gave him a skeptical look, but Spencer just shrugged.

"Face it, Rosie. You both love Zoe, which means you both will do anything it takes to keep her happy. Regardless of how fearful you may be."

Rose smiled fondly at Spencer as she reflected on what he said. She thought about how he would do anything to keep her happy without hesitation.

"Yes, I suppose that's how it works." Rose looked into the fire to hide her blush from Spencer. She decided to change the subject. "Are you ready to tell me about your sword?"

Spencer smiled broadly, "Since you asked nicely–" He unsheathed his sword and formally offered the hilt to Rose. Rose took hold of the hilt, but the weight of the folded metal pulled her downward, rolling her off her seat. She stood up, then grasped it with two hands, barely able to hold it level in front of her.

"Are you kidding me?" Her muscles strained when the sword's weight was too much to handle. "This sword is yours?"

Laughing, Spencer took it back into his hand and made a few fluid movements to show off the sword's brilliance. Then he carefully returned it to its sheath and placed it across his knees.

"Show off," Rose mumbled. Spencer didn't bother disputing it. Of course, he was showing off for her, and it was working. He slid the sword closer to present the hilt again.

"See here, Rosie," Spencer pointed to the ornate letter 'M' carved masterfully into the base of the blade. "This stands for Marconia, to which our allegiance is sworn. All soldiers in our army have this on their sword."

He pointed to both sides of the letter to show a set of three lines gradually decreasing in size. "These indicate the level of proficiency and leadership a soldier has. The more lines, the more ability."

Rose ran her fingernail into each of the six groves alongside the ornate 'M'. Then she pointed to the stars engraved above and below the letter. "And the stars, what do they mean?" She asked.

"The stars at the bottom are reserved for the generals. The general with two stars is known as the second in command, my most trusted and skilled advisor."

"*Your* advisor?" Rose couldn't believe what she just heard. "That would make you the… the…" She had trouble saying it out loud.

Spencer just smiled at her, "Yes, the star above the letter 'M' is reserved for the High Commander, the leader of the entire Marconian army."

Rose was still skeptical, "And this is… this was your sword ten years ago?"

"Don't you believe me?" he asked.

"I'm trying to, but that would mean you were commander of the troops in your early twenties!"

Spencer didn't flinch, "Twenty-one actually."

"But I thought positions like that were reserved for older, more experienced men."

"In the Marconian army, our status is based on knowledge and ability, not how old you are. Age doesn't necessarily mean wisdom."

"Spencer," Rose shook her head trying to believe him, "I've fought with you before. You could barely keep up, let alone subdue me."

That familiar sparkle touched his eyes before he answered.

"Well, truth be told, I've never had to fight a person so light on their feet as you." He saw Rose blush, "That, and I let you win."

Rose's eyes bulged and her jaw dropped in shock, "You are such a liar! I beat you fair and square." She playfully punched his shoulder.

Spencer laughed at her reaction, "It's the truth; I let you win."

"That's ridiculous. If you are so good, why would you just let me win?"

"So I could see that look on your face." His smile grew even bigger when he saw Rose blush again.

"Come on," she shook her head at him. "What's the real reason?"

Spencer spoke seriously for her, "Because after I was discharged, I never wanted to fight again. I didn't even want to touch a sword."

Rose chose her next question carefully, "Then, why did you go through all that work to get it back?"

"I told you already," He shrugged with a dismissive smile. "I like this sword."

Rose relented with her questions, "I don't blame you for that. It is a beautiful sword, especially the embellishments."

"The most important part of the sword is the engraved 'M'. Without it, it's just another sword. Every Marconian soldier knows it is more than just a letter— it's a symbol."

"Why is that?" Rose asked.

"Many people believe we swear to our king. But a Marconian soldier swears his allegiance to his country, and all that reside in it. This means it is our responsibility to ensure the protection and prosperity of all Marconians."

The meaning of Spencer's words struck rose harshly, "What if the threat is the king?"

Spencer hung his head, "It doesn't matter. Our responsibility is to the kingdom first and foremost."

"Then, why haven't you, or anyone in the army, confronted King Robert? Is he not enough of a threat to our country?"

The weight of her words settled heavily on Spencer. These were the same questions he had wrestled with for the past ten years, since the day he was discharged. He reminded himself that Rose had trusted him enough to carry her secrets, and he needed to do the same with her.

He was just about to tell her everything when he heard a rustle come from a nearby bush. He turned his attention to the sound to see a small snipe hop out of the bush. His eyes narrowed suspiciously as he continued to watch it peck at the ground for something to eat. His memories took over, and he allowed old pain and embarrassment to creep over him.

"Another time, Rosie." Spencer stoked the fire to avoid looking at Rose. "It's late, and I'm not entirely brave enough to tell you."

Rose reached out to hold his hand. Her thin fingers felt soft in his grasp. The smooth caress of her thumb relaxed him. It was a wonderful feeling Spencer didn't want to end. Next thing he knew she had opened his hand and pulled his palm gently toward her.

"What are you doing?" he asked.

"I'm looking at your palm," she answered softly.

"Why?" he asked.

"I thought reading your fortune could help," she replied.

"No thanks," Spencer insisted.

"Why not? I give good fortunes," she promised. "People journey for miles to have me tell them of their future."

Spencer gave a nonchalant shrug, "If I'm too busy thinking about my future, I find it hard to appreciate the things that are right in front of me." He smiled as he caressed her cheek down to her chin, making Rose blush despite her stubborn resolve to only be friends.

"I should probably turn in for the night," she said, changing the subject.

"Yeah, probably a good idea," he agreed.

She stood up to face her wagon, "Are you staying up?"

"Just until the coals die down, I won't be out here much longer," he smiled.

Rose smiled back just as brightly, "Goodnight, then."

"Goodnight, Rosie." He watched her return to her wagon and close the door behind her, but not without one last glance toward him. He shifted the coals farther apart as he studied the palm of his hand. He wasn't sure what kind of risks the future held for him. All he knew was right now, at this moment, he would endure it all and then some, if it meant he could be together with Rose.

Chapter 29

The first rays of morning easily woke Darien up. He had barely slept last night, and the burning in his eyes happily reminded him of it. He tried to block the light with his pillow to salvage more moments of sleep, but his mind was wide awake. Even with his eyes shut, a never-ending list of worries, concerns and responsibilities screamed for his attention. His head rolled to one side giving him a clear view of a small dresser next to the bed, on top of which was a candle burnt almost down to the stump, and Zoe's red and silver medallion. The silver gleamed bright white in the sunlight making it hard to ignore. Zoe had promised it would help to calm his dreams if he wore it, but he shoved it in his pocket instead. The pounding in his head made him think twice about his previous notions about the trinket. Darien cursed his thoughts as he begrudgingly reached out for the chain necklace and hung the medallion around his neck. Almost immediately the pounding stopped, and the pain was gone. He touched the medallion curiously. The medal felt warm when he traced the curve of the emblem with his thumb.

"It's just a lucky charm," Darien told himself, then proceeded to dress for the day.

Outside, he was greeted with an already warm morning. All was quiet and the sky still clung to a few grey hues from the night. Darien exhaled a sigh of relief. He may not be able to sleep, but he could at least find solace that no one else was awake. Except he wasn't alone. One of the campfires had been lit nearby. It took him a second to blink through the haze to notice a small foldable table in front of a woman who sat wrapped in several blankets writing on a stack of papers: Zoe.

Prince Darien wanted to go over to her immediately but hesitated instead. The last thing he said to her was a complete rejection of any help she offered to him. He couldn't erase the memory of her when he said he would find his own way to fulfill the prophecy. Zoe's face had instantly twisted up in surprise and hurt, which made his heart ache for her. She was already in such physical pain; only someone as stupid as he would think she could handle an emotional blow as well. He didn't want her to hurt anymore, but he also didn't want to risk making things worse while trying to smooth things over.

Finally, the prince decided it was foolish to hide from Zoe out of fear of what she might say. It's not like he could avoid her forever. Or could he? No, he would not do that to Zoe. He may mess everything else up in his life, but he refused to ruin what he had with her as well. Darien convinced his feet to move toward the woman he loved, but slowly... carefully. He didn't want to be a bother to her if she was too busy. She still had not moved or acknowledged him as he drew closer, which made him think he could easily turn to do something else without her even knowing he was there. But her soft voice forbade him to entertain the notion.

"Good morning, your Highness," Zoe spoke formally but did not look up from her writing. She kept on writing as if she hadn't spoken at all.

Darien was slightly unnerved by the ease of Zoe's multitasking.

"Did some prophecy tell you I would be here?" he said then looked over his shoulder stupidly. He swallowed while he considered all the many things Zoe could be capable of, thanks to her gift.

Zoe continued to write as she answered, "No, but my eyes have always been sharp."

She quickly wrote a few more words before placing a definite dot at the end of her sentence. Zoe's eyes glistened like cool pools of water when she looked up at him.

"You're up awfully early," she stated.

Darien couldn't tell if the sudden chill on his neck was from the slight morning breeze or Zoe's response. He cursed himself. Of course, it wasn't the morning breeze. The day was already far too warm for his liking. Darien rubbed the back of his neck anyway as he sat down next to Zoe.

"I couldn't sleep." He nodded at her. "What's your reason?"

Zoe flicked her pen toward the pages in front of her. "I have work."

It was then that Darien noticed almost all the pages had been filled from top to bottom with her small, delicate handwriting.

"What are you writing?" He was astonished by the amount of work she had already accomplished.

Zoe ignored his curiosity, crossed her arms, and changed the subject.

"Why couldn't you sleep, your Highness?"

The question brought his full attention back on to her, away from the papers. Ordinarily, this would be the time when he would respond with something witty or initiate a game that insisted she answer first. Thankfully, he knew better than to play those games right now. Zoe was a portrait of seriousness, so he should follow her lead. Well, loosely follow her lead anyway.

"There are several reasons. Including one about Spencer's painfully loud snores." Darien laughed nervously at his joke when Zoe didn't even crack a smile. "But I think the primary reason is: I knew you were upset with me. I'm sorry, Brizo."

She continued to look at him, revealing nothing. "Sorry for what?"

"Sorry for lying to you, and placing you in danger yesterday." Darien tried to look as remorseful as possible, hoping Zoe would pity him.

Zoe shook her head casually then gave him a shrug. "You already apologized for that, and I already forgave you yesterday."

She went back to scribbling on her pages.

Darien didn't understand, "Well, something's bothering you, Brizo. Is there something else I should be apologizing for?"

"Yup," Zoe answered. She continued working on her pages as if releasing her anger with every word.

"Will you tell me, or do you need to continue this mysterious act?" Darien tried not to sound too annoyed.

Zoe paused and looked at him thoughtfully. "I don't know if you are ready to listen."

"Come on Brizo," Darien rubbed his strained eyes. "It's too early for riddles. What is bothering you?"

Zoe put her pen down, so she could give the prince her full attention. "You're not acting like yourself."

She spoke calmly and sweetly to him, but the answer slapped him in the face. He didn't think he was acting any differently than he had previously.

"Not being myself? Since when?"

"Since we escaped from Peter… after you pulled me from the river. You've been different."

Darien was trying to recall any strange action of his but continued to draw a blank. Try as he might, he couldn't figure it out.

"Different how?" he asked as gently as possible.

Zoe gave him a look that he had never seen from her before—worry.

"Ever since we escaped yesterday, you have been insecure and directionless. You act like you are undeserving of... anything good." Zoe looked away embarrassed. "It's not like you at all."

"But, that *is* what I am," Darien was still confused. He wasn't sure if he was missing something obvious because he was still waking up, or if Zoe was trying to teach him something in her roundabout, mysterious manner.

"No, it's not. I've never seen you like this," she insisted.

"Fine, then how *do* you see me?" Darien asked. He was eager to get to the actual problem, so he could hurry up and fix it.

"You have always been confident and fearless. You know what you want and go after it head-on. There's usually this ease about you that..." She trailed off, then turned her attention back to the comfort of her writing. "Never mind, it's probably just my imagination."

Darien's heart sank. As much as he wanted to argue, Zoe was right. His love for her allowed him to welcome back that same confidence and ease he had ten years ago. After all this time searching for Brizo White, he knew the moment he laid eyes on her she was someone he could care for, someone he would protect with his life. Yesterday, when they were captured, all he could do was watch helplessly as Zoe executed their escape. Not only did he fail to protect her, but he was the one who placed her in harm's way to begin with. Then, his confession to her about his past brought back fresh reminders of his failures as a prince. Doubt and insecurity contaminated his heart as he was swallowed up in their filthy sludge. Then, when a plan had been devised to help him set things right, he had shied away again. Darien wasn't acting like himself at all.

His shoulders sagged, "Honestly, I have been depressed and afraid for so long; I carried those badges with distinction. I simply thought that was who I was now. Then I met you, Zoe. You're right. That is not the kind of person I am, and I'm embarrassed you had to see that side of me."

He now had Zoe's undivided attention again, giving him the courage to continue.

"I don't want anyone else to suffer because of King Robert. And I refuse to be a forgotten chapter in the proud history of my family's legacy. But, most importantly, I don't want anything malicious to happen to you ever again."

"I have already spoken with Spencer about my concerns last night. I have decided to go along with your plan. It's a good one; I think we can pull it off together."

Zoe tried to act nonchalant, but her beaming smile betrayed her. Darien immediately returned the gesture.

"Really?" she said. "Together?"

"That's what I said, isn't it?" Darien teased.

"I'm glad," Zoe blushed. "Otherwise, all this writing would have been a terrible waste."

Darien glanced down curiously at the pages.

"What have you been writing?" he asked.

"Oh, not much. I'm trying to work out the final part of *The King's Play* in our program. You know, the fulfillment of prophecy."

"Really?" Darien reached out for the papers when he saw his name scrawled all over them. "Let me see."

The moment his hand touched the pages, Zoe's hands also had a firm grip on them to secure them in place.

"It's nothing you don't already know," She dismissed. "Just you wandering the kingdom then finding us… you know the rest."

"If you're writing about me, then I have the right to read it." Darien's fingers tightened, crumpling the pages while pulling them away from her. He smiled when Zoe's grip did the same, pulling back in her direction. They were locked in a small game of war; both refusing to let go.

"It's not ready to be read," Zoe protested, nervously biting her lip. "It's rough, terribly rough. You wouldn't like it if you read it now. I promise… It's bad!"

Zoe looked up at Darien pleadingly, only to be met with his confidently smug, teasing grin. Her eyes narrowed as she tugged harder, crumpling the paper even more.

"You better let go or it's going to tear," Darien spoke confidently.

Zoe stared back without flinching, "Then it will tear."

"Then, you will have to rewrite everything you lost all over again." A menacing glint touched Darien's eye.

"I suppose so." Zoe still didn't back down.

Darien's brow lowered curiously. "You'll forget something. There's no way you can remember all of it."

The papers started to tear slightly under their grip, but Zoe kept her sight locked on him. Darien shifted uneasily when one corner of her mouth drew up knowingly as she began to recite.

"Rumors of the prophecy spread throughout the land, whispered in every corner, breathed down every street until it found its way to our phantom prince's ears. A flicker of hope ignited in his heart at the possibility of righting the wrongs he had to endure. The brave prince resolved to find the wise fortune teller who foretold his redemption, wanting to know every detail that would help him fulfill his destiny…"

Darien loosened his grip long enough for Zoe to free the papers from his hand and clutched them close to her chest, lovingly.

"*Wise fortune-teller?*" Prince Darien scratched his chin disapprovingly. "She sounds so old and feeble. Shouldn't you add how beautiful and accomplished this fortune teller is? Not forgetting tenacious, of course."

Zoe nervously tucked some hair behind her ear. She looked away to hide her smile. "It's not relevant to the story."

"Not relevant, how so?" he asked.

"I don't want to take time away from the action later on. The audience loves the fight at the end," Zoe explained.

"But there wouldn't be any action later if not for the profound influence you have on me now," Darien rebutted.

"Profound influence?" Zoe blushed again.

Darien laughed softly while holding her gaze. "You're the seer. Didn't you realize you were writing a romance?"

Zoe's smile beamed so brightly that Darien swore he could feel his heart melt.

"Would you like to help me then?" she asked softly. "Just to make sure I get the story right?"

Darien returned her genuine smile, "I would like nothing more."

Chapter 30

R ose had slept so soundly last night; the sun had been up for hours by the time she finally had her breakfast. She stretched in her seat just outside her wagon, sipping her tea. She saw Darien and Zoe sitting together by the fire pit carrying on as if they were the only two people in the world. She quickly looked away. Darien still bothered her, but she had come to an acceptance that he was a part of Zoe's life now—a fact she needed to accept sooner or later. Her eyes instinctively looked in the direction of Spencer's wagon. Her heart skipped when she caught sight of the man leaning casually against the wheel of his wagon. He sat comfortably, but hard at work with his pen and paper. Something about him was different. He seemed stronger than she had ever given him credit for. She watched him curiously as she continued to sip her tea.

The next thing she knew, Rose's heart was beating loudly and her hands turned clammy. She rubbed them on her hips in an attempt to mask the nervousness that was swelling up inside her. Her mouth was dry, but her mind raced with a million different things she should say. Rose mentally scolded herself. She had walked over to Spencer's wagon countless times to talk to him without any problem. Why should today be any different? Rose couldn't remember wanting something as much as she wanted this to happen, and was terrified by the possibility that he wouldn't agree. She swallowed hard and forced her breathing to slow down with a few deep breaths.

"Enough of this, Rose," she said to herself. She set her cup down, willing her legs to move.

Spencer looked up from his work to offer Rose a smile when she drew closer. Rose was grateful because his smile made it easier for her to relax, and thus finally speak.

"Hello." She tried to say more, but her mind had gone blank.

Spencer, on the other hand, smiled wider, clearly enjoying Rose's discomfort.

"Hello," he answered back slowly, as his eyes glanced at her hands.

Rose had just become aware that she was wringing her fingers nervously, and then blushed when she noticed that Spencer had noticed. She dropped her hands to her sides and forced them in her pockets. Rose didn't need them to betray herself again.

"So," Rose spoke as casually as she could. "I was curious as to the kind of evening you had planned for tonight."

Spencer sighed as he pointed toward a very thick notebook sitting next to him.

"I'm working on a speech for Darien and trying to figure out the right effects to use to emphasize the proper points to help gain support from the crowd. It's a big project. Everything has to be planned just right or it will blow up in our faces. Why? Is something going on?" He asked, welcoming her distraction.

Rose swallowed again, failing to calm her nerves. "Oh. Well, if you weren't busy, I was going to ask you to do something with me."

"What do you need?" He asked calmly.

Rose could tell by the lack of emotion on Spencer's face she wasn't being very clear.

"No, it's nothing important. Not like saving the kingdom, kind of important. I just… um… wanted to do something… together, you and me." Rose's eyes grew wild with disbelief at how ridiculous she sounded. She was about ready to turn and walk away in embarrassment when Spencer spoke.

"Rosie, are you asking me out?" He leaned onto his knees to study her carefully. "Just the two of us?"

"Yes," Rose released a large sigh of relief. "Yes, that is exactly what I'm doing."

"No," Spencer's face revealed no emotion.

Rose's muscles tensed, "No?"

"No," His face remained hard as stone. "I have been asking you time and time again to do something together, and every time you have rejected me. Now you're finally ready to give it a go, and think you can just ask me once and I'll say *yes*?"

Rose's eyes searched back and forth for an answer. "Yes?"

Spencer shook his head. "Rose, look at it this way. For the past ten years, I've been trying to be something more than just friends with you. I could have given up at any time, but I didn't. Now, you think it is okay to swoop in and snatch away my victory like it is entirely your idea." He shook his head frustrated. "No, I'm not going to allow you to do that."

He stared at her with a stone, cold look that refused to flinch. Rose folded her arms, leaning back to consider the man. Their eyes locked in a tense stare, each challenging the other to look away first. Rose broke first as her lips twitched into a smile, and she choked back a laugh. She ran her fingers through her hair then planted her fists firmly on her hips.

"Alright, Spencer," she started. "I'm not entirely sure what kind of plans you have going on in your head. However, I thought you should know, I am done running away from you. So, whenever you are ready to exact your plans, you know where I'll be."

Spencer continued to stare at her, emotionless. Rose felt nervousness creep back into her chest.

"Right then," Rose nodded resolutely. "I will leave you to your work." She turned around stiffly on her heel, then started to walk away.

After what felt like an eternity to Rose, Spencer was on his feet falling in quickly alongside her, stride for stride. He took her hand and wrapped it around his arm as he looked into her eyes.

"Rosie, I was hoping you might join me for some exploring in the woods. There's something I've been wanting to show you." Spencer's usual charm and confidence were back.

Rose relaxed. "You tease! I thought you were going to let me walk away."

"I'm the tease?" Spencer's eyes grew wide. Rose looked away embarrassed. His voice softened, "So, will you come with me, Rosie?"

Rose answered him sincerely, "Sounds interesting, so I will see you tonight?"

"Who said anything about tonight?" Spencer drew back, surprised, "I thought we could go now."

"Now?" It was Rose's turn to be surprised. "Didn't you say you had a lot of work to do?

"Yes," he admitted. "But do you think I'm going to allow you the opportunity to change your mind?"

Rose mused over his answer, allowing herself to reveal her emotions in her smile instead of holding back. "If that's what you would like, you're in charge."

Spencer was pleasantly surprised, "Wow, you are trying several new things today, aren't you?

Rose poked him squarely on his chest with her finger. "Don't get used to it."

He laughed as he put up his hands in surrender. "Okay, I won't. Why don't you get your coat, and I'll pack up the rest"

"What else do we need?" She asked, curiously.

Spencer's eye had that usual glint as he winked at her. "You will see,"

He turned to disappear into his wagon as Rose stood there wondering what Spencer was scheming in that mysterious mind of his. She decided to stop wondering, and hurried off to snatch up her coat.

Chapter 34

Rose and Spencer spent the entire afternoon hiking, tracking, climbing, and all sorts of rigorous activities they loved to do. They had come across a meadow that had somehow retained most of its green color and was spotted with wildflowers despite the heat. When Rose asked Spencer if this was what he wanted to show her, he looked around to take in the view then shrugged, unimpressed.

"The meadow is nice," He agreed, "But it is not what we came here to see."

The same could be said of a thin waterfall they had passed, an orchard of trees littered with butterflies up along their trunks, and a herd of deer they had crossed paths with. All were very beautiful to behold, but not enough to match whatever Spencer was planning.

They stopped for a late lunch, courtesy of Spencer. He had packed a generous spread of smoked meats, bread, cheese, honey, and berries.

Rose couldn't help being impressed. He had packed all her favorite snacks and even laid out a thick blanket for them to enjoy their picnic on.

"You sure know how to show a girl a good time," Rose softly laughed to herself.

Spencer paused and answered her seriously, "I know how to show *you* a good time."

His words made her pause, speechless. All she could do was respond with a warm, genuine smile. After enjoying a few more snacks, Rose finally found the confidence to speak again.

"Everything you've planned turned out to be perfect, Spencer. This was a lovely first date."

"Oh this isn't over. We haven't even got to the best part yet," Spencer answered calmly.

"And what would that be, Spence?"

"Don't rush this," Spencer looked at the horizon. "It is still too early."

Rose laughed, "Then why did we leave so early?"

"Because," Spencer took a calming breath, "to truly appreciate what I'm going to show you, you will need to hear the rest of my story."

Rose was a mixture of excitement and worry. She wanted to hear the rest of the story but didn't want Spencer to tell her if he wasn't ready.

"Do you want to tell me the rest?" she asked carefully.

Spencer donned his storyteller's voice, "Yes, it is time you knew it all."

Rose sat comfortably across from Spencer, "No theatrics please, you already have my attention."

"As you wish," Spencer smiled before sharing the rest of his past with her.

"After Prince Darien was banished, the army became agitated. Most of us weren't entirely sure how we should be feeling. We had just fought back a treacherous army that wanted to infest our beloved country like a disease and was victorious in defense of our people. But we had lost many brothers in the throes of battle. And, of course, there were the three hundred of our men whose deaths were unexplained. Then we hear talk about how Prince Darien, who had been the reason for our victory, was also the reason for the unexplained deaths. On top of all of that, the prince we had followed was stripped of his birthright and banished from his castle without so much as an inquiry.

Things grew worse when King Robert took over. We found out he had sent a small crew of counselors, as he called them, to mingle among us. They wanted to hear our concerns and opinions about recent matters to relay back to the king. I don't care what they called themselves. We all knew they were spies. I had never met one personally, but my men had told me about them. Their actual mission was not to consult but to sort out where our true allegiances lied.

Then the changes started to happen, small changes that could easily be rationalized— little tweaks here and there to sound policies and agendas that tipped the balance of power more towards the king than the people. It was all cleverly disguised under the preface that our beloved king would take care of us, and we would no longer have to worry about our struggles.

A handful of my men recognized what was happening immediately, but many were fooled by promises of an easier life. With so few of us, it was difficult to plan anything worthwhile that would right the wrongs that were happening. But, as I said, a Marconian soldier's allegiance is to the country and the protection of all those in it. It was our duty to do something; otherwise, we were breaking our oath as protectors of the land.

One day, we gathered together to confront King Robert directly. We didn't plan on a fight—just to offer our advice as we have always been encouraged to do for the king. However, thanks to the king's spies he already knew why we requested an audience with him and prepared a few surprises for us. First, he thanked us for voicing our concerns. Then we were assured that the prosperity of the kingdom was his primary concern. He also reminded us that dissension among his troops was evidence of a weakened army, and that was something he would not tolerate. That's when he stripped us all of our ranks and authorities in his military.

Instinctively we drew our weapons, not willing to be dismissed without a fight. We weren't going to give up so easily, especially when the true colors of our new king had just been revealed. But our next surprise was a small troop of assassins, loyal to the King, hiding in the shadows that appeared and surrounded us with their weapons. They had murder in their eyes, ready to fight to the death," Spencer shivered as he recalled the scene from his past.

Rose couldn't believe what she was hearing. It was hard to imagine her friend, Spencer, taking on King Robert for the sake of Marconia.

She was unable to stay silent any longer, "And did you fight?"

"No, we didn't," he answered.

"Why not?" Rose was surprised by his actions.

Spencer answered with a lesson he was taught when he was a young boy after it was known that he wanted to grow up to be in the Army. "A good soldier knows how to fight with all his heart and might, but a wise soldier knows when to walk away so they can fight another day. We were grossly outnumbered. If we had died for our convictions that day, our voices would have been completely silenced and our story never told.

King Robert showed us mercy by branding us as cowards, unfit to be a soldier in his army, and we were formally discharged to create a new life more suited to us. We were free to leave, but not without one final surprise from our gracious king. All our swords were taken away, so if we talked about anything that had happened no one would believe us."

Rose forced her mouth closed to not appear overly enthralled by Spencer's story.

"So why now?" she asked. "What made you want your sword back now?"

"Your sister gave us the prophecy about Prince Darien reclaiming the throne. Admittedly, I had reservations as to whether or not he could achieve such a goal, but if your sister prophesied it then I wanted to believe it. Yet, we still had nothing, not even a whisper to hope on, just the prophecy.

About a year ago I ran into a few of my men after one of our performances. After they got over the shock of me joining a band of gypsys, performing on stage, and my colorful outfits, we talked about the prophecy. They asked me if I believed it would happen. Since I didn't have a better answer I simply told them that if Brizo prophesied it, then it has to."

"Thank you for that," Rose added, sincerely.

He smiled at her, "Hey, I may have my doubts, but I also know how fast gossip travels. Zoe's credibility would have been ruined if people heard her lead storyteller didn't believe in prophecies." Rose nodded in agreement and Spencer continued his story. "My men doubted that Prince Darien was capable of rallying our troops. But they did confess that many of our brothers have been itching for a rematch. And more men who have seen King Robert's injustice firsthand have offered to join our cause should we ever decide to rally for the people again. After we talked more we concluded that we could fulfill the prophecy, with or without the prince, if we had someone strong enough to lead us. Then, of course, they turned to me.

I didn't make any promises that day, but I have thought about our discussion since then. I reasoned that if I was going to be the one to rally my men, I would need a symbol that united them together. The first thing that came to mind was my commander's sword. I knew I had to get it back, and that meant I had to return to the man who had taken it, King Robert.

Do you remember when I was gone for about a fortnight last year?" Spencer asked.

"Yes, you said you were going to scout out new villages for us to perform in." Rose's eyes narrowed, "Don't tell me you weren't scouting for us?"

"I scouted for you, just as I promised, while on my way to the castle. Surprisingly, King Robert accepted my request for an audience. All I did was ask for him to return my sword to me, and I promised that it was for mere sentimental purposes, and my absolute discharge would still be in effect. After studying me, he agreed to return my sword to me in exchange for his nephew, Prince Darien.

I had no idea the prince would simply stumble on your doorstep shortly after that. It was so coincidental that I began to wonder if Zoe's prophecy was actually coming true on its own. So I waited to see what Darien would do. After an entire winter with us, it was clear he had no interest in reclaiming the throne. That's when I found Peter to arrange the exchange." Spencer stretched in finality. "And the rest, sweet Rosie, you already know."

They sat in silence for a moment, allowing Rose to digest all that she heard.

"I believe I have gravely underestimated you, Spence," was all she could say.

Spencer smirked, "Don't be too hard on yourself, I have kept a lot hidden from you."

"What an interesting pair we make, huh?" Rose mumbled.

"That's what I've been saying, Rosie," Spencer teased.

They shared a small laugh, then Spencer took notice of the horizon again.

"Well, we better get going. It is almost time and I don't want you to miss it."

They quickly packed up their things, and were on their way again. Rose's curiosity grew as Spencer carefully led her up the side of a steep hill. They continued further up until they reached a flat, stony clearing near its precipice. The view was breathtaking. Rose could see the thick forest covering the rolling hills and tumbling boulders below them. The setting sun had turned the sky darker shades of blue and indigo. Rose shivered. Thanks to the lack of trees in the stone clearing, a cool wind washed over her freely, tangling her hair. Rose pulled her coat tighter to keep warm, but Spencer had already anticipated the temperature drop. He calmly wrapped a wool blanket from his pack around Rose's shoulders.

She smiled graciously at him then nodded at the view. "It's absolutely beautiful, Spencer. I've never seen a view like this although I imagine it would be better to see in the daylight."

By now the dark blue sky had turned into an ominous shade of black with slight hues of navy refusing to yield. Spencer gave Rose a wide smile as he moved behind her.

"No, Rosie. Look up." He pointed to the sky, and Rose obediently tilted her head to follow.

The moon waned thin and low on the horizon, giving off minimal light. The next thing Rose saw left her breathless. The lack of light allowed the stars to shine more brilliantly than she had ever seen. Rose had never imagined so many stars were in the sky. Even the tiny ones normally dulled out by the lights of the cities gleamed through the darkness. A brilliant flash of light streaked across the sky that made her jump. Then Rose saw another flash of light, and another and another. A shower of stars rained down towards them in the sky providing a shining display for them to enjoy.

"Oh, wow!" Rose breathed with her eyes wide with pure amazement.

"You like it?" Spencer asked excitedly.

"I love it! I had no idea there were so many stars, and so bright." She answered.

Spencer gently rested his hands on Rose's shoulders. "I try to keep track of and watch star showers like this. It always calms me, and I see things more clearly."

Rose reached up to hold Spencer's hand.

"I see what you mean." Rose gave his hand an affectionate squeeze.

Spencer squeezed her shoulders in silent response.

"Now, I need you to look down there." He turned her shoulders, so she faced where he pointed. At first, Rose could only see darkness, but there was a small flicker of light, then another, and another. They appeared in the same way the stars had appeared in the sky except, these were not stars. These were campfires. She calculated the pattern of the lights for a moment before she spoke again.

"Is that our caravan?" Rose asked.

"Yes, that is the infamous White and Red Troupe," Spencer answered fondly. "Ten years ago I was banished and had lost my way in the woods. At the time, I did not care that I was lost. Nothing mattered, until the day everything did. I no longer wanted to throw my life away just because someone else had an agenda. I knew I had to get my bearings, but I was too turned around to make sense of anything. I decided to find some higher ground, so I could use the stars to find my way. I knew they would help me think clearly, so I could figure out where to go. Unfortunately, when I made it up as far as I could go, the sky was overcast. I couldn't see anything."

Rose listened intently to Spencer's story. She always knew him as a confident, sure man. She honestly didn't think there was anything in the world that could rattle her friend. However, Rose had known very little about Spencer's past. His past was usually tucked away securely in a metaphorical box with several heavy locks strewn all over it, chained, and then wrapped up beautifully in a soft velvet cloth which he carried deep inside his heart. Now he was entrusting her with the lowest moment in his life, a vital story from that special box that he worked so hard to ignore. Her heart went out to him.

"Until I looked down," He continued. "I saw your fires, and they reminded me of the stars. I felt warm and safe. I knew I had to make my way down to the camp. That's when you found me. Saved me, actually—twice."

"Twice? I only remember helping you scare the wolves away." Rose asked.

"You saved me from the wolves," Spencer agreed. "Then you offered me a home, with your troupe. You gave me my life back. See, I had lost everything; my friends, my brothers in arms, my rank, my home, even my identity. Being a soldier was all I had ever known. Rosie, you opened my eyes to a life far richer and more fulfilling than I ever imagined. That calm and clarity you felt as you gazed at the stars, is how I feel when I gaze into your eyes. I have come to realize that it wasn't the White and Red Troupe that drew me into safety. It was you. I love my new life because you are in it."

Rose put a hand on Spencer's cheek. "Spencer, I…"

He waited patiently for Rose to finish her sentence, but she never did. Rose was distracted by something she had seen out of the corner of her eye. Rose turned and squinted to try to see the view better. She saw several small lights heading toward the large cluster of campfires.

"What does that look like to you?" She pointed to the moving lights and Spencer focused his attention on them. His soft face hardened in an instant.

"We need to get back to camp now." Spencer didn't panic, but the urgency in his voice made Rose move quickly. She knew something wrong was happening. She sensed something dark, she sensed… death. Her heartbeat quickened as they raced down the cliff, but what unsettled her the most was the faint skeletal laugh rattling in the back of her mind.

Chapter 32

"I am not putting that into the play," Zoe laughed at Darien's suggestion. It was late and they decided to move their work into her wagon for better light and to have something to eat.

"Why not?" Darien's voice was low and calm. "I think seeing your face next to mine is essential to the story."

"It's boring and will cause us to lose half our audience." she reminded him. "This is a quick play, not an epic."

"Uggh, fine," he relented, "But you need to promise you will throw something in there so the audience knows we were meant to be together."

"Again," Zoe sighed with exasperation. "Our relationship is not essential to move the story along."

"Wrong, you were the first person who believed in me. I was a lost and miserable mess before I heard about your prophecy. And then when I met you face to face, you never doubted my abilities, even when I did.

Brizo, you're the one who reminded me of who I really am, and who I can be again," Darien explained.

Zoe blushed. "Stop, you did that all on your own."

"All thanks to you," Darien continued. "You single handedly changed my perspective on life. If that is not essential to the story, then what is?"

"You keep talking about me like some kind of hero, but it was you who helped remind me of who I was, and can be again." Zoe shifted to face him squarely. "Before you, I barely left my wagon. I had been painted as some mysterious deity that everyone had to be careful around. The extent of my fun went as far as writing stories for the troupe's performances. I ended up living vicariously through them."

"And now you play a crucial role in one of those stories. So, why not allow yourself to shine a little brighter than usual?" Darien asked gently.

Zoe's shoulder's dropped when she sighed. "I don't know. I have gotten comfortable being an obscure name that everyone loves and fears. Putting a face to that name feels like a huge step for me."

"I'll say it is," Darien agreed. "When I first put the name Brizo White to your face I was blown away by your beauty. Then you spoke and your compassion was intoxicating. Meeting you face to face only added to the divinely, mysterious image I had heard of."

"You're laying it on pretty thick." Zoe's blush extended down her neck.

"I'm simply speaking the truth," Darien shrugged. "There's no sense in denying the facts at hand. I assumed that matriarchs considered all the elements of the story before making final decisions."

"Alright!" She finally gave into his argument with great reluctance. "Since you insist on playing the matriarch card against me, I will allow you to add it."

Darien's face split into a wide, satisfied smile.

"But I reserve the right to edit out any unnecessary details about us. I do not want the play to get too sweet."

Darien's smile transformed into a mischievous grin. He looked as if he was about to say something to her, but she never heard it. Zoe's world blurred into a swirl of colors as her body remained fixed in her current position. The next thing she knew, she was engulfed in the color red. The world around her materialized to reveal an elegantly decorated room with thick, red rugs and curtains, and golden furnishings accenting the walls and tables. Her eyes zeroed in on a smallish, older looking man with a pointy white beard, and ornate crown on his brow. Kneeling before him was an armed guard trying hard to look confident in front of his king.

"Why is it so hard to find a bunch of traveling performers?" King Robert spoke sharply.

"We are following up on a few leads as we speak, your Highness." The man swallowed hard to control the shake in his voice. "I am confident we will corner them any moment now."

"I hope so, for your sake," the king sneered. "Summer is almost over and the people are getting unruly. They are starting to believe they could take me on even without my beloved nephew leading them."

"Even if the prince managed to regain control of his former troops, I doubt they will be successful against our superior army." The guard spoke the words as if saying them out loud would convince himself they were true.

The king simply glared down his nose at him. "I wish I shared your optimism, but I want to be positive that this prophecy will never come true. I need some insurance to guarantee everything will play out according to my plan."

"Rest assured, your Highness, you have all the insurance you need despite our success," the guard gulped.

King Robert turned to look into the fire. "Yes, but Brizo White is too powerful to ally herself with anyone except me. With her by my side, I will be invincible."

Zoe's vision blurred again and she was lost in a swirl of colors. She jolted back into reality to Darien shaking her frantically with panic stricken eyes.

"Brizo, please say something," he begged.

"Darien," she whispered.

The shaking stopped and he brushed a few strands of hair out of her face. "Brizo, what happened, are you alright?"

"I am alright, it was just a vision," she answered calmly, breathing through the stabbing pain that cut through her middle.

"A vision?" Darien repeated. "You mean this happens all the time?"

Zoe took a few breaths to relax her muscles. "Yes, this is normal."

"That was one of the most terrifying moments of my life. You were here, but your consciousness was not. I had no idea what to do."

Zoe smiled at his concern. "Shaking me isn't the best idea. It hurts me less if I come out of a vision on my own as opposed to being pulled back by someone else."

Darien let go of her shoulders, "Oh, I'm sorry, I didn't know… what do you need?"

"Tea?" she spoke gently with another warm smile.

Darien leapt out of his chair to fix a cup for her. Zoe held back a laugh as she watched him pour the hot water over the leaves with such determination, careful to remember a touch of honey to sweeten it. He offered it to her as if it were a powerful concoction that would heal her of a terminal illness. Zoe sipped it gratefully, allowing the warmth to wash over her.

"So, what did you see?" Darien asked, then reined in his curiosity when he thought better of himself. "Unless you're not supposed to tell me. Is it some kind of secret?"

Zoe looked up at him with all seriousness, "I saw King Robert."

Darien's face paled for a moment before he spoke slowly, "What about him?"

"He's looking for the troupe. He's determined to make sure the prophecy doesn't happen."

"Don't worry Zoe, I won't allow him to capture me again," he said.

Zoe shook her head. "I don't think he's looking for you anymore."

Darien's mouth went dry. "Who is he looking for?"

"Me," Zoe uttered softly.

Darien and Zoe heard a shrill scream coming from outside the wagon.

"What was that?" they both said to one another.

Their question was answered by the door of the wagon being burst open by two king's men clad in white.

Chapter

As Rose ran closer to the caravan her heart sank and her feet turned to lead. The normal dim glow of the wagon lights had grown into a frightening blaze. Its light was bright and angry, refusing to be hidden by the forest. The only thing that kept her moving was Spencer's hand clenched tightly around her arm. When the trees cleared, Rose's fears were confirmed. Several wagon roofs were on fire, and patches of glowing embers littered the once soft grass. Spencer immediately jumped in with a group of men snuffing out each fire as fast as they could using buckets of water and blankets.

Rose shook her head, scolding herself for standing dumbstruck at the scene before her. She bolted for her wagon with one goal in mind: find her sister. Their wagon was one of the lucky ones that had not been burned, but the white paint glowed an ominous orange because of the surrounding fires. The door was broken open, and the flower pots lay smashed next to the steps.

"Zoe!" Rose screamed, jumping to the door without bothering with the steps.

The place was in ruins. Everything inside was turned over or broken from an obvious struggle. The only thing missing from the wagon: Brizo White. Everything that happened next was a blur. Rose ran all around the camp shouting for her sister. The constant roar of men barking directions to each other, babies crying, mothers humming to soothe their children, and other sounds of chaos rattled Rose's mind. Then, all went quiet and she could only hear the haunting laugh that would not leave her alone.

She crashed into Darien who grabbed her arms and held her steady in front of him.

"Rose!" shouted Darien, bringing her out of the silence. "Where have you been? They have Zoe."

Rose's wits rushed back to her, and she twisted her wrists out from Darien's grasp.

"Who has Zoe?" Rose demanded. "Where is she?"

"Some men, bearing the King's brand, charged the camp. We were in the wagon when they stormed in looking for her. I fought them off as best as I could, but there were too many of them. Next thing I knew, the whole camp was on fire and two of them left with Zoe flung over their shoulder."

"And you didn't follow her?" Rose interrupted as if Darien were to blame for everything that had happened.

Darien ignored her anger, "I did until another man knocked me out."

"Knocked you out?" Rose grabbed the collar of his shirt. "You're the prince! Why did they take her and not you?"

By this time, Spencer had found his way next to Rose and put a hand on hers to release Darien. She did, reluctantly.

Darien's eyes narrowed in on Rose. "Where were you?"

Rose opened her mouth to speak but shut it quickly. Her responsibilities crashed down on her shoulders like stones. Where was she? Her eyes cast down under the judgmental glare of Darien. He appeared much stronger, and smarter than she remembered. Rose wondered how someone she believed to be so ridiculous and uncertain could take on such a powerful countenance.

"Nowhere," she whispered. "I was nowhere."

She wanted to cry but refused to give Darien the satisfaction of seeing her so hurt. The problem was that was exactly how she felt—hurt. The one time she let her guard down, the one-time Zoe wasn't her first and last thought, this happens. She failed Zoe, she failed her mother, and she failed the Troupe. So many people relied on her for her protection and leadership. She failed them all.

Darien refused to let up. "You needed to be here! Your people needed you, and you turned your back on them."

Rose shouted back at him, tears welling up in her eyes. She refused to blink for fear of crying.

"Don't you think I know that? Don't you think I've been telling myself that over and over since the second I saw the torches heading toward the camp? No matter how fast I ran, it wasn't enough. No matter how many targets I can hit with my knives, no matter how well I can trick my enemy, it doesn't matter because I wasn't here." Rose straightened with resolve. "I am the matriarch of this troupe, and every drop of innocent blood that was spilled is on my hands. I allowed this to happen. You can scowl at me all you want about right and wrong, but this… this is my family. You cannot possibly know the pain I'm in."

Rose turned to walk away leaving the two men alone in the looming haze from the fires that had been extinguished. "Your selfish heart will never understand."

Chapter 34

Rose sat in front of her broken home on a tree stump that jutted out of the ground. On any normal day, it was the best view of the camp. You could see all the wagons circled into groups. The air would be filled with sweet and savory smells from all the dinners cooking. There would be laughter in the air from children playing, and dancing to the music of the performers practicing their songs.

Now she saw only misery. The cries and wails had died down, but the stench of smoke choked her. The entire camp was enveloped in an eerie, undead feeling. Rose sat frozen in shock, staring off into the distance at nothing in particular. She wanted to do something, but her mind was a sea of black. All she could do was imagine the poor men and women who gave their lives for the troupe tonight. No, she didn't imagine, she saw each death played out one by one. Even though she wasn't here to witness the events, she saw it all. That's when her tears finally fell. She saw each of her friend's lives cut short, wishing she could have done something more to prevent it. And that cringe-worthy laugh, as faint as the wind echoed like a siren in her head.

Rose was pulled from her thoughts when she heard footsteps approaching her. She straightened up slightly then returned to her discouraged slump when she saw it was Darien. He looked uncertain again. Except, this time there was sincere concern in his eyes.

"What do you want now?" She asked in a guarded, unimpressed voice.

Darien sat down next to Rose but remained silent. Rose saw him finger a chain that hung around his neck, while she waited for him to speak. He finally broke the silence with a soft, sympathetic tone.

"I do know." Darien looked tortured. He gathered his courage to continue. "The pain, the struggle you feel, I do know what it feels like."

Rose looked away. She was still upset with him and now disgusted that he dared to say he knew how she felt. He couldn't possibly know.

"After I was banished by my uncle, my only living family, I went into hiding. All I did was wander from place to place around my kingdom. Every day was a cruel reminder of how I failed my people. I saw how the new policies of my uncle rob everyone of not just their wealth, but their spirit and freedoms. I was face to face with my kingdom's pain, no matter where I went. The worst part was at the end of the day; all I could think about was what I should have done. I would wonder how I could have been better but wasn't. I wasn't the prince my kingdom needed me to be. I willingly handed them over to my devious uncle. It was the worst mistake of my life, and my ultimate failure."

Rose's hatred cooled, and she looked at him with sympathy.

Darien continued, "Tonight was not your fault, Rose. It was mine. Every pain and misery from my uncle's hand is my fault. King Robert's rule will haunt me for the rest of my life."

Rose wanted to touch his hand to offer some kind of comfort, but something stopped her. She felt as if the broken prince wanted the pain, and welcomed it. For the first time, she saw him as he truly was. He was a prince, tormented by his past and desperate to fix it.

She spoke slowly to him, "Zoe always told me, 'If you don't like the ending, then write another chapter.' If we had to write another chapter, what would it be about?"

Darien closed his eyes to hide his sorrow, "All I can think about is getting Brizo back."

Rose nodded in agreement, "Do you know where they might have taken her?"

"If Robert knows about her gift, and I suspect he does, then she will be taken straight to the palace to be as close to him as possible," Darien answered directly.

Rose started piecing together a plan. A sly smile curved her lips.

Darien looked at her warily, "What are you thinking?"

Rose nodded to Darien, "I'm thinking King Robert made a big mistake when he stopped seeing you as a threat."

Chapter 35

Zoe had been left alone in a beautifully decorated room with soft carpets covering the cold, hard stones of the castle, the very same room she had seen in her vision. Thick blankets and pillows adorned a long sofa and a collection of padded chairs. All were clad in the Marconian colors of deep red and gold. A shimmering chandelier hung low from the tall ceiling, along with more golden candle fixtures secured uniformly on the walls. The generous amounts of candles provided just enough light to reveal all of the room's luxurious and expensive flourishes. Any true Marconian would easily feel a sense of patriotism standing in a room such as this. It was cozy and welcoming to anyone who required rest. Zoe, however, felt uncomfortable. When her captors left her alone in the room, the hard clap of the lock in the door told her what this room was in actuality—her prison. She stepped over to the large fireplace, where warm flames danced and snapped. It took the chill off of her just fine, but it was not hot enough to rid her of the cold feeling of danger that clutched at her chest.

Zoe forced her breathing to slow down. The silence of the room washed over her as she turned her thoughts to her sister. Her eyes flickered from one direction to another, searching. Zoe found her. Rose was sitting on a stump outside of their wagon with the same glow of firelight surrounding her. Zoe gasped, knowing the glow was not a mere hearth fire. It was light from the homes and wagons that were burning in their caravan. She saw Darien approach and sit down next to Rose nervously. Zoe couldn't hear what was said, but she saw the look of resolve in her sister's eyes. The image blurred to reveal several hundred men, decked with weapons of all kinds, dressed in sturdy clothes that were dusty from traveling. All were listening to a lone man, Darien, contemplating the validity of his words.

The vision disappeared and Zoe was back in her room, now kneeling in front of the hearth. She clutched her middle and gritted her teeth. Amid her agony, she smiled to herself.

"That's it, Rose, lead him out of the shadows," she whispered. Her faith and hope in her sister breathed confidence back into her. She offered a silent prayer, willing that same confidence out to the Prince, her love.

A loud clang of the lock opening startled Zoe to her feet. The door opened to allow King Robert to enter, decorated in all his golden riches from rings on his fingers to the crown on his head. Behind him, five servants carried golden trays piled high with food and placed them carefully on a long table in the room. When the servants left and the door was shut, all that remained was Zoe and the king.

"Please," he spoke kindly, gesturing for her to join him by the table.

Zoe slowly obliged as she sat down near him. He poured her a glass of wine and then filled one up for him as well.

"The infamous Brizo White," he mused, then looked her up and down, approvingly.

"I have wanted to meet you for a long time. I have to say you are exactly how I imagined you to be." Zoe simply watched him calmly, an unreadable lack of emotion that masked the rage within. "You must be hungry. Please help yourself."

Zoe glanced at the food in thought. She was extremely hungry, but she also knew the decadent food on the table would give her more pain than she recently endured from her vision. Years of suffering had taken a toll on her insides. By now, it hurt too much to eat more than simple soups or stews. On further thought, she also knew she was a prisoner. The more she obliged the king the more control he had. Zoe folded her hands in her lap as she gazed back at the king, eye for eye, in power.

"What have you done to my caravan, Sire?" she asked. Her voice may have been soft and delicate, but she held her frame upright in a dignified manner that demanded answers—a tactic that did not go unnoticed by the king.

"My Lady, I have done nothing to your caravan."

"My people burn because of your soldiers, why?" Zoe didn't ease up, knowing he was playing games.

The king took a generous sip of wine and shifted in his chair. "So, the rumors are true. You can see things that others cannot. Tell me, what else do you see?"

"I can see you avoiding my questions," Zoe answered plainly.

King Robert was surprised by her indignation. He considered her for a moment while stroking his long beard.

"It would seem my men were a bit overzealous when I gave them the order to bring you here. I have no interest in the people in your caravan," He answered.

"Clearly," Zoe spoke out loud to him. She thought of the number of families hurt or destroyed because of his men's callousness, and the king's lack of interest. She didn't know the specifics. Her vision only showed her what was around her sister, but she knew it was bad. Rose's face said it all.

The King looked back at her intently, "I will speak to my men directly. They will be punished for their blood lust."

Zoe continued to watch Robert carefully. She knew his men wouldn't be punished just like she knew the King wanted her at the castle, with him, no matter the cost.

"Why am I here?" she asked, not entirely sure she wanted to know the answer.

A smile formed on the King's lips—kind, gentle, foreboding.

"Why, I would like to offer you a job, is all."

"A job?" Zoe clarified.

"Yes, my dear, a person such as yourself can be beneficial for the strength of this country. With your help, we can counter possible threats before they even happen," the king preached fervently on his kingdom's behalf.

"I'm afraid I won't be much help to you then," Zoe answered as meekly as she could. The king merely took another long drink as the kindness melted away from his face.

"You see," Zoe continued, "everything I prophesy inevitably happens. There is no way to avoid or change it."

"You know this as a fact?" The king simply asked.

"I do."

"Oblige me then," the king went on, "what happens when you try to change the fate of a prophecy?"

Zoe took a breath to steady her emotions, "It makes things worse, much, much worse."

The ease returned to the King's face. "How so?"

Zoe stared at the King. She hated dwelling on this topic.

"I knew a dancer once. I had seen her break her leg, and so I convinced her to be somewhere else that day. I wanted to prevent the tragedy because I knew how important dance was to her. Regardless of where she was, her leg broke anyway. She was unable to dance for several weeks."

"How is that much worse?" The king twisted his face in suspicion.

"Because," Zoe paused to push away her rage and disgust for the king for pressing the issue. "Several others nearby were also hurt in the same accident—people who would never have been hurt if I had let her continue with her original plans. Because of my gift, I knew the only reason why they were hurt was that I tried to change her fate."

The king took a sip of his wine, contemplating Zoe's vague story. "Have you attempted to change your visions since then?"

"No," Zoe said flatly. "I have no wish to make the same mistake twice."

"Nevertheless, you would be a great asset to me here, as my counselor and visionary. I desire you to remain here, as my ally."

Zoe furrowed her brow, "Do I have a choice?"

"Of course you do." The King's overly polite tone was back. "You always have a choice."

Zoe leaned back in her chair, doubtful. "Did I have a choice when you sent your men to 'invite' me here?"

King Robert grinned wildly, "Yes, I believe you and I will get along rather nicely. And, who knows, perhaps the two of us together can solve the riddle of changing your visions."

Zoe laughed, "You believe you can bend fate to your will any more than I?

"Everything bends to my will, eventually," Robert's tone was so absolute it made Zoe shudder. She stared back at him, fully aware of his control over her future at that moment. "Now, there is just one other matter I'd like to address."

"What else could concern you, Sire?" Zoe was careful not to allow the sarcasm in her thoughts to drip into her words.

"I once heard of a prophecy concerning my nephew,' King Robert paused, waiting for Zoe to respond. Zoe knew this technique all too well. Many people would come to her for information about someone else's prophecy and conveniently pause, expecting her to fill in their gaps. She would not allow herself to be tricked so easily by this little man.

"I wasn't aware you had a nephew, Highness. He is not mentioned in any of the history books."

King Robert gave a subtle smirk. "It said my nephew would take my kingdom from me this summer."

"And this troubles you?" Zoe asked.

"Should it not?"

"Summer is almost over," she answered flatly.

"Which means he could show up on my doorstep at any moment," he retorted.

A blurry vision of two armies clashing swords by the castle flickered in Zoe's mind.

"If you believe the prophecy, he very well could," she stated.

Robert leaned in closer to her, "Do you believe the prophecy?"

Zoe leaned in even closer to look at the King eye to eye. "I don't see how it matters, considering everything bends to your will eventually."

The King sat back in his chair, aggravated. "And you said your prophecies always come true."

"So?" she asked.

"So, do you not recognize your prophecy?" The King threw up his hands, unsettled.

"I don't know what you want me to say, your Highness. My name gets attached to numerous stories I never prophesied. I think it's so other troupes can sell more tickets."

The king stood up in a fit of rage, "Say whatever you want, my dear. I believe my nephew is planning something, and you know more than you care to reveal."

He clapped his hands while staring down at Zoe menacingly. Four guards marched into the room and quickly surrounded Zoe.

"Put her in the tower for a few days with only bread and water." He stepped closer to Zoe, "I suggest you use your time to consider how much better off you will be by accepting my offer."

Zoe spat in the King's face. In an instant, the guards had their hands on Zoe, dragging her away from all the lavish comforts she was offered.

Chapter

The Red and White Troupe had collected all they could salvage, and moved on from their last campsite. Rose didn't feel the need to stay put in an area that held such disastrous memories for them, and she didn't like the fact that King Robert knew exactly where they were. Away from the circle of wagons the troupe had set up all that remained of their stage. While the curtains and railings were burned by the king's men, the main platform remained sound. The rest of the troupe were sorting through their things, taking stock of what they had, and what they could offer to the families who had lost much more. Rose couldn't hide the pride she had in her family as she watched them go about their work. What happened to them only a few days ago was horrendous and unforgivable. All lost something, some more than others, and all had good reason to curse the world and harden their hearts. Instead, her troupe reached out to one another, offering what they could to combine their resources, and opened up their wagons to those without one. Amid so much pain, they still were a family and would never allow each other to endure their struggle alone.

With as much love Rose felt for her troupe, she harbored twice as much hate for herself. No one blamed her for not being around when the wagons were attacked, but she continued to feel as if she failed them. Spencer and even Darien had reminded her that even if she was there, there wasn't much she could have done to prevent the raid. Perhaps not, she admitted to herself, but she could have certainly done something instead of just being there to pick through and sort through the aftermath. If she had been there she might have been able to fight off a few of the men or might have been able to stop Zoe from being taken away. She could have done something, anything to change what had happened. But Spencer's voice butted into her thoughts, reminding her that things could have gone much worse if she was there, too. That was hard to imagine for Rose. But when she thought about it, he was right. Dwelling on the past wasn't helpful to them now. All that aside, the hurt remained, and she continued in all her best efforts to lead her troupe. It was her responsibility to help them recover, the way a good matriarch should.

Standing next to Rose was Darien, lost in thought. Spencer sat comfortably on the edge of the stage, whittling away at a new block of wood.

"Do you think this plan will work?" Darien asked Rose quietly. "Many of these men have no reason to trust me, let alone follow me into battle."

Rose saw more creases of worry form on Darien's face as he continued to allow his fears to consume him. She smiled as confidently as ever at the prince.

"It's too late for you to back out now, so make sure you give it all you got." Rose went to sit with Spencer. When Darien was no longer looking at them she leaned her head in closer to him. "Are you sure these men will listen to him?"

Spencer shrugged, "Depends."

"On what?" she asked seriously.

"On whether they will show up," Spencer mumbled.

"You don't know if anyone is even coming?" Rose's eyes were wide with panic.

"It's not like this is a formal tea party, Rosie," Spencer answered. "Those who decide to come will come."

"Yes, but…"

Spencer put his hand on hers in the hopes of calming her down. "Rosie, we got the word out to everyone we could, and Darien is willing to do his part. We have done all we can. There is nothing more to do except wait."

"Right," Rose forced herself to breathe. "Now we are waiting."

The morning rolled on into a hot afternoon. Rose had nodded off while leaning against Spencer's shoulder for support. She was jolted awake when his muscles tensed and abruptly sat up straight. Rose was about to jeer him for waking her up but held back when she saw urgency written all over his face. One hand drifted easily to the hilt of his sword nearby while the other tightened his grip on the knife he had been using to whittle with. His eyes scanned the surrounding tree line. Then he sniffed as if catching the scent of something in the air.

Spencer stood up protectively when a lone man with dark skin emerged from the forest. The man wore thick leathers that hung close to his body, along with durable, worn-in boots and gloves. On his back were two scythes about the size of his forearm, crossing each other with handles pointing up behind his shoulders. On a leather strap that hung across his chest were various types of small sharp knives. Attached to his hip was a simple sword, clearly lacking the mark of a Marconian soldier. Spencer easily placed himself in between the man and Prince Darien, holding his stance firm and head high.

"Spencer, Babeeeey!" The way he lingered on the word forced the man into showing a wide grin for Spencer. Whether it was genuine or not was still unclear to Rose.

Spencer answered calmly with a casual smirk, "Xander, my old friend."

The men embraced warmly, then grasped the back of the other's neck while touching foreheads together.

"Strength and focus, Brother," Xander spoke to his friend.

"Strength and focus," Spencer answered sincerely.

Xander glanced behind Spencer and glared at the Prince. "You didn't tell me he was going to be here."

Spencer gave Prince Darien a long look over his shoulder before turning back to Xander. "I didn't think you would come."

"And you were correct," Zander's face soured into anger. "That man has been nothing but a ghost for the past ten years. What makes you think he deserves our attention now?"

Spencer leaned in closer to his friend speaking soft yet firm, "Because we all have been ghosts lately. Don't you want that to change?"

Xander gave the prince another long look, considering him. "I don't trust that guy."

"But you trust me." It wasn't a question. Spencer was direct, refusing to let anger envelop his friend.

After a long moment, Xander clapped his hand on Spencer's shoulder giving him a genuine smile. "It is good to see you again, Brother." Xander gave three very loud and very sharp whistles through his teeth. As if on cue, more men emerged from the forest. Gradually, the few men grew into a crowd of warriors and then a small army answering their call to arms.

"What is this?" Spencer's tone was still flat and calculated, showing off a now white-knuckled grip on his sword.

Xander offered an embarrassed grin, "Well, the men weren't entirely sure if they should show up. Many have been lingering in the forest, waiting to see what everyone else would do. When I arrived they asked me to test the waters. I just signaled for them to give you a chance."

Spencer gave the crowd an approving smile as a few walked past them, offering warm handshakes and nods of acknowledgment. "You're a fine leader, Xander."

"I am fine," Xander agreed with ease, showing off his smoothest smile. "But you're a much better leader than I."

Spencer chuckled, "Debatable."

Xander laughed then directed his attention past Spencer to the brunette. Rose was suddenly uncomfortable when she realized she was the only woman in a sea of gathering men. She tried to mask her nerves, but Spencer recognized her discomfort straightaway. The two men walked over to her, and Spencer caught hold of her hand for support.

"Rose," he said confidently, trying to project some of that onto her. "This is Xander, my right hand, my second in command of the former Marconian Army. Xander, this is Egeiro Red, the Second Matriarch of the White and Red Troupe."

Xander bowed formally to Rose, taking her hand in his. "An honor and a pleasure, my beautiful flower."

Rose was surprised, "Is it?"

"It is. I have seen you perform before, and was in awe of your talents." Xander touched the hilt of one of his knives. "I never thought my knife skills could be rivaled by a matriarch."

"Thank you, but I am the one who is honored to meet a trusted friend of Spencer." Rose nodded respectfully.

Xander smiled wildly as if he was about to speak, but Spencer cut him off. "Alright you two, that's enough gushing for one day. Xander, you should see to your men, and we will see to the prince."

"This ought to be interesting," Xander breathed as he turned to walk towards his men.

"Indeed, it will," Spencer replied with confidence. He and Rose turned to walk the other way only to have a pang of fear flash over him. "Where is Darien?"

Rose looked around and couldn't find him either. She must have been too distracted by the army and Xander's conversation to notice the Prince had wandered off.

"Oh yes," she spoke sarcastically. "This is going to be very interesting."

Chapter 37

Spencer and Rose found Darien pacing behind the stage, clutching onto the chain around his neck. He looked as if he was going to be sick. Rose's initial instinct was to slap some sense into him, but surprisingly it was Spencer who approached with calm understanding.

"I get it," Spencer spoke solemnly. "I can see their faces, too."

Darien looked up at Spencer. He looked burdened and tired,—not the look of a man about to rally his troops and save the day. "How do you handle it?"

"One day at a time," Spencer said gravely. "Look, if it's still too much, I will do it for you."

"Do what?" Darien asked.

"Rally the troops and storm the castle. I can take the spotlight off of you, if you want," Spencer's voice rumbled heavily with reluctance, but his eyes still were compassionate.

Darien spoke slowly, "Do you *want* to take over?"

Spencer shook his head sure of himself, "No, but I know this is a lot to ask of a man who's still hurting. I don't want to add more weight to the burden you bear."

"I would never ask you to do something I should do for myself. This is my destiny, and I need to take hold of it." He ran his fingers angrily through his hair. "You're right though, I do carry too much death on my shoulders. So much that even Brizo admitted she cannot see past it. But what if that burden is the only thing keeping me from becoming the bloodthirsty monster I was before?"

Rose's ears perked up when she heard her sister's name. Rose realized she was the least qualified person to say anything to the prince. But she couldn't keep silent anymore. She spoke as gently as she could to the fragile prince.

"Zoe told you death is the reason why she cannot see your future?"

"Something like that." Darien shrugged.

"Interesting," Rose whispered as she tapped her finger in thought.

Spencer watched Rose carefully, "What are you thinking, Rosie?"

Rose's back straightened and her eyes focused on Prince Darien, peering deep into his soul. Her voice took on an authoritative, all-powerful, unworldly nature.

"Is it your *future* you wish to see?" Rose didn't realize how commanding her image was until she saw the prince noticeably squirm, and Spencer's eyes grow as large as saucers. She wasn't trying to intimidate them. She didn't think her question required a dramatic show for accompaniment. It just, sort of, happened, like an involuntary sneeze or cough. Rose shifted her weight to change her stance, hoping to ease her friends' nerves. She waited patiently for Darien to consider her question.

"What I want to see is what happened all those years ago." Darien looked up at Rose. "There are large gaps in my memories that remain unfilled. I wish I knew what I had done to cause my men's death."

"Maybe that's why you can't move on, because you cannot reconcile your actions with no memories to go off of," Spencer mumbled to himself.

Rose sat down in front of Prince Darien, "Let me see if I can try something."

Darien was apprehensive, "What are you going to do?"

"I'm going to try to see your past," Rose answered.

"Can she do that?" Darien asked Spencer with unbridled surprise, then he turned to look back at Rose. "Can you do that? I thought seers only saw people's future?"

Rose blushed, "Hence why I said *try*."

"But not even Brizo can see through all the death I carry. What makes you think you can?"

"I have a hunch," Rose answered with confidence.

Darien looked back at Spencer still unsure. Spencer responded bluntly, "Hey, what have you got to lose?"

"Well, okay then." Darien sat down opposite Rose while shaking his head. "This is by far the most ridiculous thing I've ever done."

Rose's jeering tone returned as she smiled, "I highly doubt that."

Darien smirked back at her when he realized her little tease relaxed him. He was much more comfortable and ready to give Rose the benefit of the doubt.

"Alright, so how are you going to see into my past?" he asked.

"Umm," Rose tried to think of a good idea, but instead her thoughts loomed on the bone-chilling sound of laughter that consumed her thoughts. The laugh started as a soft chuckle, then grew into a throaty, boisterous sound that beared down on her like a siren. Rose shouted over the laughter, trying to force all her attention on Darien. "Why don't you tell me the last thing you remember."

Darien said something to her, but she couldn't hear him. The laughter was deafening, and now she was racing through the trees at top speeds, along a river, across a plane, and abruptly stopped just outside a deep valley dotted with patches of light snow. Death was quiet now, replaced with the sounds of the wind whirling towards her. She expected to shiver, but the chill in the air never struck her. Rose was merely a shadow in the prince's memory.

A small cavalry made their way into the valley towards her. The tromp of the horse's hooves was steady and confident, as were the men riding them. Only one soldier looked worried— Prince Darien's trusted herald, riding alongside him— the only one not afraid to speak his concerns.

"Sire, do you think this is wise, splitting off from the army, all because of a hunch?"

"It's not just a hunch," Darien answered him with authority. "Intelligence says this could be the battle that could end the invasion. Naturally, the only way to ensure that end is an unquestionable display of power. We cannot just win. We need to give them a clear message that will make them question ever crossing swords with us again."

"Yes, your Highness," the soldier agreed, then continued. "But something about this doesn't feel right."

"This was the best idea my uncle could come up with. I trust him, so I have no reason to worry."

"Yes, your Highness," the soldier whispered, then glanced over his shoulder nervously.

The three hundred men rode deeper into the valley before his herald spoke up again.

"I don't mean to make you nervous, Highness, but is it much farther? I cannot shake the feeling that we are in a bad place."

Prince Darien gave the man a strong, but sympathetic look. "If it pleases you, send ten of your best riders to scout the area ahead and around us. Maybe then your fears will be laid to rest?"

The soldier breathed a sigh of relief, then pounded his fist to his chest. "Thank you, my Lord. I'll do that right away."

Before the man could turn to execute his orders, there was a sharp slice of wind and a thick arrow was lodged straight in his heart. The world seemed to slow down. Prince Darien reached out for his herald trying to process what had happened while his friend looked down at the arrow lodged in his chest.

He looked back up at his prince, eyes glazing over wide with confusion, "Wha..."

The soldier had fallen from his horse, wrenching free from the prince's grasp.

"What?" was all Prince Darien could say as the world around him had stopped at that moment. His loyal herald, his brother in arms, his friend, someone that he had grown to care for and trust throughout this war, was now dead.

The cries of war rushed over Prince Darien until their shouts of pain and wrath were deafening. The prince turned around to see the enemy charge toward them like floodwaters. Darien drew his sword and kicked his horse in the direction of those barbarians, eager for vengeance. But before he had a chance to do anything, he felt a small bite on the side of his neck. He reached up and found a tiny needle stuck in him like a pin cushion. He instantly dismissed it, but the blur of his sight and heaviness of his limbs demanded his attention. His body sagged and then fell from his horse. He hit the ground hard but did not feel much. Darien's body was numb and unmovable. His sight was blurry, but he could make out an occasional face of his men nearby.

Upon seeing their leader fall, the men screamed with rage. Instead of allowing their grief to slow them down, they mustered their strength and fought with the courage of a thousand men. Each Marconian soldier drew from hidden pools of pure vigor that allowed them to attack their foe head-on, cutting down as many opponents as possible until their ill fate caught up with them.

Prince Darien lay helpless on the ground while he watched the battle wide-eyed. The pain of not being able to fight with his men caused tears to roll down his cheeks. These men fought like bears protecting their cub as they protected their prince from any more harm. They lashed and clawed relentlessly until the bitter end.

Rose threw her hands up to her ears covering them as she squeezed her eyes tight. She wasn't sure how much more death she could endure watching. The hollow, skeletal laughter of Death rattled in her mind. It was too much. She felt as though her head would explode.

"Enough!" she shouted at the top of her lungs.

All went silent. Rose slowly opened her eyes, not sure what she was going to see next. She was still in Darien's memory standing next to him as he lay helpless on the ground. He was surrounded by a circle of men who had bravely fought in defense of their prince, all lying lifeless on the cold ground. The sight made Rose gasp, even though she already knew the fate of the men. Seeing it played before her was much different than hearing about it.

She looked around and noticed the enemy's army had suffered grievous losses as well. More than two-thirds of the enemy forces had fallen to the determination of the three hundred—an accomplishment she would have deemed impossible had she not witnessed it firsthand. Two large men, heavily armed with weapons of all kinds, strolled disrespectfully over the bodies toward the prince. They sneered down at him with revulsion, as one of them drew out a long, serrated knife.

"Let's just kill him now while we have the chance," the man hissed, bending down closer to Darien.

"No," commanded the other with a deep authoritative growl, "you know our orders. Lord Robert needs him alive for everything to go according to plan."

The first man gritted his teeth, "He is the reason why so many of our brothers are slain! Only a third of us remain after this battle alone!"

"Yes," the other agreed, "Marconian soldiers are much tougher than we expected, but we must stick to the plan if we expect to be rewarded with payment."

"I suppose fewer men means more for us in the end," sneered his friend.

"Indeed it does," the larger man said, "Knock him out, and make sure he doesn't remember anything."

The first soldier flipped the knife in his hand and gave Prince Darien a brutal whack with the butt of his knife. The world turned black.

Rose opened her eyes to find she was back in her camp sitting across from Darien while Spencer watched carefully. She was relieved, and surprised, that Darien had recovered his forgotten memories. Rose had heard stories of the three hundred over the years—how they were slaughtered like innocent lambs unable to defend themselves, while Prince Darien watched and laughed. What she saw was a different story altogether. She wanted to shout out in excitement and dance around after realizing what she had just done. But the truth that Darien's memories exposed left her somber and angry.

"That vile, treacherous, snake!" shouted Darien.

"I think calling him a snake is an insult to snakes in general," Rose stated quietly.

Darien looked at Rose, considering her words. "You're right, at least a snake has a purpose in the grand scheme of things. Robert has shown his true colors, and they are much worse."

"You know what you need to do," Rose added, still calm, still quiet.

"I've always known what I needed to do," Darien fingered the red and silver pendant around his neck deep in thought. He smiled to himself, then met Rose's powerful gaze confidently. "The difference is, now, I have the confidence to do it."

The prince got to his feet, but before he could jump up to the stage, Spencer caught his arm.

"Wait," Spencer sounded nervous, then nodded towards the large mass of soldiers that had congregated. "What do you plan to say to them?"

The question didn't even cause Darien to flinch. "Something they haven't heard in a long time… the truth!"

Chapter 38

The steady roar of the crowd dropped to a low rumble when Darien appeared on the stage. A few men threw taunts and jeers, but most of them were intrigued, willing to hear Darien out—whether or not he was convincing was another matter.

"Warriors of Marconia!" Darien shouted. "Men who have been reputed to fight with the ferocity of bears in defense of our families, our homes, and our country. You have been through too much for too long. You have lost your king, your queen, your freedoms, your confidence in your nation and its rulers. In my travels, I have seen the injustices inflicted upon you, forcing you into exile for defending the rights of the people. That is not something any warrior should have to go through."

Several men started to heckle the prince.

"Whose fault is that?"

"Where have you been?"

"Why would you allow this to happen?"

Darien looked around at the faces turned towards him. These were men that desperately wanted to do something, but lacked the power to do so. They needed a leader—one who could understand their struggle, their desires, and would see their mission through to the end. Unfortunately, these were also the faces of men who have been hardened by the politics of their country, and the harshness of the world. They would not give their trust easily. The sheer enormity of the situation settled heavily on Prince Darien once again, only this time his resolve was absolute. He would lead this band of warriors against the tyrant who had taken over, and right the wrongs he allowed to happen.

"The truth is; I have failed you all. This is entirely my fault. Instead of fighting for my birthright and standing up for you, I cowered and allowed myself to be forgotten. I allowed this evil to consume our beautiful lands. And my doubts and fears have held me back for the past decade."

Darien glanced over at Spencer, apologetically, wishing he could undo the past ten years somehow. He had failed Spencer, he failed these men, and he failed his entire kingdom. Spencer's face was calm, yet encouraging. He simply gestured for Darien to continue. Confidence welled up in the Prince's heart. He needed to keep going. He had failed these men before, but not this time. Never again.

"I cannot be still any longer. I can no longer mourn the past. It is our future I am concerned with. Warriors, you have taken an oath. You have vowed to protect your country and in protecting your country, you protect your families and their lives. You have vowed to protect Marconia from all those who wish to harm her."

The jeering shouts quieted as all listened intently to what Darien would say next.

"Today, I am going to hold you to that oath," Darien paused to ensure he had everyone's attention. "Today, I am asking you to stand against your king and all that he stands for: greed, division, and suppression.

These are things King Robert has cleverly disguised under the agenda of 'improving the lives of all.' You and I know this is a lie and have seen the limitations in our lives, making it harder to feed our families, harder to defend our homes, harder to achieve the life we strive for with our own two hands. With the might and the voice of Marconia, we can change that. We must rid our country of the very source of the poison that ruined her in the first place. We must rid her of King Robert himself; only then will we be able to reverse all the evils he has done. Gentlemen, we have been asleep for far too long, living as shadows of our former, valiant selves. I say it is time to wake up and remind the world what happens when someone crosses the Marconian Army. Together we will be as fearsome as the bear woken from hibernation as we reclaim our country, and restore her to her former glory!"

A small few continued to gauge the sincerity of Prince Darien's words. As the Prince's speech started to sink in, many men started to nod their heads in agreement. A soft cry of acceptance rippled through the crowd, gradually gaining more enthusiasm. For a slim moment, Darien thought he had succeeded in winning the men's loyalties. But Xander was the one who spoke first, arrogantly questioning all Darien had said.

"We have lost much by the hands of King Robert. But before him we lost three hundred of our best men because of you!" he shouted at the Prince.

Doubt spread like wildfire through the crowd. They recalled their brothers in arms, their friends, and their untimely demise, thanks to Darien. A few men shouted out with anger and disappointment with their Prince.

Darien clasped his hands behind his back calmly recalling the memory of the three hundred. He looked confidently into the eyes of his men, waiting patiently for them to settle down. He knew they were angry, and he wasn't going to deny them their say in all of this. The men quieted down when they realized their Prince still wasn't backing down.

"There are some inaccuracies that have spread into rumors, ugly rumors, since that night. If you are going to trust me, you will need to know what happened. We were lied to. Faulty intelligence was given to us on the day of the invasion. We were ambushed by our foe, a plan orchestrated by our very King Robert. My men, our brothers, were slaughtered before we had a chance to attack. I've tried to run from this gruesome memory, but I realize in doing so I've failed to honor my men and their sacrifice. The truth is, they protected me even after I fell. They were so fierce and so terrible—they slaughtered more than two-thirds of the army that had been sent after us." A low rumble of soldier's voices discussed the facts Darien revealed.

"It was an army of assassins, conscripted by my uncle to ensure his rise to power. They were specifically told to leave me alive to take the blame for the slaughter of my men. With no other witnesses and my vague memories, it was easy for him to start and spread several rumors concerning what happened. These rumors countered what little truth I had to offer, and I was banished. With me out of the way, Robert assumed the throne. The perfect end to his perfect scheme." The men were outraged when they heard of King Robert's treachery. It looked as if they were ready to storm the castle at that very moment. But the familiar, doubting voice spoke up again.

"And how do we know that what you say is true?" Xander shouted. "Or are these just more lies to persuade us to follow you again?"

Darien opened his mouth to answer but it was Rose who shouted in response, "How dare you stare truth in the face and call it a lie!" She shouted at Xander with a deafening boom. All the men's attention was now on her.

"Rose, no," Darien spake.

Rose held up her hand to quiet Darien, "King Robert has cheated you out of your livelihoods, stolen your confidence, stripped you of your freedoms, and robbed you of your very identities. How dare you imply he is incapable of treason for his selfish gain?"

"Darien has lied to us before," Xander retorted.

"No, he hasn't!" Rose snapped quickly back, giving Xander pause. "Everything Darien has told you about what happened is true."

"How do you know? You weren't there!" All the sweetness that Xander had for Rose when they first met had disappeared in a second. His eyes turned malicious and vindictive. "For all we know, you could be lying to us as well."

Spencer made a move to Rose's defense, but Darien was already on it. He spoke up to draw the men's attention back to him.

"More division, Xander? This is exactly what King Robert wants. Use your logic; everything I have said to you is true. Rose helped me to remember my past, and expose the true plot of King Robert to take over the kingdom."

Xander laughed openly, "She is the spinner of these lies? It would have been better if you had said Darien was a coward who hid in fear while his men were slaughtered. The fact that you made him out to be a hero, fighting the betrayal of his only family, is just too preposterous. Especially when we all know him to be a bloodthirsty, merciless monster. Or did you forget about that, Sweetie?"

Rose spoke firmly, "I know full well who Prince Darien is. Lies do not ensnare me; they submit their truth to me."

Xander openly mocked Rose with a loud pompous laugh. Darien tried to quiet Xander's jeers, but he was more concerned with the look on Rose's face. She was solemn and calm, something much more terrifying. Then her eyes went dark. Darien had seen a drop of Rose's power when she used her gift to help him recall his memories, now it was a full-on waterfall of power that engulfed her. She looked beautiful and terrifying at the same time. The blazing heat and suppressed anger had caused small beads of sweat to form on her skin—not the most important quality to notice, but combined with the afternoon light the sweat gave her an unearthly glow that would have seemed daunting to the untrained eye.

Darien suppressed a smile. Thanks to Zoe, he was able to see most of what Rose was doing was a trick or just dumb luck. However, as she began to speak he realized it was anything but.

Chapter

ose took a step closer to Xander. Her eyes narrowed, focusing her full attention on him. "Truth can be a bitter draught to swallow."

Rose's authoritative tone made Xander reexamine the woman in front of him. A chill ran up his spine when the next thing she said shook him to his core.

"I know the truth about you, Xander Gould, or should I say, Xander Goldfield. The eldest son of Philip Goldfield, a highly skilled farmer from the back parts of these lands." Rose frowned in thought when Xander's face tightened with anger. She had found her hook on the first try. Something about his family being farmers tormented this man, but why? Farmers are the legs that Marconia stands on. There is no shame in working the land to feed its people. Then the laughter of Death tickled the back of her mind, and immediately she knew far more than any talented gypsy could glean from random clues on their patron.

"That is until you gambled their land away without their knowledge." Rose squinted at the man. "You threw away the only security your parents had in this world—security that kept you and your younger brothers fed, clothed, educated, and given a chance for a prosperous life. You stole it from all of them, even yourself. When you realized the gravity of what you had done, you turned to the kindness of others for help. When friends couldn't give any more, you decided to turn to the kindness of strangers. Oh yes, Xander, you learned very easily how much you could swindle from kindhearted ladies with deep pockets, thanks to a smile laced with charm. Although every coin you made went toward your family, people started to see you for who you truly were, a swindler. No one wanted to give to a scoundrel such as you anymore. It was by pure luck you were able to conscript into the Marconian army, willing to do whatever it took to ensure a steady income for your family, although small, to save them from destitution. And even though they have scraped up a new, less fortunate life, you still send them all you can in retribution for your actions so long ago."

"How, how do you know all this?" Xander stood firm but was noticeably shaken.

Rose answered with confidence and authority, "I am Egeiro Red, sister to the loved and feared Brizo White."

There were audible gasps and whispers among the men. Xander's mouth hung open in fear. Rose smiled at Xander's discomfort then addressed all the men.

"For those of you who do not know, my sister, Brizo White, is a powerful seer of truth. She is the one who foretold the unification of the Marconian army and the inevitable dethroning of the tyrant, King Robert. Rest assured, gentlemen, everything my sister foresees will come to pass. Prince Darien will restore this country to its former glory, and right the wrongs that we have had to endure," She turned to look directly at Xander, "I am Egeiro Red, seer of all that my sister cannot. So, mark my words, and heed my warning. All of this will be for naught and turn out for the worse if you refuse to allow Prince Darien to lead you as my sister prophesied."

All eyes were on Xander as he contemplated Rose's words. His face turned satisfied as if Rose had just beaten him in a fair fistfight. He stepped forward, speaking loudly, "Then we will follow him into a new age of Good and Light! With the strength of our arms and the vigor of our hearts, we will subdue King Robert and restore Prince Darien to the throne!"

The army roared with agreement. Cheers and dancing started up, and the higher-ranked soldiers congregated together to plot their strategy. Darien raised his fists high in the air, encouraging the men to lift their cheers even louder. Then he saw Rose holding on to Spencer's arm, noticeably weak. As Darien approached them, she smiled brightly at the prince.

"Your smile would be a bit sincerer if you weren't so weak after that stunt you just pulled," Darien said.

Rose straightened and stood on her own. "I am well enough, and my smile is real."

Darien eyed her suspiciously. "Keep this up and you're going to make Spencer jealous."

Spencer coughed a dubious laugh, drawing closer to Rose. She shook her head at the prince.

"Are you still so insecure that you cannot accept a small amount of praise, or can you just not accept it from me?" Rose teased.

"Keep in mind, you have never offered me praise before. All I did was exactly what you wanted me to do."

Rose raised an eyebrow at him defensively, "Come now, Prince Darien, you and I both know you never do anything just because I tell you to."

"Then why the smile?" Darien furrowed his brow.

"Because," Rose shrugged as if it were unimportant, "You managed to do the one thing I have been wanting you to do since we first met."

"And what is that?" Darien looked at her suspiciously, waiting for some sarcastic remark that he would need to rebut. Instead, Rose's face softened.

"You surprised me." Rose spread her ornate skirt into a deep curtsey fit for a king.

The importance of this small gesture was not lost on Prince Darien. At that moment, in one motion, Rose formally recognized him as her sovereign ruler. She was now his ally. No matter how much they bickered with each other, Rose was now someone the prince could trust to have his back. Darien returned the formal gesture to Rose, offering a sincere smile.

"Thank you, Rose," he beamed. "Now, if you excuse me, I have some planning to do."

Spencer shook his friend's hand proudly before Darien left to join the officers. Then Spencer instinctively put his arm around Rose's waist. She responded to his gesture by leaning her head onto his shoulder. It was a long minute before he finally spoke up.

"So Rosie, that was an interesting stunt you pulled off."

"Yeah, I'm sorry for singling out your friend. I didn't think I would have to defend my abilities to the entire Army, or anyone, for that matter," Rose cowered a little with embarrassment.

"That doesn't bother me. Xander is a better fighter when he has a bruised ego anyway," Spencer confided.

Rose chuckled, "Glad I could help."

"I am interested to know if that was a real show of your gift or if it was just a trick." Spencer's face was serious as he waited for her answer.

"It started as just a trick, but then my gift sort of took over. It was as if I was no longer in control of what was happening. All of a sudden I knew things, personal things, about him— things no one else knew, and he wanted to keep secret. But I couldn't keep them a secret. I had spoken the words before I even realized what was happening," Rose shivered, despite Spencer's warm arm around her.

Spencer twitched at her answer, not at all the response she had hoped for. "That's disturbing."

Rose spoke up defensively, "I know it was a little strange, but in the end we got the job done. The least you could do is congratulate me for helping Darien."

"Congratulate you? Why would I congratulate you for doing something you could have easily done without the use of your gift?" Spencer was trying not to raise his voice, but he couldn't hide the anger that frothed up inside of him. "You keep putting your own life in danger for the sake of everyone else. You don't know how quickly the consequences of using your gift will come on you. It could be one huge rush, catching up for lost time. The next time you use it could be the death of you."

"Everything hinged on gaining the confidence of the army. What I did was necessary to give Darien the chance he needed to succeed."

"How fortunate for all of us you have learned to use more of your gift... except for you."

"I shouldn't have to remind you that my gift is necessary for the prosperity of our troupe." Her eyes were cold as her words bit back at him.

"I refuse to believe that for a second." His answer was so absolute it gave Rose pause, forcing her to listen to him. "Your life is just as important as everyone else's here. I will concede that fate may not be inescapable, but the path you take to get there is entirely your own... through your own choices."

"But we have tried..." Rose started to answer softly but was immediately cut off by Spencer.

"Then, try harder. I'm not giving up, and neither should you," he answered pointedly, then walked away to join his army.

Chapter 40

Zoe woke reluctantly when the sunlight hit her squarely in the eyes, thanks to a small cut-out from the top of the wall near the roof. She guessed its primary purpose was to let fresh air into the room, instead of mercilessly waking her up. Zoe sat up from a pile of straw that had served as her bed ever since King Robert imprisoned her in the tower. It was the only real thing of interest around her aside from a metal tray and cup that held a fresh serving of bread and water. The straw wouldn't seem like much to the average person; but to Zoe, who had been in this room for almost two weeks on the cold stone floor, the straw was better than gold. She crept over to her meal and gingerly sipped the water as she nibbled her bread. She would never admit it to the King, but his simple bread and water was the perfect thing for her to eat in strenuous situations such as this. Had she eaten much of the decadent food he had served her in the beautifully comfortable room downstairs, she would have been in much more pain than she usually had to endure. Yet when she nibbled on simple bread, it was far more delightful than any elaborate feast the king may have requested. All for the chance to win over her allegiance. She smiled to herself when she considered the irony.

Zoe stretched and flexed her muscles, then her vision blurred and her body turned rigid. Her eyes were distant as she saw something much different than the walls of her room. She saw trees blurring beneath her and clouds swirling above making her feel like she was flying through the air. In front of her, Zoe could see King Robert's castle gradually growing larger. She flew closer to it, then she raced up the stone walls, higher and higher until she glimpsed in through a crack in the stone. She saw herself nestled comfortably on her pile of straw. Zoe winced; she looked so frail and sickly. Her pale skin looked practically inhuman in comparison to the already pale stone walls she leaned up against. Zoe looked at herself in disgust wondering how anyone could love someone so helpless and, quite frankly, so ugly. But then she thought about Darien and how much he did love her already. She remembered all the tender words he had for her to ensure she knew how important she was to him. Zoe smiled when she thought of Darien. She longed to be with him.

Thinking about Darien caused Zoe to soar off to the west, over a few hills until she came upon a large army clad in dark reds. The next thing Zoe saw both terrified and excited her. She was face to face with her beloved Darien, eyes fixed, jaw set, and fearless. Next to him was Spencer, just as alert and focused on the inevitable battle that loomed ahead of them. A glint of concern betrayed Spencer's hardened appearance as he reached to his left to take the hand of Rose, squeezing it for comfort. Prince Darien whispered to himself as he clutched the charm Zoe had given him.

"For you, Brizo White," He gripped the hilt of his sword tightly and quickened their pace to the castle.

Zoe was back in her tower room, now cold and gasping for breath. The pain in her side screamed at her, but she ignored it. Knowing that Darien was coming breathed new confidence inside her. Zoe made her way back to her straw bed to finish her slice of bread.

It was mere seconds after Zoe finished her meal that her tower door banged open to reveal two guards clad in chainmail and weapons. They each grabbed one of Zoe's arms and proceeded to drag her down the stairs into the main part of the castle. The three of them stormed into a large, round room decked in red and gold tapestries and a large, decorated carpet that took up the majority of the room. There were several wooden desks set up, each strewn with piles of papers and scrolls. When they entered, Zoe saw King Robert was reading a small page of scribblings that looked like it was written in haste. He stood in front of a vast window carved out of the stone that led to a simple terrace. The King immediately crumpled the note in his hand and waved his fist at one of his advisors.

"You wait until now to tell me this?"

The small advisor trembled with fear, "I'm sorry, my Lord. We just heard about it ourselves."

"Peter is never this slow about information. How did he not know about this?" the king demanded.

"My Lord," The advisor bowed lower to his king to avoid looking into his eyes. "Peter has deserted us. We haven't heard anything from him since he sent word of the seer's last location. We only learned about this because one of the palace scouts stumbled upon them."

"Desert me? That fool. When we are through here, I will seek him out and make him suffer for his cowardice."

The advisor bowed several times while cautiously backing away toward the safety of the door. King Robert directed his anger onto Zoe, pointing the piece of paper at her.

"Did you know about this?"

Zoe stared at the crumpled paper unsure how to answer, "Exactly what are you referring to?"

King Robert gave an exasperated sigh as he grabbed Zoe's arm and yanked her over to the terrace. For a split second, she feared he was going to throw her over the railing for asking such a question. Instead, he shoved her off to the side where a spyglass was set up then motioned for her to look through it. She bent over to see what the king was talking about and allowed a faint smile to cross her lips. She had a clear image of Darien cresting the hill, on his horse with the red army following after him.

"Did you know about this?" King Robert asked again, biting back his rage.

Zoe lifted her eyebrows innocently, "I know many things your Highness, sometimes it's hard to sort out what is insignificant and what is..."

"Don't you dare pretend to be coy with me, Witch!" Robert interrupted her. "Answer me plainly; did you know my nephew was coming?"

Zoe obliged the king, allowing her anger to surface. "Of course I did, Peter is not a fool, you are! I know far more than you can imagine. Locking me up in a tower cell doesn't change any of that."

The king spoke gently, "If you had told me of his whereabouts I could have given you a more comfortable room with all that you desire."

Zoe glared at the man with disgust, "What I desire is for you to throw yourself over that railing and rid us all of your filth."

King Robert gritted his teeth. "If you claim to know so much then you would know to watch your tone when you are around me."

"Why should I?" Zoe mocked, "I am far more powerful than your minuscule mind can comprehend. If you knew what I was capable of, *you* would watch *your* tone around *me!*"

King Robert's lips curved into a sneer, "So powerful, and yet still unable to change a fortune to benefit another. I wonder why that is? Maybe you're not as powerful as you think you are."

Zoe merely stood there with hatred in her eyes. She wished she had an answer for him or some deep hidden power she could use that would make him cower in fear. She had nothing.

"Oh, did I strike just the right chord for you?" Robert smiled in triumph. "Why don't you prove how powerful you are? Change the prophecy! Make me the victor of this war! Together we will be an undeniable force that no one will challenge!"

"Never," Zoe whispered. "Darien has come for you, and you will lose. No power in this world can change it."

King Robert made a small motion to his guards. Zoe watched their approach only to realize too late what was about to happen. As one of the big men grabbed her, the other landed a heavy blow to her stomach before she had a chance to brace herself or try to put up some defense. She cried out in pain as the guard's fist connected painfully with her body. The other guard held onto her firmly, making it impossible to just sink to the ground and curl up in a ball. The strain from her side added to the repeated blows from the assailants' fists, knees, and boots. Neither showed mercy when bruises formed on her flesh nor when her blood began to stain the floor.

The king merely looked out the window in the direction of the Red army. "Try if you must, Darien, but will not hand back this kingdom to you."

Chapter

Rose sat on her mare at the top of the hill next to Prince Darien. They were waiting for the rest of the Army to gather into their lines. After many protests from Darien and Spencer, Rose insisted there was no way they were going after her sister without her coming along. Spencer had ridden to the back of the army to help keep all the men moving steadily to the castle. He hadn't spoken to Rose since Darien's rousing speech. That revelatory, exciting day for Rose turned out to be a tragic one for Spencer. He was convinced that the day she tapped into her gift's full potential would be the day that her body would fail her. If Rose was being honest with herself, he had every right to be angry. It is, after all, what happened when Zoe started using her gift. However, Spencer was always so focused on her wellbeing. He never stopped to look at the larger picture. Rose wished she could convince him that this was their best option. More people would benefit if she saw this prophecy through. Despite her efforts, none of her arguments would work on that stubborn man. He continued to insist there had to be another way to help everyone without Zoe's death and Rose sacrificing her health. Rose wanted more than anything for Spencer to be right but had yet to discover what else she could do. The finality of the situation irritated Rose at first, then she had come to peace with what she needed to do. Perhaps that's just what Spencer needed to—time.

As Rose scanned the dead plains lying in front of her, and King Robert's army clad in white and gold congregating between them and the castle, reality sunk in. The vast number of people they eventually would have to fight made Rose's stomach twist in fear. She relaxed a little when she scanned Prince Darien's troops behind them. She had seen these men, gathered in a crowd, frustrated and despondent a few days ago. They had been looking for something to happen, looking for someone to lead them. Now they were armed to the teeth with old weapons or anything that could be used to fight. Their armor had been pulled out of chests and closets and was donned once more with bright red paint marking the warriors siding with Prince Darien, the warriors of Marconia. Eyes set and determined, these men looked hungry—hungry to correct so many wrongs that weighed them down for so long. Then the world spun for a moment as the menacing echo of a laugh rattled in her head again.

Rose felt a sickening twinge of recollection. The vision she had almost a year ago was being fulfilled… today. In an instant, the gravity of her predicament struck her like lightning. Rose's mouth went dry and her heart wrenched when her vision played out in front of her again, blow after blow, concluding with Spencer's body thudding lifelessly in front of her. Hearing Death's mirthful laughter chaffed Rose to no end. She wished she didn't know how her best friend would die. More importantly, she ached to be able to do something… anything… to prevent it. Her sister's warnings to never change a vision rang in her memory. Gritting her teeth, she closed her eyes. Even that relative darkness held no comfort for her. The darkness only heightened her gruesome memory. The shouts, the clash of the swords, the smell of the dirt, the pain in her heart—all too real.

When she felt as if she couldn't endure much more, Death's laugh returned. This time the sound accompanied visions of men's bloodied faces displayed before her. Rose knew instantly that Death was teasing her by listing who would be joining him today. She couldn't breathe. The images were relentless and more terrible with every second. Tears flowed freely around Rose's cheeks. She tried to process the images but couldn't.

Shaking her head to scatter her thoughts, the unspoken anxiety was all too much for her.

"I am aware that good people will die today," Rose spoke out loud. "You don't have to gloat about it!"

A hand touched Rose on her shoulder, and a voice called out her name, "Rose?"

Instinctively, she drew one of her knives and held it to her assailant's neck.

Rose opened her eyes to see Darien frozen in shock while he eyed her blade carefully. She instantly retracted her knife from her friend and was once again aware of her surroundings. The field between the two armies was still empty. No one was hurt—not yet anyway.

"Are you alright?" Darien asked.

Rose put her knife away and wiped her face to remove the wet tears still clinging to her cheeks. She composed herself before answering.

"Oh, of course." She managed a weak smile. "I am alright."

"Who were you talking to?" Darien still looked concerned about her, and even frightened.

"Um, nobody," she shook her head, silently scolding herself for being stupid. "Myself, I guess. It's no big deal."

Rose tried to shrug it off as nothing, but Darien's stare still lingered while he sat tense and ready to act.

Rose's voice softened, "What about you? Do I finally get to see the monster everyone says you are?"

"Not today, and never again. The man I was is not who I am today," he answered confidently.

"Perhaps not, but he is still a part of you. Instead of ignoring those feelings, perhaps you should embrace them," she said.

Darien arched an eyebrow at her. "Are you saying I should allow the monster to take over?"

"No," Rose corrected. "I'm saying your past ferocity combined with your newfound wisdom could make you stronger than ever. If you allow it."

Before Darien could press the matter, Xander and Spencer rode up on their mounts and stopped alongside Rose.

"Everyone is in formation, Your Highness," Xander spoke formally. "They are waiting for your word."

Prince Darien looked out across the wide lifeless plain where King Robert's army stood, clad in white hues. They stood forming a fearsome border around the castle in defense of their king. Even from this distance, the look of determination and confidence in their army could be seen. Rose looked around the red army and noted their resolve. These men would give their lives to defend their country and their prince. Rose had to take a deep breath to compose herself, shutting out the faint rattle of laughter as best she could.

"Any last thoughts, before we do this?" Prince Darien asked rhetorically.

Without skipping a beat Rose blurted out, "They're going to come at us hard on our right. This may make us retreat through that ravine, which will thin us out."

Darien and Spencer stared at Rose, completely caught off guard by her comment.

"Woah, woman, how about we take orders from someone who's done this before," Xander blurted out.

Spencer held his head in his hand, shaking it back and forth, while Darien looked between Xander and Rose uneasily. Rose noticed a shift in Darien's posture as if he were remembering he had the final say in all matters at that moment.

"Why do you say that, Rose?" he asked stoically, while ignoring Xander's protests.

"It makes sense that if our right side was hurt badly enough, we may accidentally retreat towards…"

"What makes you think our right flank is in danger," Xander interrupted rudely.

Rose didn't skip a beat before defending herself. "I saw several faces of our men who would die. Men I know are holding the line on the right."

Spencer remained still as stone as he watched the interaction play out. He caught Rose's eye and they stared angrily at each other in a wordless argument. Finally, Darien nodded to Xander to follow through with Rose's suggestions.

Xander spoke boldly to two of his men nearby, "Take your men and fortify the right side. Make sure you spread the word that *I* told them to be extra vigilant. Tell them to expect the worst, and be ready."

"Yes sir!" The men shouted as they rode off to carry out their orders.

"You should get in position as well, Commander, and wait for my signal to attack," Darien added. Xander pounded a fist to his chest and rode off.

Spencer reeled in on Rose with a hushed whisper, "You need to stop doing that. You're being reckless."

"You think I'm being reckless?" Blood boiled inside of Rose, tinting her face red with restrained anger. "First of all, I'm not doing this on purpose. I have no control over what I see and don't see. Second of all, I don't care if I can't change their fate, I can't just sit around knowing something terrible is going to happen without doing everything in my power to stop it."

Rose expected Spencer to continue to argue; instead, he reached out to hold her hand gently in his. His stony face softened allowing Rose to see fear clearly in his eyes.

"Bold words," he whispered gently. "I wish you listened to them too."

Rose was speechless as Spencer led his horse between Darien and her. Darien had paid no attention to their hushed conversation. His jaw was set and his eyes fixed on the castle. He was as fearless as ever. In his hands, he held a thin necklace with a round, disc-like charm strung on it. Rose recognized it immediately as the red and white emblem of her family.

"Where did you get that?" she asked.

Darien was jolted out of his thoughts, "Brizo gave it to me to help with my dreams."

"Your dreams?" Rose shook her head. "What does our family's emblem have to do with your dreams?"

Darien was caught off guard by her comment. "Brizo told me it is a symbol that shows the coexistence of light and dark together. If I find meaning in the dark, then I can. ."

"Thrive in the light." Rose finished.

"Exactly," he nodded.

Rose blinked as the words fell on her heavily.

"Is there something wrong?" He asked.

"Not at all," Rose answered slowly. "I'm glad she gave it to you."

He nodded respectfully then turned his attention back on to the charm. He caressed it reverently with his thumb then Rose heard him mutter to himself, "For you, Brizo White." Then he brought the disc to his lips, kissed it gently, and then returned the chain to his neck. In one fluid movement, his hand caught hold of his sword, unsheathing it and raising it high over his head.

"For Marconia!" Prince Darien shouted. His army joined the cry, lifting their banners and weapons high over their heads, driving fear into their enemy. Their horses leaped forward, leading the front line down the hill towards the castle as if they were hungry wolves on the hunt. These men were hungry for a win, a win that would save their beautiful country from being run down by the tyranny and greed of their king.

The men were ravenous, desperate for redemption. This was their second chance to do some good for their country. Every movement of their swords testified their resolve with calculated, careful blows inflicting damage efficiently and almost gracefully. Rose didn't have time to linger in awe at the skill of the soldiers she fought with. She sped straightway to the right flank to offer any help she could. She winced when she realized her offer of help seemed insignificant in comparison to the combat skills of each soldier. Regardless, Rose hurried her horse faster to the men, certain there was something she could do.

She charged directly through the middle of a group clad in white, who were about to overpower some of her men. She used a shield to knock away several swords and managed to knock a few men off their feet. When she saw how much of a help that was, she continued to barrel through the men in white, offering her soldiers the time they needed to gain the upper hand. All was going well until one of the larger soldiers caught Rose by the foot, causing her to hit the ground hard. Before she had a chance to catch her breath she saw a shadow of a man looming over her with his sword held high. Rose instinctively rolled away and sprang to her feet. She turned to face him just in time to see Spencer sink his battle-ax in the back of her assailants' armor, and watch him fall to the ground still. Rose stared at the man, a faint laugh of Death rattling in her head.

Spencer grabbed Rose, furiously pulling her to face him, "Foolish woman! You don't ride straight into the middle of a battle! You have no idea what these people can-"

Rose saw movement in the corner of her eye. She didn't have time to argue, so she shoved him back abruptly. Spencer took a few steps back from the momentum only to see a sword slice straight down in front of him. It hit the ground with a loud *'thunk!'* separating the two, just barely missing Spencer. Spencer elbowed the man in the face while Rose stabbed him with her knife. The two of them made eye contact for a moment before Spencer nodded and turned to encounter the next obstacle. Rose moved away from their fallen enemy and made herself as useful as possible. She quickly learned that the castle soldiers were more concerned with fighting the stronger, heavily armed men than a fragile little woman much smaller than they. She made good use of this by using quick and fluid movements to inflict small but deadly cuts to her enemy while their attention was occupied by the Red soldiers. Rose continued to work until she ducked instinctively, barely saving herself from a mace swinging past and almost grazing the top of her head.

Where did that come from, she thought as she rolled away from the fight as best as she could. Then she heard a sound that made her blood run cold and her body freeze in place.

"Rose!" Spencer shouted in desperation. Fear overcame Rose as she realized what was playing out in front of her. Spencer continued to cut and slice at each man who confronted him until he had another spare second to shout to her. "Rose, get out of here! It's too dangerous!"

All Rose could do was shake her head in denial, whispering, "No, no, no, this cannot be happening." Anger and determination grew inside her allowing her the strength to stand.

"Never!" she called back. "I'm not leaving you!"

Rose tightened her grip on her sword then sprinted towards Spencer.

"Don't argue with me, Woman! Run for —"

Rose recoiled in terror when the next thing she saw was exactly what she remembered. Spencer's eyes were fixed on her, making him blind to the man lunging for him with his sword.

"Look out!" Rose shrieked, causing Spencer to pivot. It wasn't enough. The enemy laughed as his sword hit Spencer's chest. Rose knew in an instant it wasn't the soldier's laughter she heard. It was the laughter of Death.

Chapter

"**S**pencer!" Rose saw her love fall helpless to the ground in front of her, fulfilling her dreaded vision. Spencer was so concerned with keeping her safe that he was distracted when the crippling blow struck him down. Her gaze targeted and locked on to Spencer's conquering opponent. Before she had a chance to think, Rose sprang toward him with her knives. This was personal, and she wanted to be as close to the man as possible to see her vengeance executed. Rose managed to slice his face before he knocked her to the side.

Then, the most peculiar thing happened. Rose could see the soldier's next move, and then the next, and his next. She lunged again anticipating his attacks and responded in kind. She had managed to find every soft spot in the man's armor using only one of her knives.

The soldier was surprised to see a woman half his size dodging every one of his blows. The sight only kindled his rage, upping his game with more complex fighting techniques. Rose tried to see more and more to keep one step ahead of the man. She dipped, slashed, and dodged with ease until she accidentally dwelt too long in the future to see the man's next move.

Rose wasn't prepared for the crushing blow to her chest from his elbow. She fell flat on her back, struggling to breathe. The man loomed over her, blocking out the sun as he held his sword high, ready to strike his final blow. In the last fight for her life, Rose groped for a dagger that lay nearby and threw it as hard as she could at the man.

The soldier was frozen in place, arm still held high, looking down at her. Rose could see blood dripping from the corners of his mouth. Her dagger was lodged in his left shoulder, not the crippling blow she had hoped for. But the only movements the man-made were occasional twitches and winces of pain. The light dimmed from his eyes when he looked down to expose a spearhead thrust clean through his middle. Rose remained still as the bloody man fell to the side to reveal her savior.

"Spencer!" Rose choked, still catching her breath.

Spencer dropped the end of the spear then fell beside Rose to help her sit up. She breathed deeply and allowed his arms to encircle her.

"Are you hurt?" He asked, worried. "Did he get a piece of you?"

"Me?" Rose gasped. "I saw him kill you! He stabbed you. You fell!"

Spencer couldn't help smiling as he pulled Rose to her feet. "That's why I wear armor, Rosie."

"But..." Rose tried to protest.

"It was the blow that knocked me down. The blade only cut me a little. I'll see to it later." He shrugged.

Rose touched his armor, uncertain. "Are you really alright? You're not dead? You're not going to die from this?"

Spencer took her hands in his. "Rosie, I finally have you. Why would I do a stupid thing like that?"

She thought she had lost him, along with any future of happiness. It was that moment she realized she had always loved him. Since the night she found him in the woods, and every night since then, she was in love with Spencer. Rose threw her arms around his neck and kissed him with all her might. She was never going to hold back her feelings from him again. Spencer pulled her in tightly, not allowing her to let go.

Chapter 43

"ouldn't you wait until after the fight for your romance?" Darien called out as he approached them on his horse. "Are you trying to get killed?"

His mind was focused on the fighting. The last thing he expected was to have to interrupt such an intimate moment between Rose and Spencer. He didn't bother trying to hide his annoyance with the couple.

Spencer let go of Rose just in time to block a swing from an enemy's sword allowing Rose the opportunity to stab the man in the side. He fell to the ground, helpless. Spencer backed closer to Darien's position ready to defend his prince, with his other hand keeping Rose close to his side. The extra help that was sent to the right flank was just what the men needed. Darien's soldiers successfully thinned out King Robert's army in the surrounding area and sent them retreating to other parts of the battle to regroup. Darien shouted orders at his men to continue to push the enemy back. The warriors readily obeyed, and their line continued to press forward onto the White army, driving toward the castle.

Darien, Spencer, and Rose stayed behind the front in case someone broke through and attacked from behind.

Darien dismounted his horse and stormed over to Spencer. "You better get your head on straight, Spencer. I don't need a love-struck storyteller right now. I need a warrior!"

"Sorry. Darien. I got lost in the moment. I'm sure you understand." Spencer shrugged, not allowing Darien to cast a pall on their kiss. Rose smiled at his calm reaction.

But her smile turned to alarm when Darien grabbed her arm. "What I understand is your sister is still locked up somewhere. I don't understand how a visionary woman, such as yourself, cannot see into the future to find out where she is!"

Rose immediately shouted back at Darien. "I never said I was a visionary like Zoe. I'm still learning how to control my gift. Even so, I have read my cards several times! All they tell me is Zoe is with Robert."

"So read them again, Rose," Darien insisted.

"Excuse me?" Rose blinked.

Darien drew closer to her, "Get out your cards, and read them again."

Rose shook her head, "The answer will be the same."

Darien's tone was vicious, "Then you keep trying and trying until they say something new."

"It doesn't work that way, Your Highness," Rose spoke his title as if it were an insult. "The cards are never absolute. They don't give details."

"Just the kind of talk I would expect from a gypsy— using your words to trick us into thinking you know so much more about the world than the rest of us. I should have known to expect this kind of scheme from you." Darien scowled at her with contempt.

Rose's countenance darkened. "The woman you are trying to rescue is a gypsy. Choose your next words carefully, Your Highness."

"Did the cards even tell you if she was alive?" Darien mocked Rose's lack of information.

Rose flinched in fear at the possibility of seeing her sister's death. She had seen the three hundred soldiers die in Darien's memory. She had been taunted with faces of men who would die, and had seen enemy soldiers fall by the hand of their Red army. She even thought she saw Spencer's death, a scene that tormented her for months, but thankfully worked out for the better. But none of that could prepare her to see Zoe's death.

Her confidence boiled back up into a controlled rage, "She is alive."

"How do you know?" Darien continued to mock.

"She is my sister. I would know if she were dead," Rose said with complete seriousness.

"Then as her sister, I would think you would be doing your absolute best to help us find her. Have you, Rose? Can you honestly say you have done absolutely everything you can, and even a little more to save your dear sister?" Darien demanded.

Rose's face went pale while Spencer spoke up in her defense.

"It sounds to me like you're angry, and you are taking it out on the wrong person." Spencer stepped in between Rose and Darien so he was nose to nose with the prince.

"The wrong person? Look at her! She wanted to come to help save her sister. But she has done nothing to improve Brizo's situation in any way."

"She may not have seen Zoe yet, but she has been invaluable on the battlefield!" Spencer was losing his calm with every word. "She knew Robert would come at us hard on the right, and had you send extra troops to help. She has commanded this part of your army with ease and has suffered miraculously few casualties as of yet. For someone who has never had to endure the pain of battle, she is a natural. You should be thanking her. Instead, you shout at her telling her it's not enough?"

"He's right," Rose spoke softly. The two men arguing nose to nose turned to Rose in surprise. She looked Prince Darien squarely in the eye. "You're right, Darien. It is not enough."

She turned her gaze onto Spencer for a long moment as her face softened lovingly. She smiled, then closed her eyes, took a deep breath, and opened them. Her demeanor had changed. She held herself erect and proud with her feet planted strong beneath her. Her countenance radiated authority as she fixed a stone-cold stare back on Spencer.

"I'll need some time to work. Make sure your men hold their line; I'll be defenseless if any of Robert's men get through. After I find Zoe, you'll need to get to her quickly. Don't wait for me."

Rose looked behind her and found a small rock jutting out of the hillside. She calmly walked over to sit beside it. A small gust of wind tangled her hair, muffling the sounds of war nearby. She took her tarot cards from her pocket, eyes set with resolve.

"No!" Spencer bolted after her and dropped to his knee, grabbing her shoulders.

"What's she doing?" Darien asked, unsure of the gravity of Rose's unspoken plan. Spencer knew what was about to happen, and if it upset him then it couldn't be good.

"No, Rosie," Spencer shook her. "You don't have to do this!"

Rose held back tears, "Yes, I do. She is my sister. A tree cannot thrive without existing in the light and the dark.'"

"What does that even mean?" Spencer shook his head with concern.

"It means, I need to give into the darkness if I want Zoe to live."

"No," Spencer breathed. "No, you do not have to do this, this cannot be the answer."

"But it is the answer. *'What one has, the other must also.'*" A corner of her mouth slid into a small smile as she recalled her mother's words. "It has always been the answer."

"We have no idea what may happen if you fully harness your gift." Spencer swallowed hard. "You could find yourself in the same situation as Zoe. You could die, too!"

Rose touched his cheek. "Then I'll need you to take over the troupe for us. Don't let our family fall apart. You will need to keep them united."

Spencer shook his head, refusing to accept her charge. "I can't, I won't! There is no point in staying if you are no longer with me."

"You must, Spencer." A tear rolled down her cheek. "We are united as a family. I will always be with you."

He held her close, hoping she would change her mind, but he knew it would be in vain. Spencer kissed her forehead before standing then joining Darien again. Rose remained seated completely focused on what needed to be done.

Darien looked at Spencer, his friend, his rock, who had always kept him on the right path. Spencer looked broken. His entire frame seemed weighed down with grief as his whole existence began to slip out of his grasp like sand. Prince Darien put a hand on his friend's shoulder.

"Is she going to die?" He carefully asked.

Spencer looked away, towards the battle to regain his composure. "No more than Zoe."

"Is there anything we can do?" Darien looked back at Rose over his shoulder. Despite all the banter and arguments the two had endured, the prince had grown quite fond of Rose. Deep in his chest, he could feel a protective, brotherly love for her that roused concern for Rose's future.

Spencer's eyes were cold as steel while he scanned for possible threats. He was once again the unyielding, focused soldier who would protect his country and family at the cost of his life.

"Death comes for us all. What matters is how we meet it. Rose has accepted it wholeheartedly for the sake of Zoe…" He paused to look at Darien, "… and you."

Darien looked at the raven-haired woman shuffling her cards with new eyes. He immediately felt horrible for guilting her into this. He had essentially demanded she lay down her own life so he could save her sister. He wished he could take it all back, but it was too late for apologies. He saw Rose sitting as regal as ever as the severity of her situation pressed down heavily on her shoulders.

Darien offered a half-smile to his friend, "She's good for you. I hope to be a leader half as good as she is."

"Don't just hope for it, Darien, be it."

Prince Darien nodded as he drew his sword, ready to protect Rose until the end.

Chapter 44

"Two shuffles and a cut," Rose told herself. She thought of the lessons Zoe tried to teach her. Rose took a deep breath, embracing the warmth of the sun, the tickle of the breeze on her neck, and the soft grass beneath her.

"Clear my mind and focus on one question," she told herself the same way Zoe always spoke to her. Rose took a cleansing breath and focused on her sister. "Where is Zoe?"

Rose's thoughts echoed over and over in the empty void of her mind. The words built on top of themselves, layer by layer, until it felt like a crowd was shouting at her. Then, in an instant, there was only silence. Rose saw King Robert in a tall castle tower watching over the battle as if it were a play set up to entertain him. Her vision cut out abruptly and was replaced with darkness.

Rose snapped her eyes open and lifted her hands in disbelief. "I don't want to see the king!" She shouted at herself. She looked down at the cards she had dealt. They told her nothing. Rose sighed as she gathered them up, reshuffled, and tried again.

"Okay, okay," She whispered, "something more meaningful." Rose entered the quiet of her mind again and asked the only question that mattered. "Is my sister dead?"

The question echoed in her thoughts until… nothing—no vision, no voice—only the quiet darkness of her mind. Rose's cards still revealed nothing to her. However, Rose noticed the 'Death' card facing her again. The skeleton's toothy grin mocked her as she stared into its empty eye sockets. She could almost hear the skeleton laughing at her continued failure. Rose shook her head.

"Again," she told herself.

Rose tried a third time, and still nothing, nothing except for Death staring at her again. The card didn't scare her. The death card rarely meant actual death. Usually, it meant a great change was coming.

"Yes, I know!" she insisted as if the cards could hear her. "We are fighting, right now, for Darien to take control of the kingdom. You don't have to tell me about death, or any kind of change. It's already happening."

Again she scooped up the cards, again she tried to find her sister, and again she saw nothing. Over and over, she sought the power of her gift, and over and over she failed. But her failure always showed Death being dealt among her cards. Every hand, every attempt ended with Death grinning up at her.

Every failed effort only made Rose angrier. How could she be so incapable of this small little thing? Wasn't she born with the gift too? Wasn't she supposed to share in all her sister has? Why couldn't she help? What was she doing wrong? The villainous laughter returned to her mind. It was real. She didn't imagine it. Death was laughing at her. He taunted and he teased her. He was practically giddy with excitement as he watched her try and fail over and over again. In Rose's mind, she saw Death whooping and hollering with such mirth that his bones strained to keep from shaking apart into a shapeless heap. Fury and rage exploded out from Rose.

"Enough!" she shouted out loud to silence the laughter in her head.

She saw Spencer and Darien both freeze in surprise, but Rose continued to speak in a thunderous voice.

"I am Egeiro Red, Daughter of Rebekah, second Matriarch of the White and Red Troupe, Seer of Death, Commander of Lies, and Guardian of all that is Dark. I command you to end this nonsense and show me what I must know."

The laughing skeleton of death in her mind quieted and bowed humbly in respect to Egeiro Red, Seer of Death.

The darkness in Rose's mind was replaced with the scene she saw earlier of King Robert standing in a tower. This time, he was staring at his prisoner, Zoe. At least it looked like her sister. Zoe's entire presence was different from what Rose was used to seeing. Zoe was standing up straight, not doubled over in pain. Her cheeks had color and were fleshed out instead of hollow. Zoe looked strong and untouchable.

Before Rose could dwell on the miracle of her sister's health, she saw both of them turn their heads toward a thud that emanated from the main door.

Chapter 45

King Robert stood with his arms folded comfortably across his chest, projecting as much power and authority he could muster. He stared down at Zoe lying on the floor beaten, in pain, and bleeding. She struggled to coordinate her battered body to stand up but failed, collapsing to the floor again. Robert smirked as his captive tried to rise once more, gloating over her continual failure, proving he was the one in control of her.

"I think by now you have come to realize what true power looks like, my dear," he boasted.

Zoe struggled to stand again, unsuccessfully.

"There is no future for you if not by my side." The king's voice turned malevolent, "I'll make sure of that.'

Zoe's head hung in shame as tears stung her eyes.

"My future," she whispered to herself.

Then her eyes opened wide with complete clarity. Zoe felt something that she had not felt in a long time: strength. She was keenly aware of the dull pain from her bruises and the piercing sting from her cuts. Parts of her body throbbed from being beaten, but none of it hurt anymore.

The constant pain she had endured for the majority of her life— the pain that was always there because of her gift— the looming pain she had learned to accept as a part of her identity, was gone. Strength filled her muscles as she flexed them. Warmth engulfed her body as she could feel the color flood to her cheeks. Her heart steadied to a calming rhythm, and she could sense waves of energy washing over her. Zoe's mind was buzzing with possible reasons that could explain what was happening to her. None of them were convincing.

She was still sore from her physical wounds, but the pain dwarfed in comparison to what she had to endure for so long. That chronic and exhausting sensation no longer plagued her.

Zoe couldn't explain how it happened. Nevertheless, she said a silent prayer of thanks for it all. She was determined to use her strength to her fullest capacity. This was a promise she would hold herself to, especially when she had no way of knowing how long her reprieve would last.

"My future?" Zoe questioned herself as if asking a phantasmal being around her for confirmation of her thoughts.

"My future!" Zoe spoke with confidence and knowledge that she had a future to look forward to. She looked up at Robert with cold, steely eyes.

She was able to maneuver herself to her knees, causing Robert to burst into a toothy, covetous smile. However, his mirth was stolen away as Zoe rocked back onto her heels. She slowly, steadily rose to stand upright in complete defiance.

"I am Brizo White, daughter of Rebekah, first Matriarch of the White and Red Troupe, Seer of Truth and Sentinel of all that is Light. I have more power inside me than you have in your entire army. I will not bow to someone as small and menial as you."

The king's complexion turned purple. With a clenched jaw and bared teeth, he tried to advance on Zoe. His feet refused to move. Something inside him kept him rooted to the floor as the seer continued to speak.

"You, King Robert, son of Tobias the True, brother to Alastair the Courageous, I see you as you really are: small, angry, a mere dwarf of a man clawing at the ground to find his riches. Your love of attention and power is second only to your love for yourself. Thus, you have been painted into a lonely corner. There is no one left to offer you the love you so desperately desire."

Zoe took an assertive step forward, causing the king to flinch. "Eyes clouded with envy of your brother's reign, you do nothing but take. You hurt all those in your kingdom who wanted to love you. Now, they loathe you with every breath. You rain down misery and destruction on all you come to meet, and delight in bringing them down lower just so you can feel mighty. Your strength is hollow, a mere shadow of the strength your predecessors wielded."

She looked at the once-proud king as if he were an inconsequential insect. "Your power appears intimidating, but when challenged, it will crumble to nothingness. You will inevitably lose all that you have desperately tried to acquire to validate your self-worth."

At first, the King looked as if he believed every word Zoe spoke. She wondered if he might have mistaken some of her words for prophecy. If that were true, then escape should be fairly easy for her. Her hopes of an easy exit from the King's clutches were destroyed when his face resumed its usual undisturbed superiority.

"My past does not scare me, Witch. What matters is now, and right now you have yet to mention my future. If you're scared to mention my future it can only mean it is a good one for me." Zoe stared at the king with seething hatred. Robert's eyes widened with understanding as the possible truth struck him.

"Or, could it be, that you are incapable of seeing my future? Could it be that the great 'Seer of Truth' knows no more than anyone else concerning my fate?"

His grin faded to anger and then contempt as Zoe's face blossomed into a smile. Her mirth continued to grow until she roared with laughter, and tears streamed from her eyes.

"Oh, your Highness, your future is indeed hidden from me; but that is not a good thing. It means your future holds the one thing I cannot see: death."

Her smirk teased and taunted King Robert in ways he never imagined. Animosity blazed inside him resulting in one strong, powerful blow to Zoe's head sending her spinning to the floor, unconscious.

King Robert straightened his robe then turned to the nearest guard. "You there, send my order to double the guards surrounding the castle doors. No one breaches this room, understand?"

"As you command, my King!" The guard bowed and hastened from the room.

Robert approached the balcony to view the ongoing battle. It appeared he still had the upper hand, and the lies of the white witch were trivial attempts to rattle his confidence. He stared back at her lying in a helpless heap on the floor. Even if she was telling the truth about his death, he would not allow it. He has gained too much just to have something as trivial as death take it away.

Chapter

With Darien's men pushing King Robert's army further and further away, Spencer took the opportunity to glance back to see how Rose was doing. His blood ran cold when he saw a vague, unfocused look in her eyes and her rigid body. He left Darien's side in the hopes that he could help her... somehow.

"Don't touch her," Darien called after him, stopping his friend. "Zoe told me about this. It's best just to wait her out until she is coherent again, otherwise, you could hurt her."

A flash of terror struck Spencer as he hesitated for a moment. He knelt next to her and tucked a lock of hair behind her ear. Spencer felt tortured. He was delighted Rose was able to tap into her gift, just like she wanted. On the other hand, he knew her life would never again be the same. He knew the gift of prophecy Zoe, and now Rose, possessed came with painful repercussions. It drained their energy, their life, and caused extensive physical pain inside their bodies. All the dancing, acrobatics, exploring, hunting, tracking—everything that made Rose who she was—was over. Even just being outside for too long would be a struggle for her. She would be condemned to the life her sister had been living. She would have to be shut up inside, cold, tired, frail, and everything she feared would become a reality.

Spencer felt useless. He wasn't sure what to do, or how he could help her. How would he manage to soldier on without her if she couldn't handle the pain? Right now, he didn't care about the battle, he didn't care about Prince Darien, or Zoe, or King Robert. He didn't care about anything except for Rose. The only place he wanted to be was next to her. No matter what may happen next, he would never leave her side.

* * * * *

Zoe smiled broadly at King Robert, "I believe you have a visitor."

Robert's face twisted in disgust. "It can't be…"

The door was kicked in to reveal Prince Darien, sword in hand, ready for a fight. He smiled slightly when he saw Zoe, but his eyes narrowed when he found bruises all over her exposed skin.

"I'll be fine," Zoe whispered, touching her cheek tenderly with a grimace.

Darien's vengeful glare burrowed into his uncle. "You're going to pay for what you've done to her."

"She's fine, she knows how to take a hit," King Robert spoke easily.

"And for what you've done to the very people you swore to serve when you became king."

"I never promised to serve. I became King to lead them."

"Lead them where, into oppression?" Darien spoke boldly, "You have failed them. You took away their freedoms, their very identity. And now, they want it back."

"These people are like children; they aren't smart enough to take care of themselves. They need me to tell them what they want and what to do. Without me, there was nothing but anarchy."

"You have taken away the very essence of life, their freedom to choose for themselves. The wisest king is but a mere servant to his kingdom, doing all he can to ensure their prosperity."

"That's how your father ran things," Robert sneered. "You remember what happened to him. He died in his prime, an unhappy, unfulfilled life with no legacy."

"My father had a great legacy. The people loved him, and most importantly he had my mother and me. We were his ultimate joy. He wanted you to be a part of that, but no. You chose your own misery by staying away, alone with your hatred..."

Rose blinked and was overcome with dizziness. As her body started to descend toward the ground, she felt two long, muscular arms gently catch her. When her vision focused, she saw Spencer sitting next to her with his brow creased with worry.

"Rosie, are you alright? How do you feel?" he asked as softly as he could.

"What did you see?" Darien interjected as if commanding her to speak.

Spencer snarled at the Prince, "Give her a moment, I beg you!"

"We don't have a moment!" Darien insisted.

Rose spoke up once her head stopped spinning. "I saw Zoe. She is alive and she is safe."

Spencer's face was still tight with concern.

"Rose, you called yourself the Seer of Death," he whispered.

"Can you tell us what you saw?" Darien asked again, slightly less commanding.

"I saw your uncle, and I saw you," she answered. Her eyes searched into the space in front of her for what she should say next. She appeared defeated as she allowed her shoulders to sag. "To win back your crown, you killed King Robert."

Everyone was still for a moment as the words echoed dissonantly in the breeze.

"I do what?" Darien dared Rose not to change her answer with a glare.

Rose took Darien's glare and used it to fuel her confidence. "I saw your uncle with your father's crown set upon his brow. You found him in a room filled with tapestries with a large window that allows him to keep an eye on the battle with Zoe nearby. Robert knew he was in trouble when he saw you, so he unsheathed his sword to defend himself. You deflected every attack easily. It was only a matter of seconds before your blade found its home in your uncle's heart."

Darien quietly stared at her for a moment, seething hatred frothed in his eyes.

"I will not kill my uncle." His tone was soft but his words were sharp as knives toward Rose. "I know he is vile, and a tyrant, but he is the only family I have left. I will not run him through with any blade."

Spencer tried to redirect Darien's anger away from Rose. "Darien, I hate to say it, but if Rose has seen it, then… whether you like it or not…"

"No. No, I reject your prophecy. I would never harm my family. I'll find another way."

Rose was unshaken by the prince's words. She spoke the facts, directly and plainly to the prince with no added flair or emotion. "There is no other way; you must kill King Robert if this is to end."

"This will end," Darien maintained, "but not with me taking my uncle's life."

Rose continued flatly, "If you don't, all we are trying to do will be for naught. All the suffering and pain your kingdom had to endure will seem like paradise compared to the bloody reign that *will* come by Robert's hand."

Darien reared on her, unbelieving. "What was it you called yourself, Seer of Death? That must be who you are now, right?"

Rose's poise began to fade at the mention of her new, self-proclaimed title. Darien was the first to notice and refused to relent.

"I think you wish everyone would see themselves as dark and evil. Just like you."

Spencer tried to defend her, "Now wait a minute! Rose isn't…"

Darien ignored him, "I will not grant you that wish. I am not what you say. Your prophecy is nothing but a lie."

Darien spied his horse nearby. He easily approached and settled onto the saddle. "I know the tapestry room you saw. This will end, but it will end on my terms—the right way." Darien maneuvered his horse around and rode off, full speed, to the castle leaving Spencer and Rose alone.

Spencer turned to face Rose and tensed when he saw conflict stirring within her.

"Rosie, tell me what to do. Do you need anything? Are you in pain?"

"No, I'm not in pain. I'm fine." Confusion enveloped her. "It is odd; I feel exactly the same as I always have."

Spencer breathed an audible sigh of relief. Instead of being relieved with him, Rose bowed her head. Her hands clutched large fistfuls of her hair, as the tears began to fall.

"What is it, Rosie?" Spencer was afraid for her.

Rose looked up, emotionally pained. "Is this who I am now? The dreadful 'Seer of Death and Darkness'? I harnessed my gift so I could help my sister, but at what cost? I don't want to be a 'Commander of Lies.'"

Spencer gathered Rose up into his arms to hold her, to remind her how much he loved her. He put his hand on her cheek and focused his eyes on hers.

"Listen to me. Just because you see darkness, doesn't make you evil." Rose tried to protest but he continued undeterred. "You are good. You have a light inside you. The only reason you used your gift is because of your love for Zoe. That means you are worthy to hold the responsibility of this gift. Only love can quell the darkness, so the *notorious Seer of Death* should also see love. You must embrace it. It is what makes you mighty. It is what makes you good."

Rose's face relaxed a little. "How can you be so sure?"

Spencer brushed a few strands of hair out of her face. "Because, If there is one thing in this world I know I can be sure of, it's you."

Rose smiled at Spencer and took hold of his hand.

"Now, let's set aside this emotional revelation and go help Darien." Spencer gradually turned back into the experienced general as he refocused on the battle. "It won't be easy for him to kill his uncle."

"No," Rose stated. "No, Darien will be fine. He will do exactly what he said. He will find a way to end this on his own terms. What he needs is time. We should continue to hold the front. The kings' army needs to stay out here, away from the castle."

"But you just said Robert had to die. Darien won't be able to do that. He will need our help."

"Yeah, I have a hunch. I don't think my prophecies are set in stone. Unlike Zoe, I think, my visions can change."

Spencer tried to understand what Rose was saying. "But, wouldn't something as ultimate as death be unchangeable?"

Rose spoke slowly as the answer seemed to come to her from a hidden source. "I saw a version of Robert's death. And now that I have told Darien about it, I don't believe it is set in stone. Robert's death, yes, will happen. But when and how—that's entirely up to Darien."

Spencer smiled proudly at the magnificent woman that stood next to him. The realization of what she had done warmed his heart.

"You told him the absolute truth knowing he wouldn't like it, knowing he would want to change it."

Rose blushed shyly. Spencer pulled her close and kissed her.

"Well then, we will let Darien do his own thing, and we will take care of the front for him. Sounds like a good plan, Commander *of Lies*."

Rose laughed as Spencer mocked her new menacing title. She had a feeling he was going to tease her about this from now on. She couldn't be happier. I t will be a constant reminder that she was in control of her fate. That darkness may exist in her, but she would never allow it to control her.

Spencer wrangled two horses and helped Rose up on her mare before mounting his. He scanned the battle with a calculated glare and opened his mouth to speak. He paused, then looked at Rose with that all too familiar glint in his eye.

"Alright, Seer of Death," Spencer teased. Rose couldn't help rolling her eyes at him. "What do you see?"

Rose scanned the scene in front of her while calling on Death's help again. The dancing skeleton was no longer a burden to her; she had recognized him for what he was, a friend. For so long he had been ignored by members of her family because he was thought of as dark and evil. Now he was alive again, with purpose and meaning, all because of Rose. She was the Master of Death, not because she commanded it, but because she was not afraid and offered respect instead.

Rose was shown glimpses of faces, as before. But now, she was also able to see events of the entire battle play out, just as she was able to see her opponents' next move while she was fighting. Rose pointed to several locations, revealing current and future happenings in each area. Then, she pointed at the ravine that worried her before the battle started.

"There, we need to use the ravine to our advantage. We need to force them to bottleneck there. Only then will they accept we have won and offer their surrender."

As she spoke, Spencer shuffled his military strategies around in his head to account for his new intelligence. Spencer kicked his horse forward with Rose following behind. He got the attention of a handful of cavalrymen, and within seconds had sent them all off to different areas of the battle with new orders. All had their specific instructions, but all were given the overall order to drive their opponent toward the ravine to make their last stand. The men fanned out in different directions while Spencer and Rose stayed behind on the right flank to help maneuver the king's army to exactly where they needed to be.

Chapter 47

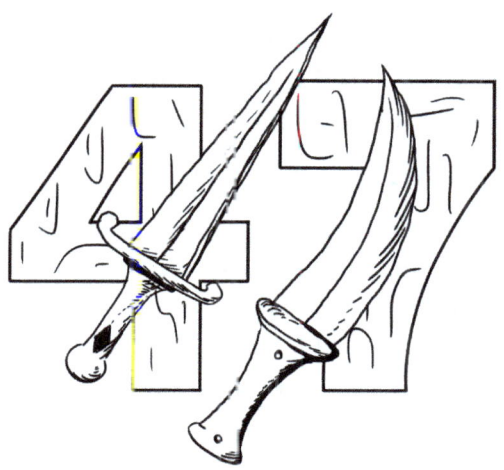

oe's eyes snapped open at the sound of King Robert yelling at his advisors. Her head was throbbing, but the enduring pain from using her gift was still gone. She flexed her muscles and realized her wrists and ankles were tightly bound with ropes. Yet, even bound, Zoe's curiosity grew in proportion to Robert's shouting. She remained as still as possible to secretly listen in on the latest report.

"How can a tiny, out-of-shape army be doing this well?" she heard Robert yell. "My army has more men, more practice, and more motivation than they do!"

Zoe heard a councilor's falsetto voice trying to answer the king. "I… I cannot explain it. Somehow, no matter what we plan, the men are thwarted before they can carry out their order. They are faster, smarter as if Fate herself is on their side."

"Fate," King Robert spat in disgust. Zoe remained as still as ever, hoping Robert wouldn't look too closely in her direction. "Or is it just luck?"

Zoe stopped listening. She tried to reason out her answer. She was overjoyed that Darien's army was a formidable opponent against the king's forces. But there was something more going on. There were too many coincidences, too many good breaks for it to just be luck. Additionally, Zoe knew for a fact it wasn't fate, because she would have been able to see something herself.

That could only mean one thing; it had to be Rose.

Zoe kept her eyes closed as she allowed herself to be swept up in a mere visualization of her surroundings. She whispered her sister's name in her mind, and her vision blurred as it raced down the side of the castle, across the meadow, and up the hill until she finally closed in on her sister's location. Zoe had found her sister in this fashion countless times, but this time was different. As Zoe inched closer to her target, Rose turned around abruptly to meet her sister face to face.

"Rose?" Zoe asked.

"Zoe?" Rose whispered back.

"You... you can see me?" Zoe couldn't believe what was happening.

Rose smiled excitedly, "I can see you! Are you alright? How are you feeling?"

Zoe smiled broadly, "I feel amazing. I don't know what you're doing, but it must be right. King Robert is furious with the way this battle is going."

Rose's excitement faded to stone, "Is he with you?"

"Yes, we are in–"

"A room full of tapestries overlooking the battle to the west," Rose finished for Zoe.

"Yes, how did you..." but Zoe was interrupted again

"Stay where you are, Darien is on his way. One way or another, this has to end with Darien."

Rose looked as if she had matured overnight. This was not the untrusting, temperamental sister Zoe had grown up with. Rose had an air of confidence and control about her that commanded Zoe's attention.

"I understand, sister," Zoe answered.

Rose nodded and her image immediately blurred, and Zoe was back in the tower, back to reality.

Zoe risked opening her eyes just a crack to assess her surroundings. King Robert had moved out onto the balcony overlooking the battle, still yelling at two of his advisors. He was screaming something about more money for the men if they would turn the fight back to their favor while the advisors nervously wrote everything down. Zoe continued to look around the room. She saw the door they all entered earlier. That entrance to the room was guarded by one soldier standing tall. His hand rested comfortably on the hilt of his sword, and he stood alert listening for any approaching footsteps. Brightly colored tapestries depicting noteworthy events in Marconian history covered the walls giving the illusion the room was bigger than it was. There were several desks holding piles of paper, a large circular rug that covered most of the room, and one more soldier standing directly in front of her.

At the moment, the guard's attention was on the king throwing a terrible temper tantrum, so she seized the opportunity to wriggle out of the ropes that bound her. Then slowly, steadily, she reached up to the man's belt and carefully pulled a dagger free from its sheath. She lay back down with the dagger hidden in her hands, pretending to be unconscious. The next thing she heard was the advisor's feet shuffling away towards the door. She peeked through her eyelashes to see. Once they were gone and the door was locked again with a loud *'clang!'*, she knew it was her chance.

In a blink of an eye, Zoe had stabbed her guard behind his knee with the dagger, then banged the hilt on the side of his head as he crumpled to the ground. By the time the second guard realized what was happening, Zoe had thrown her dagger and buried it in his shoulder. The man barreled toward her angrily. However, before he could unsheathe his sword, Zoe had grabbed a candlestick from a nearby desk. She pounded it straight into his face, knocking him out.

When Zoe looked up she saw King Robert holding a broad sword aimed at her, ready to fight. Zoe took her time to take a sword from one of the men and draw the dagger out of the other.

"Exactly where did you learn to fight like that, my dear?" The king asked in a patronizing tone.

Zoe's eyes narrowed, "You really should have watched our show for yourself. At the very least you would know we are not so ignorant when it comes to weapons."

"Or knots," King Robert motioned to the ropes lying by her feet.

Zoe simply shrugged, refusing to take her eyes off of her enemy. "I am a gypsy after all. I know how to turn a trick or two."

Robert sneered, "We will see."

He leaped, lunging the sword towards her middle. Zoe easily deflected his advance, causing him to veer to the left. She spun on her ankle and sliced with the sword, drawing blood from his arm. Robert grabbed the cut in disbelief then faced her again with pure rage.

Blinded by fury, Robert rushed at the smaller woman. Zoe stood as if ready to match his strengths and fend off his blow. Just before Robert lunged, Zoe dropped the sword and smoothly slid out of the way. She stepped in close, slashing her dagger fluidly across his side, drawing more blood. With a quick snatch, she unsheathed the King's own dagger and spun it around in her fingers. Her hands remembered their strength and she couldn't resist a smile. The flash of light off the naked blade caught the King's attention. He paused and checked his belt then gaped at the woman in front of him—only now realizing the woman was not as frail as she appeared to be. With an animalistic howl, all the advantages of decades of training and years of experience abandoned the king. His movements became predictable as he rushed at Zoe, trying, and repeatedly failing, to hack her to pieces with his sword. As if following the motions of a familiar dance, Zoe easily maneuvered around each of Robert's charges and used his blind rage to inflict a plethora of small wounds that stung with every move. It didn't take long for Robert's breathing to turn heavy and labored. This allowed Zoe to corner him in front of one of the tapestries. She stood directly in between King Robert and the only door out of the tower, daggers at the ready as she watched the beaten man try to convince himself he still had the upper hand.

Zoe was pleased with herself. It has been a long time since she has been able to work her muscles as hard as she just did. All her training from various plays from when she was younger came back to her as easily as whistling. It was an exhilarating feeling. But the joy was fleeting when King Robert started to smile as well. The sight made her nervous as she quickly scanned around her to see if she was missing something.

"Ah yes, very well done, my dear," the king spoke breathlessly. "But you see, you're not the only one who knows how to turn a trick."

King Robert lifted his sword and cut one of the ropes that held the tapestry behind him in place. The cloth fell easily to reveal a small door hiding behind it. He mocked Zoe with a formal bow then turned to open the door. Zoe ran to charge him but skidded to a stop after only a few steps. As King Robert opened the door, he froze mid-step, dropping the sword from his hands. He was face to face with his nephew, Prince Darien.

Chapter 48

King Robert swallowed nervously with the tip of Darien's sword barely grazing his nose. Darien's face was a mask of stone, unyielding. Not even a relieved sigh from Zoe disturbed his focus from Robert.

"Hello, Uncle," Darien growled softly.

"Darien," King Robert sputtered in stark surprise. The Prince's razor-sharp blade urged his uncle back to the center of the room, away from either entrance.

"Sorry I didn't use the main door, I got turned around somewhere… in my own home." Darien's last few words cut at the king, causing him to physically shrink in shame.

"Darien," Robert's voice was now soft and submissive. "I can't believe it is you! There were rumors you were dead, and I had to do something…"

"Don't you dare go on to speak as if you didn't start those rumors yourself," Darien may have been played like a pawn by his uncle in the past, but he wasn't going to allow it today. "You're going to pay for what you've done."

"What exactly have I done?" Robert asked innocently.

"You mean, aside from framing me for the murder of three hundred innocent lives and conspiring with neighboring assassins to wage war with Marconia?" Robert's eyes went wide with fear. "That's right, I remember exactly how it all happened."

"How could you possibly remember what happened?" Robert's voice was skeptical, but the truth rested heavily on his shoulders.

Darien's gaze flickered to Zoe for an instant, "I had some help from someone who knows a thing or two about death."

King Robert turned to face Zoe who had a satisfied smirk on her face. The king's anger flared. "Lying witch! You insisted you couldn't see death."

Zoe's look darkened, but her smile remained, "I can't see death, but my sister can."

King Robert's face twisted into wrath as the reality of his fate struck him like lightning.

"All family issues aside, Uncle," Darien spoke with all the authority of a king. "You have failed the people of Marconia. You led them into oppression, took away their freedoms. Now, they want it back."

"They don't deserve it!" Robert shouted. With the flick of his blade, Robert knocked Darien's sword away from his face. He ran away a few steps only to be met by Zoe, intent on stopping him. Robert was no longer in an entertaining mood. He swung with his sword as hard as possible, breaking hers close to the hilt. His small frame barreled into her like a cannonball knocking her to the floor. He continued to run to the other door for freedom, but was slowed down by a dagger whizzing in front of him and then a sword hilt flying through the air. He was forced to jump back to avoid getting hit, allowing Darien the chance to cut him off.

"How long did these people grieve your parents' death, their king and queen?" Robert boldly asked. Darien angrily slashed with his sword only to be blocked by his Uncle.

"How quickly did your people turn on you when they heard the rumors?" Robert continued.

Darien offered more blows with his sword only to be blocked again.

"These people don't deserve freedom. They are nothing without the monarchy telling them what to think, to do. They are ungrateful worms that owe us everything!" Robert yelled as he lunged toward Darien angrily. Darien deflected his attack easily allowing Robert to slide past him. Darien spun to attack Robert from behind. Robert managed to block him, but Darien could see his uncle was slowing. The prince slashed, again and again, faster and faster, refusing to relent until he changed his attack at the last moment to strike the old man's legs instead. King Robert fell to the floor in excruciating pain, grabbing the bloody wound near his knee. The blow wouldn't kill him, but it did immobilize him for the moment. Darien remained still, sword at the ready, but restrained.

"You're wrong," Darien spoke calmly to his uncle. "Our people don't owe us anything, we owe them. They are smart, resilient, and capable people. Our responsibility is to lead them in the direction where those qualities make our kingdom better and stronger as a whole. We don't give them anything; we help them with what they have. Respect and honor for the monarchy only come when they offer it to us freely, because of the service we have given. I will see to that!"

"So you will try to earn their respect by killing me?" King Robert looked defeated as he hung his head waiting for the final blow from his nephew.

"Everyone tells me I need to kill you, but I will not," Darien threw his sword down with a loud clatter.

"What?" Robert sounded disappointed, insulted even.

"I've seen more than enough death to last a lifetime, haven't you?" Darien raised an eyebrow at the little man. Robert simply grumbled under his breath. Darien looked at his uncle squarely in the eye. "Besides, you're my uncle; the only family I have left. I won't kill you. I command you to leave Marconia, and live out your remaining days in peace."

"Even if you win this battle, and banish me, I will never stop trying to tear you back down," Robert vowed.

Robert's oath didn't faze Darien at all. "Yes Uncle, I have been told you would say something like that by a very, very, annoying woman that I've come to know. The worst part about it is, she's right. I am a fool for letting you go. I believe you will do exactly what you say."

Darien leaned in closer as his tone turned dark and serious. As he spoke, his words echoed in the seemingly small room emphasizing every word. "But you better believe me when I say: I'll be ready for you. Every whisper you start, I will snuff it out. Every plan you set into motion, my men will extinguish. Every mischievous glance will be pecked out. No matter what you plot, I will be there to ensure your inevitable failure. I will always be one step ahead of you, waiting, ready to pounce. If you don't believe me, then please try. I relish the day you do."

Robert stared at the prince with eyes wide as saucers. The man was now crumpled on the floor in front of Darien. His mouth hung open as he managed to whisper three strained words, "I believe you."

Darien hurried over to Zoe leaving the defeated king behind them. She scrambled to her feet and flung her arms around Darien allowing herself to be drawn into a long-awaited kiss. For the first time since appearing in the room, genuine concern crumpled his brow as he examined the cuts and bruises on her face.

"I was worried I wasn't going to get here in time," he whispered.

Zoe smiled proudly, "And yet, when you arrived, I had him on a silver platter for you."

"Yes, you did!" Darien chuckled as he shook his head. "You are a remarkable woman, Brizo White."

Zoe beamed at him, then glanced toward Robert who was still kneeling motionless in the center of the room. She whispered to him even more quietly, "Speaking of remarkable, nice trick."

"Well, I learned from the best," he nodded to her with adoration. Zoe's cheeks flushed. It was a new color for her. Her face looked warm and healthy, not at all like her usual pale, hollow appearance. He touched her cheek gently, taking in her entire countenance.

"Listen, please don't tell Rose I said she was right," Darien shifted awkwardly, "She will never let me live it down"

"Rose!" Zoe shouted as if remembering something. She ran to the balcony, followed closely by Darien. Then she pointed toward a narrow ravine, "Over there!"

Darien squinted but it was hard to decipher what was happening among the muddle of soldiers all congregating in one area. He stepped behind the spyglass and peered through it for a better look.

He saw his men holding their weapons over their heads shouting. The remainder of Robert's army was retreating at full speed along the ravine, with no hope of returning victorious. He saw several celebrations break out amongst his army, and a few men drop to their knees in relief. All were overjoyed to have reclaimed the kingdom for the powers of good and to have restored honor and purpose to their lives.

"They did it!" Darien turned to look at Zoe. "The army is defeated."

"What about Rose?" Zoe insisted, "Did you see Rose?"

Darien looked back into the spyglass and scanned for her. He found Rose standing at the crest of the hill next to Spencer. They were the only ones not celebrating. Spencer's attention was fixed on the retreating army, watching each soldier carefully for any last-minute acts of heroism. Rose had the same frown of concentration on her face, not quite ready to celebrate. Then, unexpectedly, Rose tore her eyes from the retreating army and looked abruptly toward the castle. It took Darien a second to realize that she wasn't looking at the castle—she was looking directly at *him*. This unsettled Darien. *She couldn't possibly know that I was watching her, could she?* That notion was ridiculous the more Darien pondered it. Rose called herself the Seer of Death, not the Seer of Everything. Not even Zoe was capable of that. Then why would her attention be drawn directly to him?

"Look out!" Zoe shouted as she threw all her weight onto Darien, shoving him away from the spyglass. The following seconds seemed to be stretched out as time slowed down. As Darien fell, he watched his Uncle Robert barely miss them with his thrusting sword barreling straight toward them. Before he and Zoe had hit the ground, Darien noticed his uncle's feet tangling in both his and Zoe's outstretched legs. His uncle disappeared over the balcony. Surprise and terror contorted his face as he fell. The prince rushed over to the railing. He leaned over it, desperately searching for his uncle. His shoulders fell as he finally identified where the man was, just in time to see him hit the ground. Darien stared dumbfounded, trying to make sense of what happened... "I... I didn't even see him coming."

"I'm glad I did," Zoe breathed in relief.

Darien looked at her confused, "How can that be?"

Zoe looked at him just as perplexed, "Darien, I still have eyes."

Darien breathed a sigh of relief as he embraced Zoe tightly. "Someday I'll figure out the difference between you using your gift, and you just being amazing."

He couldn't believe how, but somehow he had managed to fulfill his prophecy. He had taken back his kingdom and extracted the evil that poisoned the crown. The prince was no longer a ghost wandering around his people. He was their king. Thanks to Zoe, Spencer, Rose, and all his loyal men, Darien had never felt more alive.

Chapter 49

"What is it, Rosie?" Spencer asked when he saw her attention turn to the castle.

Rose stood still for a moment then gave a satisfied smile, "Darien did it; the battle is over!"

Spencer looked towards the castle wondering what Rose saw, but then he understood. "You mean, he killed his Uncle?"

"No, he didn't," Rose answered proudly.

"But, didn't you say the only way this would end was with King Robert's death?" Spencer asked.

"The king is dead. Robert died because of his own wrath and greed, not by the hand of his nephew."

"He did it?" Spencer whispered to himself. Then he spoke again more confidently, "He did it!"

"Yes," Rose beamed at him.

"It's really over!" Spencer said excitedly.

"Yes!" Rose laughed.

Spencer shouted at the top of his lungs for all to hear, "Prince Darien has done it! The battle is over!"

A fresh wave of cheers and hollers of triumph rolled through the troops. Chants of *Marcoria!* and *Long live King Darien!* were taken up throughout the throng, echoing over the hills.

* * * * *

Rose was resting comfortably by a small fire Spencer was stoking outside her wagon. The sun had gone down and the usual soft sounds of music from her gypsy troupe hung in the air. The responsibility of the troupe still clung to her shoulders, but she never felt lighter. At this moment she was completely at peace with the world.

Spencer settled in next to Rose with his arm resting comfortably around her. "You seem happy for someone who is supposed to be the Guardian of Darkness."

Rose sighed, slightly annoyed with him. "How much longer are you going to poke fun at my gift?"

"Well I could say that was the last time, but you already know I'd be lying," Spencer beamed.

"Ok, well I'm officially asking you to stop."

"My dear Commander of Lies, you know I can't do that," Spencer answered smugly.

"You need to stop because you're going to drive me crazy," Rose admitted.

Spencer laughed, "That's kind of the idea, Rosie."

Rose laughed with him as she shook her head. "Fine, play your game. You will get bored with it eventually."

"Will I?" Spencer stroked his chin thoughtfully. "That sounds like a challenge."

Worry creased Rose's brow, "No, it's not."

"I do love a challenge," he smiled

"It's not a challenge," she insisted.

Spencer donned his dramatic, storyteller voice. "I vow this night to make it my mission to tease the Seer of Death whenever I can. No matter how great and terrible she may seem, I shall never fail." He added a malicious laugh for emphasis

Rose laughed, "Alright, alright, I get it."

A snap of a branch made them both cut their laughs short and look behind them. Rose let go of her knife when her sister stepped into the light, hand in hand with Darien.

"Zoe!" Rose gasped as she hugged her sister. "What are you doing here? I thought you would stay at the castle with Darien."

"Please, did you honestly think I wasn't going to check in on my only sister?" Zoe asked.

"Of course I didn't, but I wasn't expecting to see you here, in person," Rose answered honestly.

"Well," Darien spoke up, "I also wanted to see you two before the troupe moved on."

"You already know we won't turn away a visit from you." Spencer shook Darien's hand warmly and invited them over to the fire. "Come, have dinner with us."

Within moments the four of them were laughing, and having a wonderful time recalling memories of the latest events.

Rose raised her cup to offer a toast, "To Darien. Who despite all odds, took hold of his destiny, won over the love of his life, and defeated his uncle to reclaim the throne."

Spencer and Zoe lifted their cups in agreement and offered sincere praises to him. Darien accepted their kind words graciously then grew very serious.

"I know Robert is dead, but you need to know that I didn't kill him, Rose," Darien spoke plainly.

"Yes, I know," Rose answered happily.

Darien stared back at her emotionless, "You know? What do you know?"

"He tripped and fell on his own," Rose added.

"Yes, he…" Darien looked up at Rose confused. "How do you know what happened? You weren't there."

Rose tapped her temple with her finger while giving him a coy smile. "Seer of Death, remember?"

Spencer choked back a laugh, "Yes, you should never question the Seer of Death."

Rose stared at Spencer baffled, "Really?"

Spencer remained silent but continued to smile wildly at Rose, causing her to chuckle.

"Wait," Darien interrupted, "I thought you saw me kill my uncle."

Rose's confidence vanished as she looked at Spencer; not sure what to say. Spencer gave her an encouraging nod.

"I did see you kill your uncle," Rose admitted. Darien blinked at her in surprise. "But I knew it was a future you didn't want. So instead of telling you nothing, I told you the truth. I thought if you knew the truth, you would want to change it."

"But I thought visions weren't able to be changed?" Zoe asked, worried.

"That's what I thought too," Rose looked nervously at Spencer. "That is until I saw you die."

"Rosie, we've been through this," he took her hand and looked her in the eye, "The guy just knocked me down. I didn't die."

"No, you didn't." Rose couldn't resist smiling at Spencer, then looked back at her sister, "But back before Darien arrived at our camp, I had a vision that he did."

All three of her companions spoke at once.

"What, why didn't you tell me?" asked Zoe.

"You saw him die?" Darien was shocked.

"This explains everything," Spencer nodded in understanding.

Everyone paused to look at Spencer, completely lost as to why he was so calm about all this. He looked back with a small amount of panic then easily smoothed his face into a comfortable smile.

"It explains something else. It's not important," Spencer dismissed the attention with a wave of his hand. Then he gestured to Rose.

"As I was saying, it all happened the same as my vision. Except, you didn't die today. I don't know what, but something must have gone differently to change the course of events. I just can't figure it out," Rose admitted.

Spencer looked at Rose with that familiar glint in his eye. "I should think the answer is pretty obvious."

"What, so now you're an expert on my visions?" Rose asked, slightly perturbed.

"When it comes to visions about me, yes!" Spencer rebutted with a laugh.

"Tell us then," Zoe begged.

"Well, could it be that I had something to live for?" Spencer smiled at Rose then winked at her.

Rose blushed but tried to dismiss it as nothing, "Well, there's no way to know for sure."

"Answer me this: if you didn't see me die, would you have opened up to me as much as you have?" Rose was annoyed that Spencer wouldn't let this subject go. But the more she thought about it the harder the truth hit her. Her cheeks darkened to a deeper shade of rose. Of course, that only led to Spencer giving her a bigger smile, making her blush deeper and deeper.

"The look on your face, that right there tells me you know I'm right," Spencer stated proudly with a knowing glint in his eye.

"The point!" Rose shouted, directing her attention back to Zoe and Darien. "The point I was trying to make is: that was the moment I realized my visions could be changed. And that is why I told you the true vision I saw because I knew you would want to change it. And it is also why the battle went so well in your favor."

Zoe's mouth hung open as the full power of her sister's gift settled on her. "You could see the casualties before they happened, so you knew where to send reinforcements."

Rose spread her hands in appreciation, "Among other things, yes."

Darien wasn't sure how to respond to her. "You did that, for me?"

Rose glanced at Spencer again and then her sister. "Just because I see darkness doesn't mean I am evil."

Darien leaned toward Rose and put a hand on her shoulder. "Thank you, Rose."

Rose smiled back at him, honored by his gratitude. Then she slapped his hand off of her and donned a stern face.

"But, mark my words, Your Highness, if you ever call me a *witch* again I won't even bother to prophesy your death. I'll do it myself."

Darien simply folded his arms, refusing to back down. He gave her a genuine smile, one he had never given her before.

"Aww, would you look at this? I think we just became friends." Rose couldn't hold onto her anger much longer as she started to laugh with Darien. Darien turned back to Zoe.

"Now that you are no longer in mortal peril, there's something I've been meaning to ask you."

"What's that?" Zoe softly asked.

"After we escaped by the river, you mentioned that you couldn't see my future because I was too consumed by my men's death."

"I did say that," Zoe answered evenly.

"But you prophesied I would take back the kingdom. You already knew all of this was going to happen."

Zoe was silent for a long moment before she finally said, "It was all a lie. The whole prophecy we have been performing, about you saving us all… I made it up."

Darien's jaw dropped. He looked over at Spencer and Rose who did not look surprised at all.

"Did you know about this?" They both nodded their heads while responding with dumb, incoherent answers. Darrien turned back to Zoe looking slightly hurt. "Was it all a lie?"

"I'm so sorry. It was meant to give hope back to your people. And even after I learned your true identity, I didn't see any reason to take that hope away, so I kept up the charade for you. I had no way of knowing if you would go through with it or not."

"But you did know," Spencer interrupted. "You believed Darien was going to take back the kingdom even after you admitted it wasn't real."

"Why?" Darien asked.

Zoe gave Darien a genuine smile, "Because people are ruled by their hearts. Your heart has been unsure ever since you were banished. Until…" Zoe paused looking embarrassed.

"Until when?" Darien asked.

"Until the day we were alone in the forest," Zoe took a breath to gather some confidence. "That was when the visions surrounding you began to solidify, even if it was only for a moment. That is when you started to believe you were a good man and were capable of doing good things. You proved it when you rescued me from the water. That is when your heart started to focus on the kind of person you wanted to be—who you truly are."

"So, *did* you know this all would happen?" Darien asked while scratching his head.

Zoe smiled as she patiently waited to answer him, "I didn't know what you would do, but I did know your heart would make sure it was the right thing. So, that was enough for me to believe in you."

"I believed in your so-called prophecy, but in the end, it was just you believing in me." Darien tapped his fingers in thought. "Did I just make your story an actual prophecy?"

"Indeed you did," Zoe confirmed.

"So I was told the truth from the Commander of Lies and a lie from the Seer of Truth?" asked Darien. Rose and Zoe looked at each other, slightly embarrassed. Darien looked past the flames to see the rest of the troupe enjoying the evening in their playful way, complete with laughter and music. He looked back over at Zoe and put his arm around her smiling. "It doesn't matter. We made our own future, and I like what I see."

Chapter

nd so, thanks to the help of a loyal army and the tenacity of Brizo White and Egeiro Red, Prince Darien was able to defeat King Robert, and restore peace and harmony to his Kingdom!" Spencer proclaimed, once again donned in his brilliant blue and green storyteller outfit. The crowd he looked down on from his humble stage roared with cheers of delight. Confetti was thrown by members of the troupe to add extra flair, making everyone clap harder and cheer louder than before. Dancers on stage twirled and whirled behind Spencer, putting on a grand display that would impress even their more distinguished guests.

Spencer spread his arms to the crowd, hushing them down to a low roar. "But our story doesn't end there, ladies and gentlemen." The crowd applauded with satisfaction then quickly hushed to hear what was next. "That's right, Marconia, you know us all too well. We are not just any traveling band of gypsies, are we?"

"NO!" The congregation shouted back with joy.

"Of course we are not!" Spencer puffed up his chest with pride. "Ladies and gentlemen, we are the White and Red Troup of Gypsies!"

The crowd whistled and cheered with all their might when the troop's name was announced. A chant of *White and Red!* was taken up, and Spencer allowed them to continue for a minute or so before raising his hand again.

"Aren't you wondering what became of the breathtakingly beautiful Egeiro Red?" He paused to allow more cheers to swell. Spencer shot a meaningful gaze across the stage at Rose who was waiting behind the curtain for her cue. He wanted to make sure she understood just how important and critical her role was in all of this, and the people of Marconia knew it, too. When the energy of the crowd was at its peak, Spencer nodded to cue her on stage. Rose leaped out of the curtains and twirled over next to Spencer with a grand flourish. She gave him a dramatic curtsy as he bowed formally in return. He took her hand to stand up together, and saw her blush and smile more brilliantly than ever at him. The audience raged on with excitement, and many of the women swooned when Spencer kissed Rose's hand tenderly.

"The incredibly gifted Egeiro Red returned to her troupe to assume the role of head Matriarch. She carries on her family's tradition of spreading joy and hope to all those who gather for their shows, always offering you a show unlike any other, full of excitement, talent and more surprises!" The crowd offered more cheers of encouragement.

"The honor of leading the Marconian army was given to Xander." A proud Xander marched on to the stage and gave a small wave for the audience. In return, the crowd offered him deep whoops of appreciation. Spencer gave his friend a respectful bow, then continued. "He earned the men's respect by reminding them of their strength and honor, and vowed to hold them to their oaths as soldiers of Marconia."

Cheers of patriotism bloomed from the crowd to show their love for the Army and their devotion.

"And our devilishly handsome, *former* Commander of the Marconian Army," the crowd roared even louder, causing Spencer to hold out his hands for them to quiet down. "He gave up his sword to live a much simpler, happier life as a traveling gypsy, and most importantly, alongside the woman he loves."

He kissed Rose's hand gently allowing the crowd's cheers to rise again. Rose blushed again when Spencer glanced at her with that all too familiar smile. He laughed at her, knowing no one else was aware of her embarrassment but him.

"But enough about them." Spencer waved his hand dismissively to move on with the story. "We all know who you really want to hear about."

The audience quieted immediately, dripping with anticipation. Spencer raised his hands gesturing to the couple who sat on their own ornately decorated stage watching the performance, behind the mass of onlookers.

"It is my deepest honor to announce the union of the respected and beloved Brizo White with our honorable and compassionate King Darien of Marconia, two of my dearest friends who not only have found true love with one another but will share that love with all of you. Yes, fellow Marconians, these two, side by side will lead us into an era of prosperity and fortitude, igniting the proud spark in our hearts for this beloved country. Under their guidance, we will restore our kingdom to its former glory and build ourselves up to be better than we ever have been."

Spencer and Rose bowed deeply to the King and Queen, their family, their friends, hearts full of love and respect for each other. They were joined by the rest of the White and Red Troupe all dropping to one knee solemnly. Darien and Zoe rose from their seats and returned the heartfelt gesture with their own equally elaborate bow of love and respect for the performers, their friends, and their family.

The band of performers on stage broke out into a lively song and dance in honor of their beloved King Darien and his new Queen. The audience swayed along with them, clapping their hands and hollering cheers for the White and Red Troupe. Spencer and Rose gave another elaborate twirl off the stage to allow the performers to take over the grand finale of the show. Offstage, they caught a glimpse of the King and Queen through one of their curtains. Brizo White's hair sparkled beautifully in the sunlight. She looked strong and healthy. Now that Rose had accepted and begun to use her gift, death was no longer a plague to Zoe, but a friend to Rose. Zoe sat next to Darien, her true love, all traces of her infirmities now gone. Together they looked at home, sitting side by side on their thrones. Brizo's eyes turned to meet Rose's, swelling with tears of joy and love for her sister. Rose smiled deeply, trying to swallow her own tears. The silent conversation of sisters would mean nothing to any random onlooker, but to them they both recalled their promise from so long ago, ringing more true than ever.

"We will never leave each other. You will never be alone," Zoe promised.

"Never, as long as we live, I will be there for you," Rose promised just as sincerely.

The End

www.ingramcontent.com/pod-product-compliance
Lightning Source LLC
LaVergne TN
LVHW011929070526
838202LV00054B/4558